OUTLAWS AND SORROWS

CHARLES NODIER (1780-1844) was one of the pioneers of French Romantic prose; his salon at the Bibliothèque de l'Arsenal, begun in 1824 and known as *Le Cénacle*, brought together many of the key figures in the Movement and spun off other *cénacles* in which it was anchored, including Victor Hugo's. His best work consists of short stories and novellas.

BRIAN STABLEFORD'S scholarly work includes *New Atlantis: A Narrative History of Scientific Romance* (Wildside Press, 2016), *The Plurality of Imaginary Worlds: The Evolution of French roman scientifique* (Black Coat Press, 2017) and *Tales of Enchantment and Disenchantment: A History of Faerie* (Black Coat Press, 2019). In support of the latter projects he has translated more than a hundred volumes of *roman scientifique* and more than twenty volumes of *contes de fées* into English. He has edited *Decadence and Symbolism: A Showcase Anthology* (Snuggly Books, 2018), and is busy translating more Symbolist and Decadent fiction.

His recent fiction, in the genre of metaphysical fantasy, includes a trilogy of novels set in West Wales, consisting of *Spirits of the Vasty Deep* (2018), *The Insubstantial Pageant* (2018) and *The Truths of Darkness* (2019), published by Snuggly Books, and a trilogy set in Paris and the south of France, consisting of *The Painter of Spirits, The Quiet Dead* and *Living with the Dead*, all published by Black Coat Press in 2019.

SNUGGLY BOOKS

CHARLES NODIER

Outlaws and Sorrows

TRANSLATED AND WITH AN INTRODUCTION BY

BRIAN STABLEFORD

THIS IS A SNUGGLY BOOK

ISBN: 978-1-64525-048-7

Contents

Introduction

This collection assembles the works of fiction that Charles Nodier published during the first of the three distinct phases into which his troubled literary career was divided, all of which were published during the years when France was ruled by Napoléon Bonaparte, initially as First Consul and eventually as Emperor. A companion collection, *Jean Sbogar and Other Stories*, contains translations of the three novellas that he published after ten years of exile from Paris in 1818-1820, during the first phase of the Restoration that followed Napoléon's fall, prior to a second hiatus, while the more abundant work that he published after the July Revolution of 1830 is sampled in further volumes.

Nodier is now recognized as one of the great pioneers of the French Romantic Movement, of which he formed an initial Parisian core with the younger Alphonse de Lamartine and the much younger Victor Hugo in the early 1820s, but when the stories in the present volume were published in the first few years of the nineteenth century there was no such movement, and the term *romanticisme* was yet to be popularized in France by Madame de Staël's *De l'Allemagne* (1813), although she had already begun to develop her ideas in such texts a *De l'influence des passions sur le bonheur des individus et des nations* [On the Influence of the Passions on the Wellbeing of Individuals and Nations] (1796) and *De la littérature dans ses rapports avec les institutions sociales* [On Literature in its Relationships with Social Institutions] (1799).

There is no evidence that Nodier ever met Madame de Staël (1766-1817), and he rarely included any of her works among the citations that he often included in his essays and stories, but the two of them had an important common acquaintance in Benjamin Constant (1767-1830). Nodier and Constant did not become close friends until the latter's return to Paris in 1814, likewise following ten years of exile from the capital, but Constant and Staël, then closely allied, were in Paris in 1800-1803, while Nodier was making his first attempt to make a living as a writer there. They moved in more elevated social circles, and probably did not encounter him directly, although they might well have become aware of him in 1803, when he admitted to the authorship of the poem *La Napoléone*, first published as a pamphlet in 1802, which led to his brief imprisonment and banishment from the capital.

Les Proscrits (1802; reprinted in 1820 and thereafter as *Stella, ou Les Proscrits,* here translated as "The Outlaws"), Nodier's first work of fiction[1] to achieve publication, was written before Nodier went to Paris, when he had no idea that he would become a *proscrit* himself—the title refers to the royalists

1 Bibliographies routinely refer to several of Nodier's individually-published works as "novels," understandably, given problems in translating the French term *roman,* which came to be used as the French equivalent of the English "novel," but at the time it was far looser in meaning, more accurately translatable as "work of fiction" or as "romance." The longest of Nodier's works of fiction is less than forty thousand words in length, and the majority of those he published in volume form are less than twenty thousand. I have elected to describe the longer ones as "novellas" and those of lesser but still substantial length as "novelettes." Nodier said at one point, looking back on his fiction late in life, perhaps a trifle disingenuously, that he had never set out to write a *livre* [book] but only to write *episodes.* The episodic construction of *Les Proscrits* and *Le Peintre de Saltzbourg,* as well as the fragments in *Les Tristes,* permit them to be likened to poems in prose, and it is significant that the pioneering collection of prose poems *Gaspard de la nuit* (1842) by Aloysius [i.e. Louis] Bertrand includes a dedication to Nodier.

outlawed by the Revolutionaries in the 1790s—and no notion of the fact that he was planting an important foundation-stone for the development of Romantic prose fiction. It is entirely likely that Constant and Staël did not read it at the time, but the parallelism of their ideas is retrospectively significant, and it is possible that Madame de Staël's *Corinne* (1807) and Constant's *Adolphe* (1816), two pioneering Romantic novels, both took some inspiration from *Les Proscrits* as well as from René de Chateaubriand's novella *René* (1802), a much more widely-read and much more loudly-praised foundation-stone.

Compared with the exquisitely mannered *René*, *Les Proscrits* seems crude and melodramatic, and Nodier appears to have become dissatisfied with it even before its publication, but there is a sense in which its raw naivety and the near-hysteria of its tone are much closer to the essence and rhetoric of Romanticism, and many later commentators would regard Chateaubriand as a precursor of Romanticism rather than an exemplar of it; Nodier, on the other hand, became one of its paradigms, because, rather than in spite of, the unashamed extravagance of his work, which became more controlled and more composed in the later phases of his career, but never sacrificed his insatiable appetite for the display of sentimental excess.

Because most of Nodier's fiction is written in the first person, by narrators who routinely seem to be *alter egos*, sometimes even having his name, readers were often explicitly invited to consider them as autobiographical, reflecting his own ideas and sentiments even when particular incidents were clearly invented, and there is some evidence that he sometimes became confused himself as to the extent of the overlap between his real self and his fictional "selves," but the latter were always fantasies, transfigured, exaggerated and sometimes deliberately framed in opposition to his own estate. They are almost always of higher social status than he was, and possessed of finer—if often fatal—qualities. There is a strong element of wish-fulfilment in his representations of his fictional protagonists, but it is a curiously perverse and paradoxical kind of wish-fulfilment; the relevant characters are invariably "rewarded" by the providence of his plots with loss, despair and temporary insanity, and they are often tempted by suicide, even though they tend to be devout to the extent of considering suicide to be an exceedingly deadly sin.

That perversity and paradoxicality are developed with much greater artistry in Nodier's later works, but the stories in the present collection exhibit it, so to speak, in its raw, unrefined state and are thus more revealing in their primitive fashion. It is difficult to appreciate some of his later representations of the tragic nature of amour fully without having these early works available for comparison and contrast, and it is difficult to appreciate the early works fully without some understanding of the very particular biographical context from which they emerged. That biographical context was, of course, invisible to contemporary readers, and remained largely invisible even to the many commentators who attempted to depict and evaluate his life after he became famous, including his own daughter. Twentieth-century methods of research enabled further data to be unearthed that were difficult to access in the nineteenth, but only clarified the picture to a degree; it still remains inevitably confused by the misinformation contained in the accounts of his past life that Nodier often attached to introductions of reprints of his works.

All biography is, to some degree, speculative fiction, imposing hypothetical accounts of motivation on data that is rarely completely reliable, and all autobiography is, to an even greater degree, calculated mendacity aimed at self-justification and self-aggrandisement, albeit sometimes with calculated perversity. (All modesty is false, but some modesties are more ingenious than others.) The stories that Nodier's biographers have made up about him, and those he made up about himself, are selective and hazardous, as all stories are, but "the truth" is in there somewhere, just as it is in his fiction, because rather than in spite of the fact that the fiction consists of manifest artifices while the biographies pretend otherwise. The real man can only be glimpsed with uncertainty, but the glimpses can nevertheless be telling, and are greatly advantageous, if not vital, to a full understanding of his work.

Charles Nodier was born in Besançon in south-east France in 1780, nine years before the precipitation of the great Revolution, by which life in Besançon, although it was a long way from Paris, was inevitably transformed drastically. His father, Antoine-Melchior Nodier, was a lawyer who became an enthusiastic Jacobin and obtained promotion as a result to the status of the town's chief magistrate after the Revolution, becoming an important man and the administrator of the local guillotine. Charles was one of two children born out of wedlock as a consequence of his father's affair with an illiterate housekeeper, the other being his sister Elise, and although the children were subsequently legitimized by the couple's marriage, that presumably did not prevent Besançon society from considering Charles as a bastard, or deter his contemporaries from applying that insult to him, all the more readily because, as a very precocious child, he quickly became convinced of his own genius. That was more than enough to allow him to imagine himself, from a very early age, as a kind of outcast, a pariah undeserving of the social scorn inflicted on him by prejudice.

Charles was initially educated at home by his father, who had bold but eccentric ideas regarding the program of instruction he ought to follow. Charles collaborated with that program with a complete commitment to learning, revering his father and the other teachers with which he was provided on a somewhat *ad hoc* and temporary basis in his teens. By contrast, he did not revere his mother, and if he did not actually hate her, such evidence of their relationship as survives suggests that his attitude to her varied between indifference and contempt. Exactly what relevance that had to his subsequent problematic relationships with women, and the obsession with impossible ideal amour that fueled much of his literary work, must remain a matter for conjecture, but it is notable that the mothers of his protagonists generally get a bad press in his fiction, often being absent, indifferent or inconveniently tyrannical, while the heroes are envious of the loving mothers of their friends.

Caught up in the fervor of the moment, Charles also joined his father's Jacobin Club, where his youth and precocity made him something of a star, but he and his father were both devout, and although they were fully in favor of the Revolution's political aims, as they conceived them, they could not approve of the Revolutionaries' hostility to the Catholic religion and their destruction of many of its institutions in France. Thus, their sympathies were somewhat divided during the Vendean counter-revolution of the 1790s, because the royalists were fighting for their religion as well as their king. In fact, Charles always represented himself as a diehard enemy of tyranny rather than royalty *per se*, and it was not difficult for him, imaginatively, to cast royalist *proscits* as heroic rebels against a new kind of tyranny, as he routinely did in his fiction, always preferring to imagine his literary alter egos as royalist gentlemen rather than plebeian Jacobins. He also reacted against the violence of the Revolution, especially the employment of the guillotine, which, as his father's son, he eventually had the opportunity to see in operation, and which horrified him; it is routinely subject to scathing attack in his fiction and his non-fiction alike.

Antoine Nodier was very enthusiastic for his son to study for qualifications in law, and did his best to provide appropriate tutelage to supplement his own, but the circumstances were awkward, because of the Revolutionaries' disruption of the educational system, which had previously been dominated by religious institutions. His efforts included taking his son to Strasbourg for a brief excursion, but mostly he simply arranged for him to study under the guidance of friends. Charles took advantage of the relative informality of his education to specialize in aspects of it that fascinated him. He became passionately fond of words and their etymology, and built up an enormous vocabulary in several languages; that fascination was not unconnected with the strong interest in entomology that he also developed, under the influence one of his tutors who was a keen naturalist. His study in the latter science included a strong interest in taxonomy and nomenclature; many of the specimens he collected assiduously were still in the process of being organized into species, genera and families and given Latin names within a disciplined system.

Nodier wrote very little about entomology *per se* after collaborating on a brief dissertation on insect antennae published in 1798 but his fascination with systematic nomenclature led him to cultivate various academic projects throughout his career; although the grand plans that he routinely formed rarely came to full fruition, he published numerous fragmentary studies, including a *Dictionnare raisonné des onomatopées françaises* [An Explanatory Dictionary of French Onomatopeias] in 1808 and an *Examen critique des dictionnaires de la langue française* [A Critical Survey of Dictionaries of the French Language] in 1828.

Nodier was able to continue his various studies at the École Centrale of the département of Doubs in the late 1790s, where he dabbled in literature and played politics in a vague but ardent fashion, protesting against the policies of the Directoire, which had assumed control of the government in Paris in 1795, ending the worst phase of the Terror but still feeding the guillotine. In 1798 he obtained a position within the college as deputy librarian, but he lost it temporarily in 1799 when the Directoire attempted to clamp down on dissidents. Although his father was still an enthusiastic Jacobin, Charles and his friends undertook to satirize them in a public performance, and he went on the run when it was broken up by the police. Although nothing came of the pursuit and the Directoire was abolished by Napoléon only a few months later, the troubles continued and the father and son were subjected to further criticism and harassment, on somewhat different grounds.

The scandal of Nodier's dubious politics was further complicated by personal scandals. Exactly what those scandals amounted to is difficult to determine; very different pictures are provided by his quasi-autobiographical fiction, which often casts his alter egos as Don Juans, but his most recent biographers, including Richard Oliver, suggest that the profound disinterest that young women had in him led him to compensate by lying outrageously and slanderously about imaginary sexual conquests. One way or another, however, his early amorous career was problematic. When Antoine Nodier was demoted to a minor position during an administrative reorganization in 1800 he seems to have thought that his son's behavior was partly to blame, and Charles seems to have retained the same suspicion, and to have felt guilty about it.

When Nodier first left Besançon to sample life in Paris in December 1800, therefore, he left under something of a cloud. Although he came back after three months, when his money ran out, he evidently felt that his future lay in the capital and could hardly wait to return there in the autumn. The establishment of the Consulate offered many new possibilities for the future and he seems to have tried hard to find a more lucrative position, while attempting very earnestly to publish his literary work and begin building a reputation. The belated publication of *Les Proscrits* in 1802—he had written it in Besançon in 1800—was a small beginning, but it was a beginning, and it paved the way for the publication of a second novelette, *Le Peintre de Saltzbourg, journal des émotions d'un coeur souffrant* (tr. herein as "The Painter of Salzburg"), in 1803, as well as an anonymous item of hackwork, *Le dernier chapitre de mon roman* (tr. herein as "The Last Chapter of my Romance"), issued in the same year, before things went catastrophically awry.

The plot of *Le Peintre de Saltzbourg*, like that of *Les Proscrits*, is undoubtedly based in part on one of the complications that the author's amorous career had encountered. At some point before leaving Besançon he met and became infatuated with Lucile Messageot, the stepdaughter of a colleague of his father's, who was a judge in the nearby town of Dole. She married a painter, Jean-Pierre Francque, much to Nodier's disappointment, and moved to Paris, where he sought her out when he went there in his turn; still infatuated, he befriended Francque, thus maintaining a relationship of sorts with his lost love until she died prematurely, in between Nodier's writing of the two novelettes. In *Le Peintre de Saltzbourg*, unlike *Les Proscrits* and reality, the heroine's husband dies, apparently clearing the way for the disappointed lover to resume his relationship with his beloved, but that is not what happens, by virtue of a remarkable moral determination of the author. Exactly why Nodier made that narrative move—which must have seemed perverse to many readers—is anyone's guess, but it was echoed, with many variations, throughout his literary career, which produced a long series of novelettes and novellas in which fervent amours are similarly frustrated, even when all apparent obstacles have been cleared out of the way.

To some extent, that nihilistic ending is simply a repetition of the pattern of *Les Proscrits*, the heroine of which is already married, hence making a licit consummation of the protagonist's infatuation impossible, but the extra twist changes the tenor of the tragedy considerably. Nodier knew at the time, and must have been advised repeatedly, that ending his stories in that fashion was a dangerous move for a writer desirous of courting popularity, because it flew in the face of reader expectation and demand. He already knew that he was swimming against a tide by placing so much emphasis on the sentiment of his protagonists, because his romanticism (although it did not yet have that label) was at odds with a contemporary philosophical trend toward representing and championing the role of reason in human affairs—sense rather than sensibility, as Jane Austen was later to encapsulate the conflict of priorities in England, or, as Nodier preferred to put it, "positive" thinking rather than spontaneous feeling. That Nodier decided to champion sentimentality uncompromisingly was not particularly odd in itself; many other writers did the same, following in the philosophical footsteps of Jean-Jacques Rousseau, but they routinely did so on the grounds, or at least on the hopeful assumption, that it was a road to happiness. Nodier's fiction carries the opposite implication: that true, ideal amour is a recipe for disaster, which cannot lead to fulfillment but only to despair or death, no matter how much circumstances seem to favor a fortunate outcome.

Only one of Nodier's many works of fiction breaks that pattern, and that is the one that he published immediately after *Le Peintre de Saltzbourg*, which he subsequently refused to acknowledge as his, omitting it from his collected works and denying, in the introductions to reprints of his early stories, having written any fiction except for the items he did allow into that ensemble. In a way, however, precisely because of its exclusion and opposition, *Le Dernier chapitre de mon roman* is just as revealing of its author's peculiar psychology as his romanticist works. In the chapter set at a masked ball Nodier provides his protagonist with not one but two brief portraits of his *alter egos*, one an ambitious young writer too proud and idealistic to follow fashion—his present self, as it were—and the other a "Wertherian" writing under the powerful influence of J. W. Goethe's *Die Leiden des jungen Werther* (1774; tr. as *The Sorrows of Young Werther*), an identity he was already preparing to put behind him. The latter is represented as being carried to unreasonable excess by his sympathy for Goethe's hero, and the analysis of his plight is complicated by the unkind judgment that he is perversely seeking rejection in his amorous courtships, in order to justify his affectation of despair, losing interest completely in the objects of his infatuation as soon as they yield to his entreaties.

That Wertherian is obviously a caricature, and it would be wrong to read too much into it, but the observation refers to a psychological phenomenon that is not unfamiliar. In a society that puts a high price on female "purity," the romantic ideal of a sentimental young man is likely to be a woman who is stern in refusing to yield to passionate entreaties, even his own. Conventionally, the solution to that predicament is marriage, which has long been the conventional end-point of all "romances," but in extreme cases of romanticism, marriage is seen as licit corruption, failure rather than success. In the tacit and explicit narrative viewpoints of the vast majority of Nodier's works, the only true consummation that an ideal amour can have is celestial rather than mundane, conceivable in the afterlife but not in earthly existence. The assumption of his narratives, covertly or overtly, is that posthumous consummation is the sole objective toward which his heroes ought to work, based on the firm faith that it is both attainable and necessary. The extent to which Nodier really believed that is debatable, but he was exceedingly fond of the affectation.

The protagonist of *Le Dernier chapitre de mon roman* shows no interest in that ideal; his interest in marriage is purely "positive" and he sees no reason for it to inhibit his pursuit of haphazard seductions on the way. Few readers can have been astonished by the particular twist that winds the plot into a neat ironic knot, but some, at least, might have been surprised by the jaundiced tone of that eventual conclusion, From a modern viewpoint, the most interesting part of the coy account of the protagonist's easy sexual conquests is the timing of the breaking of the heroine's hymen, which offers an unusual if exceedingly vague insight into the precise nature of the various sexual encounters involved.

The fact that Nodier refused to admit to the authorship of *Le Dernier chapitre de mon roman*—although there can be no doubt that it really is his work—raises the possibility that he might have published other unsigned works during the first phase of his career that were not subsequently revealed to be his. The catalogue of contemporary works appended to the first edition of *Les Proscrits* offers an interesting snapshot of the publishing practices of the day, featuring numerous anonymous works and more than one falsely claiming to be "translated from the English": imitations of the popular "Gothic novels" of Ann Radcliffe. Nodier would have been as capable of that kind of imitation as he was of imitating the genre of "libertine fiction" to which *Le Dernier chapitre de mon roman* belongs, but no evidence survives that he might have done so. He did, however, issue one other anonymous work shortly after that novelette, of which he subsequently admitted the authorship fairly rapidly, and disastrously.

The work in question was a *libelle*—a slanderous satirical pamphlet of a kind that had a prolific history in eighteenth-century France—containing a brief poem, described as an "ode," that being a term to which the etymologically-sensitive Nodier attached a particular meaning, as a sort of condensed epic. *La Napoléone* (tr. herein as "The Napoléonad") is, in fact, a caricature of an epic lampooning Napoléon. Later editions—it was reissued in 1814, with the author's signature, as soon as Napoléon was defeated and banished to Elba—date its composition as February 1802 but it probably existed before then, at least in draft form. Nodier and his publisher must have been well aware of the danger of publishing a sharp admonition to the First Consul at a time when his police were making strenuous efforts to suppress dissidence, and cannot have been surprised when they took an interest as sales of the pamphlet slowly began to pick up. The publisher was arrested, but it is not obvious that there would have been any further consequences, nor that the publisher would have revealed the name of the author under interrogation; in fact, Nodier did not wait for that to happen, but turned himself in to the police, offering himself as a martyr to his cause.

In later commentaries and stories Nodier made a good deal of literary capital out of his brief imprisonment, but the details of it were difficult for his biographers to recover. His daughter Marie related that he once pointed at a high window in a big building and told her that it was "his bedroom," the edifice in question being Saint-Pelagie, but he was only there very briefly. Recent biographers allege that he was actually sent to the prison hospital in La Force after his initial interrogation, in order to receive treatment for a dose of gonorrhea that he had recently contacted from a Palais-Royal prostitute. When questioned, he apologized profusely for his error in penning the ode, and offered the excuse that he had been temporarily unhinged by grief because of two recent deaths, that of Lucile Francque and that of Maurice Quaï, a mystic with whom he had formed a brief but close friendship after being introduced to him and his followers by Lucile's husband.

Other people who wrote letters at Antoine Nodier's request attempting to excuse Charles Nodier's error offered more elaborate accounts of his supposed aberration, including neurasthenia brought on by excessive use of opium. They did not mention the venereal disease, which Nodier was trying to keep secret, although it is not unlikely that the symptoms of the malady had prompted him to take laudanum medicinally, perhaps to excess. Nodier's best friend in Besançon, Charles Weiss, waxed particularly eloquent on that point, insisting that Nodier had frequently been driven to the edge of insanity by his vivid imagination and that increasing doses of opium—which had supplied him with literary inspiration as well as dulling his pain—had eventually made him violently ill, damaging his nervous system permanently.

It is possible that what Weiss wrote was mere hyperbole, but Nodier was already something of a career invalid, suffering occasional bouts of serious illness that led him to suspect that he was epileptic—which, in the vocabulary of the time, was much the same thing as alleging madness. The physicians of the day were incapable of diagnosing the trouble accurately, so it remains open to conjecture, but modern biographers suggest, plausibly, that his symptoms might have been caused by hypoadrenalism, commonly known as Addison's disease, inherited from his mother. At any rate, he struggled with recurrent bouts of illness for much of his life. Whether that had anything to do with the composition of *La Napoléone* is dubious, but there are certainly grounds to wonder how much the many accounts of hallucinations and delusions and the numerous surreal episodes contained in his work might owe to his self-medication.

Exactly what role the pleas made on Nodier's behalf played in his release is unclear, but anecdotal evidence gives the principal credit to the fact that he was prompted to write a new ode, *Prophétie contre Albion* [Prophecy Against Albion], celebrating Napoléon's plan to invade England, in which he praised the future emperor to the skies. General Lefebvre, a friend of Antoine Nodier, allegedly showed the manuscript to the First Consul, who ordered its author's release, unaware when he signed the order that he was also releasing the author of *La Napoléone*. Many years later, when Nodier's name was brought to Napoléon's attention again on Saint Helena, the ex-emperor was reported to have said that he remembered it as that of the author of a eulogistic ode written in his honor, apparently having diplomatically forgotten that the item in question was one of a contrasting pair. Nodier's release in January 1804 was, however, conditional; he was placed under official police surveillance and ordered to leave Paris and return to Besançon.

Effectively, Nodier was now a *proscrit*, and the continuation of his literary career became even more difficult than before. He pursued it as best he could, publishing various essays, but only one volume containing a number of items of short fiction, *Les Tristes, ou Mélanges tirés des tablettes d'un suicide* (tr. herein as "Sorrows: Miscellanies taken from the notebooks of a suicide"), attributed to a dead vagabond. The title page of the volume has the by-line "published by Charles Nodier," but that only meant that the author was posing as the editor of the dead vagabond's works, the actual publisher being the colorfully-named Antoine Demonville.

Like the two novelettes, the short pieces collected in *Tristes* were written under the powerful influence of Goethe's *Werther*, and they exaggerated the extent to which he saw himself in Goethe's distraught and disillusioned hero, just as they exaggerated the extent to which he conceived of himself as an outlaw and a pariah. He had actually left his Wertherian phase behind, to the extent that he could poke fun at it in *Le Dernier chapitre de mon roman*, but he never abandoned the pose entirely, and sometimes seems to have been slightly puzzled by the fact that he had always resisted the temptation to commit suicide, in spite of the powerful arguments leveled against it in *Le Peintre de Saltzbourg*. His more recent biographers allege that he had, in fact, once attempted suicide in Besançon when the extent of his lies was revealed, but that his friends—including Charles Weiss—had wrested the knife with which he had stabbed himself away from him before he could do any irreparable harm.

The fact that he was politically suspect from 1804 onwards was a covert ball and chain that Nodier had to drag around for the rest of his life, long after the official surveillance was removed ten years later. The suspicion hanging over his reputation seems to have been ironically unaffected by changes in regime, because he had no clear political stance of his own, and was perennially cast as a potential subversive no matter what form of government was in office. That made it difficult for him to find employment, and certainly did not help his attempts to find publishers willing to issue his work. He lived a somewhat peripatetic existence for a while, writing and doing a little teaching, but not publishing very much.

In 1808 his personal situation changed markedly. His father died in that year, soon after Charles married the sixteen-year-old Désirée Charve, the youngest daughter of Lucile Francque's mother, by her second marriage. Prior to the marriage he seems to have been attracted to her elder sister Frances, who is said by his biographers to have resembled Lucile, and it is conceivable that Désirée always suspected that she was something of a substitute for one or both of them. In one of the several memoirs written about Nodier after his death in 1844, by Jules Janin—who was acquainted with him and his family for more than twenty years and knew him as well as anyone—Janin insists very forcefully that Nodier loved his wife and daughter dearly, and was loved equally dearly by them, and there is no reason to doubt his sincerity or his judgment, but the very force of his insistence might permit a suspicion that Nodier was not entirely convinced of it himself.

In all probability, Janin's assessment—fully endorsed by Marie Mennessier-Nodier in her own memoir of her father—was accurate, and Nodier's constant lifelong assertion that he was the most unfortunate of men was a psychological quirk rather than a serious evaluation, but it remains the case that Nodier's marriage, however beneficial it was to him in real life, did not have a very noticeable effect on the downbeat tenor of his work. Although he never reproduced the near-hysteria of *Les Proscrits* and *Le Peintre de Saltzbourg*, that progress reflected the steady sophistication of his style and his narrative construction, not a basic change of attitude or subject-matter. The story of his life and work after 1808 will, however, be more conveniently taken up in *Jean Sbogar and Other Stories*, which will detail and illustrate the second phase of his published fiction.

The translations of *Les Proscrits, Le Peintre de Saltzbourg, Le Dernier Chapitre de mon roman* and *La Napoléone* were all made from versions of those texts reproduced on the Bibliothèque National website *gallica*. The translation of *Tristes* was made from the version of the text reproduced on Google Books.

Outlaws and Sorrows

The Outlaws

Preface

"Your work will not have the suffrage of men of taste."

I'm afraid not.

"You've tried to be original . . ."

That's true.

"But you've only been eccentric . . ."

That's possible.

"Your style has been found to be uneven . . ."

So are the passions.

"And strewn with repetitions . . ."

The language of the heart isn't rich.

"Your hero strives to resemble Werther . . ."

There is sometimes a hint of that.

"Your Stella doesn't resemble anyone . . ."

That's why I'm consecrating a monument to her.

"Your madman is seen everywhere . . ."

There are so many unfortunates.

"In sum, your characters are badly chosen . . ."

I didn't choose them.

"Your incidents are poorly invented . . ."

I haven't invented anything.

"And you've written a bad work of fiction . . ."

It isn't fiction.

Chapter I

I Shall Write

I shall write. The memory of past dolors is almost as sweet as that of an old friend.

For a long time, my life was agitated by the storms of woe; but it became accustomed to tempests and it found its strength in its chagrins. Today, I love to talk about my disasters, as an old soldier likes to indicate with his finger, on the map, the place where he was wounded.

However, I have not formed the prideful design of writing for glory. I have lived a great deal, suffered a great deal, loved a great deal, and I have made a book with my heart.

Do not read me, happy generation who will have a career embellished by the illusions of fortune; surround your existence with cheerful gracious scenes by Albane.[1] I have sailed on an infidel sea and I only paint reefs.

Do not read me, pretty women, who smile at the brilliant swarm of your young adorers and who only occupy the present in counting the enjoyments of the past and looking out for future happiness.

---

1 Albane was the name by which the Italian baroque painter Francesco Albani (1578-1660) was known in France; he was notorious for the lush lyricism of his religious and mythological paintings, replete with cherubim.

Roses of the morning, sway in the breath of the zephyrs on your perfumed stems. Stella was a rose like you, but she blossomed under a burning sun, and she died.

It is for you that I am writing, impetuous and sensitive beings who have been shriveled early by the shock of passions and whose souls are nourished by lessons in misfortune.

You have only found around your youth seduction and perfidy. Dolorous regrets have followed you into maturity; society has rejected you, men hate you, and your sweet errors have been effaced like the fugitive furrow that a light wind traces in a wave.

Come to my heart; I will love you, I will soften your chagrins by sharing them, and we will weep together, if we still have tears to shed.

Chapter II

Proscription and Solitude

I was twenty years old; the last flowers were blooming in the last rays of the month of May, and I fled my pleasant fatherland. Thus, the funereal spirit that was hovering over France enveloped in its immense proscriptions the age and months of amours.

Oh, if I wrote as I feel, I would depict in rapid strokes the convulsions of those days of mourning, and you would shiver at the memory of your own woes; but I do not criticize providence, like the unjust and irreflective crowd whose members would rather calumniate Heaven than seek the truth.

Revolutions are great maladies that afflict the human species, and which have to develop at marked times. It is by them that nations are purified and history becomes the school of posterity

No, this upheaval is not a work of darkness prepared in the shadow of a few nights by a handful of fanatics and seditious individuals; it is the work of all the centuries, the essential and inevitable result of all past events, and in order for this result not to have been produced, it would have been necessary for the eternal order of the universe to be violated.

Moan again, moan forever, you who have lost, in the midst of the horrors of this scourge, the objects of your dearest affections, but do not murmur vengeance any longer; raise cypresses over the tomb of your parents' assassins, and do not sacrifice human victims thereto; the Manes are peaceful gods who do not drink blood.

Forgive, for that is the most just as well as the gentlest act of power; I believe that the culpable are few. Fever and the passions render furious, but men are only evil when they are ill.

I arrived at the foot of the mountain, and I saw on the slope the bell-tower of Sainte-Marie, which was lost in the pines. I sat down on a tree trunk that the storm had felled a few feet from a stream that descended through the fissures of a rock and wandered in the distance in the valley.

"Is it such a great evil," I cried, "to quit cities thus and to find oneself alone? I am free, and nothing constrains my thought," I added, proudly; "it is as independent as the air I breathe.

"These woods that rise in an amphitheater over a closed agrarian sea, might perhaps contain some hospitable cabin. I shall lie down there on a mat that I have woven, and I shall nourish myself on simple aliments that I have prepared. I shall savor the tumultuous pleasures that blunt sensibility without satisfying it; but nothing will trouble my repose, and I shall enjoy a mild peace, while my peers are tearing one another apart for the sake of vague abstractions."

I leaned my head on my hands and I sensed tears of grief rolling in my eyes; I raised my eyes toward the heavens, and they became tears of gratitude. It was five o'clock in the evening; the sky was pure; the sunlight was trembling in the foliage and sparkling on the snow of the high mountains; no other sound could be heard but the quivering of the heather, and that vast and profound calm was in harmony with my heart.

I was not an illustrious victim, and my name was lost in the host of outlaws, but I dreamed of the glory of Barneveld and Sydnei,[1] and my soul was uplifted.

---

1 The references are to Johan van Oldenbarnevelt (1547-1618), a Dutch

There are moments when the blood flows with more activity, when a mild warmth animates all the organs; the faculties are augmented; the imagination is embellished, sensations crowd together and are confounded; one lives more rapidly, and one lives better.

I was in one of those moments of exaltation, and it seemed to me that nature was an immense domain, from which I had long been banished, and which I had just reconquered.

---

statesman who played a leading role in the liberation of the States of Holland from Spain, and the English parliamentarian Algernon Sidney (1622-1682), who was executed for treason following the Restoration; his treatise on political philosophy *Discourses on Government* (1680) was cited as evidence at his trial and he was hailed as a martyr by subsequent liberal politicians

Chapter III

The Madman of Sainte-Marie

I got up and I followed the banks of the stream toward its source; its murmur maintained my soul in a delectable languor, and the sentiment of my existence was multiplied a hundredfold. Perhaps I would not have rendered reason to the mildness of my emotions, but they were vivid and pure; no object occupied me particularly, but all of them affected my senses agreeably; eventually, I could no longer be sufficient for the rapid succession of my sensations; they oppressed me gently, and my heart experienced the kind of grip that squeezes without wounding.

In a place where the wood became thicker, hiding the stream from my view, I leaned against a fir tree and sighed; all the powers of my soul rose up toward the creator, and I felt the need to offer a solemn prayer.

"Repose and wellbeing!" I said, aloud.

"Poor Lovely, no more repose, no more wellbeing!" replied a touching voice

"There are suffering individuals, then!" I exclaimed. My felicity was so complete that its expansion had to fill all of nature!

I approached, and I saw a young man sitting on a boulder detached from the mountain, who appeared to be about twenty-five years old; his blond hair fell over his shoulders, without styling but without disorder; his face was as interesting as his voice. A long habit of chagrin had scourged it without robbing it of its native expression of nobility and pride. It was evident by the derangement of his features that they had once been deformed by the irritations of despair, but his physiognomy expressed the calm of a reflective sadness; it no longer exhibited the kind of violent and impetuous dolor that devours itself, but the august character of the melancholy that laments over a tomb.

I had had time to make those reflections because we were staring at one another without speaking. I have observed that when two men who ought to know one another perceive one another for the first time, their souls appear in their eyes with a simultaneous movement, seeking and studying with an anxious gaze, interrogating one another in order to judge one another. I had already appreciated Lovely in that silent contemplation; I found his eyes and I read an expression there so eloquent that I felt, without a doubt, that we were made for one another; and that was not the effect of a vague prejudice of an irresistible and profound conviction that cried to me: *Embrace the brother that providence has chosen for you!*

Who would dare to doubt providence? It has furnished all our needs abundantly; it has placed on the trees the fruit that nourishes us and slakes our thirst; it has given us the wool of animals with which to clothe ourselves, the shade of the woods to protect us from the fires of the sun; and in that multitude of generous cares, would it have forgotten to prepare a friend for us?

Make no mistake, it is not without purpose that it has combined, with such a perfect accord, all the parts of two different organizations, and even if you only consider my system as the paradox of a good heart seeking to attach itself to life by the gentlest of bonds, I will sustain, against all the dreamers of that desperate metaphysics, that every time the creative spirit has formed two beings who suit one another, it destines them to join together and to love one another.

I do not know whether Lovely's thinking faculties were exercised by the same reasoning, but he drew the same conclusions, and at the same instant, we each made a spontaneous movement toward the other in order to hug one another. A rapid reflection repressed that involuntary impulse. In me that reflection related to social decorum; in Lovely, it was produced by the apprehension of misfortune.

I sat down beside him. I looked at him with interest, and I repeated his words effusively . . .

"No more repose. No more wellbeing . . ."

"Never," Lovely replied.

Never. It is frightful to despair of the future thus, and to have used up all the possibilities of happiness in the flower of one's years. That sentiment chilled me.

Lovely perceived that and was touched by my pity.

"I've suffered a great deal," he added, "but I'm no longer suffering . . ."

And he strove to make a consolatory smile pass into my soul, as if to apologize for having afflicted me.

Good Lovely!

It is barbaric to integrate the unhappy and to reopen wounds that are still bloody by an indiscreet compassion, but there are gazes that have a significance more extensive than all the words in the vocabulary, and Lovely understood me.

"Suffered a great deal," he said, crossing his hands over his inflated bosom and slowly lifting his eyelids. "I have lived in cities, and all the refined pleasures, which one purchases at such a high price, are only hideous skeletons under sumptuous clothing. I've sought others in my heart, but my heart was simple and confident, and my heart was betrayed . . . Amour!"

He articulated that word with a sigh; his face became animated, his eyes wild; his muscles were clenched and his voice died away in sobs.

"And amity," I said placing my hand on his heart, which was beating precipitately . . .

"Do those who suffer still have friends?" said Lovely.

Oh, if I had been his friend!

I already was. Lovely let a burning tear fall on to my hand.

We understood one another, and we had nothing more to tell one another.

Chapter IV

I Have a Brother

Lovely's mother surprised us; she was searching for her son with a tender anxiety, and as soon as she saw him she came to him, without seeing me.

I was glad that she did not see me; that tender expansion of the purest affection cannot have witnesses.

Lovely covered his mother with caresses.

That spectacle moved me but it did not astonish me. The unfortunate are more loving; melancholy is more tender, more confident and more communicative than pleasure, if melancholy is not the pleasure of those who no longer have any.

How electrified I was! If the divine power had transported me at that moment to my mother's knees, how gently I would have pressed them! How I would have imprinted respectful kisses on her feet. I have never groaned with more bitterness over the chagrins with which I had sometimes troubled her slumber. I have never felt more keenly the sweetness of that delectable piety, which would be a joy if gratitude had not made it a duty.

How I pity the unfortunate who is carried by the tempests of life far from the threshold of his paternal hearth and who is abandoned to himself in an unknown world. When the heart is sickened by dolor, and he no longer knows where to repose his head, he will say: "I would have reposed my head on my mother's bosom . . ." and he will groan at having quit her, and perhaps he will die without having been able to refresh his blood by means of a reparative kiss.

"Oh, my mother!"

Lovely's mother was struck by that involuntary exclamation, and turned to where I was sitting.

The character of virtue was imprinted in her physiognomy in such a respectable manner that the sentiment to which the sight of her gave birth in me was confounded, without my thinking about it, with the memory of my mother.

I stood up and I bowed

"Lovely's Mother," I said to her, "you only have one son?"

"Only one," she replied; and all her soul was fixed on Lovely.

"In the name of Heaven, have two sons . . . !"

Lovely's mother considered me attentively.

"Don't refuse my prayer," I said to her. "Give shelter to an unfortunate, a brother to Lovely."

She smiled at me tenderly, and leaned on me in order to return to the cottage.

Tell me, proud dominators of the world, whether such a noble candor ever consecrated your treaties. I have just acquired a wealth a thousand times more precious than all the splendor of your glory, and it is guaranteed by a smile.

While your arrogant souls render the world dependent on their pride, and shake it for vain formalities, here nature bears all the expenses of etiquette, and confidence ratifies the engagements of virtue.

"I have a brother," said Lovely, putting his arm around my neck.

Chapter V

The Savage Island

Yes, solitude is a friend that renders the soul its original temper and the imprint effaced by the frictions of society, but it is a friend that is insufficient; we only turn to it in our distress, when the tender communications of society are forbidden to us. Humans are not born to be alone, like the wild beasts of the desert, with no other relationships than those of need, with no other interest than that of existence; whoever is able to sustain that desolating doctrine is a blasphemer who dishonors humanity or a sophist playing with his reason.

An instant before I had been happy in my solitude, but the sensations were rapidly effaced and now I would no longer have found anything but a void in my heart.

There are no enjoyments but those one can spread; one only multiplies one's wellbeing by multiplying its links, and the only man who has been fortunate on earth is one who has left many regrets there.

I have often tried to imagine a man cast up by a tempest on the shore of a savage isle and isolated from all others, without any hope of seeing them again.

Sometimes, he walks sadly over the abandoned shores, fearing to let his gaze fall upon those uncultivated areas that no industrious hand will ever render fertile.

Sometimes he remains standing, contemplating the vast extent of the sea, and while he calculates the immense obstacle that separates him from everything that he has loved, a dolorous sigh escapes from his heart, breaking it.

Sometimes, he thinks he perceives a ship deploying its sails in the distance; he attaches his gaze to it; he trembles to lose sight of it; he lies down on the ground; he holds his breath; he hopes . . . he hesitates . . . he prays; and when the sun in setting comes to dissolve those fantastic forms, he would like to grasp them again, and prolong until the next day the error that seduces him.

Often, he writes on the sand, with a piece of wood sharpened with difficulty, the names of his parents, his friends and his mistress, whom he has lost forever. Often he pronounces it; he converses with their cherished memory; and when the echo repeats his voice, he thinks that he has heard them.

When a profound sleep has calmed the agitation of his thought for a few hours, he wakes up and summons them again . . . A beneficent dream had brought him back to his anxious family; he had seen the sweet tears of his beloved sister, and it seems to him that their damp trace is still moistening his bosom.

He weeps too, but his tears fall into the dust. He is alone!

Soon I see him lying on arid sand, motionless with exhaustion and dolor, suffering the long anguish of death. Malady has hollowed out his cheeks; his eyes are bloodshot; his breast is heaving with a painful respiration; his lips, desiccated by an ardent thirst, exhale a fiery breath; and when he senses that all the springs of his existence are broken, he parades a sinister gaze around him, which regrets not finding a friend.

A friend would have prepared a bed of moss for him; a friend would have expressed into his cup the juice of salutary plants; a friend would have thrown his garment over him to shield him from the fires of the sun and the freshness of the dew; the cares of a friend embellish death; but he is alone.

The movement of his heart accelerates, is interrupted, stops . . . his blood burns, and then freezes, and remains suspended in his veins; his eyelids tremble and close; he says: "I'm thirsty!" and he expires, without anyone having responded to him.

Chapter VI

Another Friend

When the sun rose I was sitting outside the cottage, on a stone that served as a bench.

The view was not extensive; it was only over the crowns of trees and between the peaks of rocks that the beautiful plains of Alsace were visible in the distance, the indefinite limits of which were confounded with the vapor of the clouds in the east. The other points of the horizon were occupied, either by confused clumps of pines and larches, or by rocks that time detaches from the summits of mountains and heaps up at random.

The human eye contemplates with a religious fear those great debris of creation, and the yew that extends its horizontal branches over them, crowning them with majesty. The ruins of art are imposing; those of nature are sublime.

That is because there is nothing more legitimate and nothing more august than a glorious misfortune, and there is no sentiment more innate than the profound veneration inspired by the idea of grandeur allied with the idea of destruction.

I don't know . . . but I would not want for a friend a man who saw without emotion an old oak broken by lightning and who would give alms to Belisarius without respect.[1]

---

1 Jacques-Louis David's famous painting of *Belisarius Begging for Alms*

In any case, my landscape would not, perhaps, have furnished an Idyll to Gessner[1] and a painting to Claude Lorrain, but it had the solemn, inspiring and consoling charm that puts dolor to sleep and magnifies the forces of thought.

I recognized that I had a soul. Lovely came to join me, and I felt, in giving him a fraternal kiss, that the two of us were only one.

I had only glimpsed the interior of the cottage the day before; I went back into it with him; it was simple. But maternal love smiled at filial love there; it was inhabited by virtue; it was open for hospitality, and I took it for a temple.

My eyes paused on a few works that comprised Lovely's library.

The first of books, the Bible, had the first rank; next to it was placed Klopstock's *Messiah*—the poem of religions beside its annals.[2] Lower down, I distinguished Montaigne, who is the philosopher of the human heart, between Shakespeare, who is its painter, and Richardson, who is its historian; Rousseau, Sterne and a small number of other authors came next.

Lovely squeezed my hand gently, looked at me with a mysterious expression, took an ebony box from its shelf, opened it with precaution and took out a volume wrapped in crepe.

(1781), based on an apocryphal anecdote about the Byzantine general, would have been familiar to Nodier even if his friend Jean-Pierre Franque had not been one of David's pupils.

1 The Swiss painter Salomon Gessner (1730-1788), an important pioneer of Romanticism in art.

2 *Der Messias* [The Messiah] (1748-73) by Friedrich Gottlieb Klopstock (1724-1803) is an epic poem inspired by Milton's *Paradise Lost.* It was enormously successful in Germany, but also very controversial, offending conservative minds by its use of blank verse as well as the fervor of its imagery in promoting the author's particular notion of redemption and his vision of the Last Judgment. It became a central document of German Romanticism and a powerful influence on French Romanticism, but had little influence in Britain, which already had Milton.

"Another friend," he said, presenting it to me. It was *Werther*. I admit it; I was twenty years old and I was seeing *Werther* for the first time. Lovely shook his head and sighed.

"I'll read your *Werther!*" I cried.

"See how worn these pages are," he said. "When my reason went astray and I came to roam the mountains, that friend remained to me; I bore it next to my heart; I moistened it with my tears; I attached my eyes and my burning lips to it by turns; I read it aloud, and it populated my solitude.

"Yes, Lovely, I'll read your *Werther*."

"We'll reread it together," Lovely said. "We'll reread it often."

One day, I went out with *Werther* and plunged into the wood.

Chapter VII

She

"Why can this book no longer be sufficient for me," I said, closing it dolorously.

"Why have my pleasures lost their charm? Why do I no longer love the noise of the stream, or the sunset, or the innocent memories of my childhood? Since I have opened that fatal book, it seems to me that I have put on the robe of Créuse[1] and only respire a burning air.

"I am no longer happy."

I sat down on the edge of the wood and I interrogated my heart; I needed to love; that idea astonished me, like an unexpected light, but it relieved me of a long oppression and I respired with more liberty; soon, I anticipated the future, and I found it surrounded by all the illusions of happiness. That enchanting illusion gradually extended over the present; it gave a new aspect to what surrounded me; the daylight seemed purer, the landscape more cheerful, the foliage more gently moving; my soul opened to amour, and that is only born once.

Every minute revealed new sensations to me and taught me other pleasures; my rapid imagination went astray in its brilliant hopes, and lulled me with a thousand bright chimeras. Already, it was no longer a dream . . .

---

1 The murderous garment featured in Corneille's *Médée* (1635), by means of which the sorceress in question exacts her fiery revenge on her husband's new love.

I saw the adored woman who would double my existence; I painted her in vivid colors; I took pleasure in combining in her all the attractions of youth and beauty, ornamented by the expression of virtue; her eyes respired candor and her mouth sensuality; all her actions respired grace . . .

A naïve modesty colored her complexion with a chaste incarnadine; she was the masterpiece of nature, animated by the breath of amour.

I approached, and I was able to grasp even the piquant disorder of her hair, even the movements of her heart, which lifted as it palpitated the gauze by which it was compressed . . .

She was reading; I took a few more steps, and I heard the rustle of the page that slid under her fingers, the sigh that a touching phrase extracted from her . . . I saw a tear that fell along her cheek, and I would have thrown myself down at her knees if I had not feared imitating Pygmalion in adoring my own work . . .

No! It was not a dream . . .

I had seen her; and if I were to live for centuries, that moment would always be present to me . . .

I would always see her there, as I saw her for the first time, when she raised her eyelids upon me and my staring eyes found her first gaze . . .

And now, when I have been broken by so many disasters; now, when I have nourished such painful regrets, and a funereal cloud obscures my memories, I still believe I see her as I saw her that day . . .

It is there that she was sitting, at the bottom of that little field, on the hillside, near the eglantine bush. When she saw me she let her book fall into the broom; old Brigitte smiled to reassure me, and I was more troubled than before. Brigitte leaned toward Stella, leaned on her crutch and said in a whisper: "An outlaw perhaps . . . yes, an outlaw."

If all the living beings who inhabit space had been in accord at that moment to salute me as their king, my pride would have been less flattered than by that woman saluting me as an outlaw.

Chapter VIII

Stella's Cottage

"Yes," I replied, "an outlaw . . .

"But," I added, "this is where happiness is."

"With a pure heart and memories that make no reproach, happiness is everywhere," said Stella.

"I think so too." That was not, however what I had meant to say, and she perceived it.

She did not invite me to sit beside her, but she made a slight sideways movement in order to make room for me there; I sat down; I touched her, and a sensual frisson ran through my entire being; the void in my heart was filled.

Although we had never seen one another before, we had many things to say to one another, and yet we remained silent . . . but that momentary silence told us both more than a long conversation. Stella was emotional, embarrassed, perhaps tender . . . she sought a diversion, and her hand brought her book back to her knees; it opened at the place where Werther sees Charlotte for the first time, for it was also a copy of *Werther*. I attached my sight to that prophetic page, and then returned it to Stella. Stella sighed. My gaze had been expressive; Stella's sigh was eloquent.[1]

---

1 In *Werther*, Charlotte is engaged to be married, so Werther's love for her is doomed from the start; in cultivating a friendship with Jean-Pierre Francque, Nodier was doing exactly what Werther does in Goethe's story,

"*Werther* again," I said, presenting Lovely's book to her.

"The friend of the unfortunate," said Stella.

"You have loved, then?" I said, swiftly; and that question was so irreflective that I blushed.

Stella did not respond; she detached a wild rose from the eglantine bush and pulled the petals from it. When she returned her eyes to me, she doubtless saw, by the trouble that agitated me, that I had divined her fatal allegory, and she squeezed my hand tenderly, in order for the unfortunate love to be divined. I collected the rose petals and I deposited them on my heart; they withered a long time ago, but they are still there with one of her gloves, her ballad and her green ribbon.[1]

When the sun set behind the mountain, Brigitte warned Stella that it was time to return to the cottage; I would have given an empire to accompany Stella, but I would rather have lost a thousand times over the life that displeased her; I consulted her with a discreet gaze, and she seemed to reply: *Why not?* That is because mistrust is foreign to good hearts.

I have hardly savored the favors of amour. I know that some are burning, which suspend all the faculties, intoxicate all the senses and cast the soul into a delectable ecstasy and which cause a light of apotheosis to shine over our life. But I doubt that amour has anything sweeter than the delicate and pure pleasures that are still desire, and which are already happiness. Enjoyment has something bitter and dolorous; the more perfect and the more overwhelming it is, when one savors it one does not have the strength to grasp it, and as soon as one can grasp it, it disappears; it is a flame that devours and is extinguished.

Oh, I regret even more the moment when Stella climbed the difficult path to the cottage with me. She was leaning on

---

but he had not yet done that when he wrote the present story.

1 Shredded eglantines and green ribbons crop up repeatedly in Nodier's works, to such an extent that one is tempted to wonder whether they recall an actual incident to which he attached a particular personal significance.

my arm, which pressed her breast; her breath brushed my cheek; I respired her life, and our souls were confounded in a narrow union of thought. I was so happy!

The cottage was surrounded by honeysuckle and flowering laburnum, which hid it from view; the interior was simply ornamented, but the modest furniture was not devoid of elegance; there was even luxury in Stella's cottage—the luxury of misfortune that surrounds itself with consolatory arts. I noticed a harp there, books, music and a few drawings, which represented the most beautiful sites of the mountain.

I suspected as much.

"Another outlaw," I whispered.

She interrupted me by placing her hand over my mouth, and I imprinted a fiery kiss on it.

It was late. I asked for permission to come back.

"Often," said Stella.

"Every day," I replied.

"Soon," she said

"Oh, tomorrow . . ."

And the night appeared so long to me!

I left, and her eyes followed me until I went back into the wood.

Chapter IX

The Return

It was a poetic night . . .

The fir tree agitated by the wind, the murmurous steam and the cooing dove . . . everything there spoke of Stella.

When I arrived at the cottage I opened my window; I pronounced her name softly, and I believed that all of nature had heard.

Chapter X

Interview

But what if she loved someone else? No, that fatal suspicion could not wither my happiness; I rejected those images, the cruel illusion of which tarnished the charm of my days. Stella had not yet loved.

I arrived at the eglantine bush. Mechanically, I picked a rose, and I shredded it involuntarily. I picked another, and then a third, and I stripped the whole bush. I remembered Stella's mute response. I tried to take myself back to the moment that she had made it, and I studied her soul at a distance, in order to explain the mysterious emblem that had seemed so simple the day before.

It's probable, I said, thrusting away with chagrin the roses I had scattered under my feet, *that I divined it poorly.*

From the moment that I had quit her to that one, I had only been occupied with her, and had not formed any other desire than to see her again; and when I perceived the cottage, I was struck by an involuntary dread and a shudder of terror. I remained motionless with fear, as if I had read on the door of the peaceful dwelling, inhabited by an angelic creature, the inscription of Dante's *Inferno*.[1]

---

1 All hope abandon, ye who enter here.

What, then, is the nature of the vague presentiment that enables the misfortunes of the future to appear around us and which foresees the edicts of destiny, in order to pursue us with an absent penalty?

Stella was sitting and drawing. I advanced on tiptoe and stopped behind her. She turned round and greeted me with a smile. My disturbance had calmed slightly; or, rather, it had given way to a milder disturbance; but Stella's smile annihilated me.

There is in amour a turbulent and feverish crisis that shakes mental organization forcefully and absorbs all ordinary impressions. Uncertain and confused ideas no longer leave traces in the memory, the body collapses, the eyes are veiled, the blood turns and precipitates, seething, toward the heart . . .

"You're not tranquil," Stella said to me.

I seized her hand, and an electric spark is no more prompt than the simultaneous commotion that confounded all our sensations. I took a few steps in the room and came to sit beside her.

Her eyes were fixed on her drawing; I fixed mine on it, for I dared not turn them toward her, and I found some pleasure in seeing what she was seeing; it seemed to me that her gaze left a particular imprint there, which spoke to my thoughts, a secret character that I was able to read.

Imagine my astonishment when I recognized in that drawing the sketch of our first interview at the bottom of Brigitte's field.

"What!" I said. "Stella deigns to occupy herself . . ."

"The viewpoint is agreeable," she said, blushing.

"And the imitation ravishing!"

"I intended it for you" she replied.

I wrote underneath: *Monument* . . . and the pen escaped my fingers.

"Monument to amity," said Stella, and she wrote. If she had not evaded my transports, I would have fallen at her feet.

She approached her harp; she drew a few touching sounds from it, which appeased the tumult of my passions, and caused a profound emotion to succeed that painful frenzy. I have never heard music without thinking that I feel better. I tried to envisage Stella, and the sentiment she inspired in me was as pure as her. The celestial expression that animated her face and was distributed over her entire person would have constrained to respect, by the ascendancy of virtue, the most degraded hearts. I felt that I was tranquil, and then she quit her harp I was still listening.

Tenderness disposes to confidence, and a moment of abandon surmounts all the conventions of society. I talked to her about my parents, my sister and Lovely; we wept together, and we learned that we could no longer do without one another.

One loves rapidly when there are only two people in the world and one needs to love. When the ardor of the sun had been tempered slightly by the approach of dusk, we went out of the cottage and walked in the surrounding area.

There is a large flower on the mountain that only grows in steep places and in sand; it is the columbine, whose blue cup, suspended from a frail and slender stem, suddenly falls back toward the ground, as if it were fatigued by its weight; and that plant is the emblem of a life that has ceased to be happy. Stella loved that sad flower, and she pointed one out to me, inclined over the rock.

I climbed up to it and I picked it, but when I returned, as the loose stones shifted under my steps, I clung on to some brambles, which wounded me slightly, and a drop of my blood fell on to the azure of the columbine. I tried to throw it away.

Stella grabbed it eagerly, and attached it to her breast.

Chapter XI

Poor Lovely!

One day I went out early and walked at random in the wood. Lovely perceived me and came toward me, but I was thinking too much about Stella to see anything. He seized my hand.

"You're suffering," he said.

I bore his hand to my breast.

"You're in love," Lovely added, and he considered me with an anxious pity; that idea had irritated the most delicate fibers of his heart. "You're in love! Oh, woe betide you, woe betide everything in nature that loves!"

His heart was breaking; the sound of his voice had something dolorous, and when the echo repeated that imprecation, like a lugubrious groan, a terrifying frisson chilled my blood.

"Yes, woe betide everything that loves. Do you know that fatal passion, which burns, which devours, which wears away all the faculties and does harm everywhere? Have you placed your lips on that cup of bitterness? Have you glimpsed the reefs on which your life is about to break?

"Like you, when the first flash of pleasure came to warm my senses, I smiled at the future, and I went to sleep in happiness; but it was a childish dream, for there is no happy amour on earth.

"See rather how it is traversed by all events, how it is crumpled by all storms, how it seems struck by destiny with an eternal anathema! See how everything is conjured to poison its purity, to soil its brightness and to change its sweetness into anguish!

"Have you ever imagined your beloved, lying on her deathbed, struggling against the pain that is pursuing her, the death that is pressing her, seeking to grasp the existence that is escaping her, raising a hand toward you that can no longer find you, turning a gaze toward you that can no longer see you, and exhaling a sigh that will no longer be followed by another sigh?"

"Stop, Lovely!" I cried. "You're tearing me apart!"

"Oh, if you had known the furies of jealousy, if you had groaned over amour deceived, and you were able to compare to those torments what one experiences in weeping over the ashes of a lover, I believe that the scene that is making you pale would seem as mild as a spring morning.

"But to be separated from half of one's soul by the blackest of perfidies, to interrogate a heart that no longer remembers what felt its tears enclose in its bosom, while that of the infidel woman is quivering with sensuality under the lips of a new lover, to languish abandoned while she exists for another, to be alone while she is two . . . that complete the misfortune . . . ! And reflect for a moment! Who knows whether she has not already welcomed a rival? Who knows whether she is crowning him with the flowers you wove her yesterday, and whether she is palpitating in his arms, with a perjured tenderness?"

"Lovely," I said, pushing him away, "leave me alone; you're wounding me!"

"You no longer love me," said Lovely.

"No, I no longer love you . . ."

And I cursed myself for that imposture; but Lovely was already far away.

That sin weighs cruelly upon my heart. He was suffering and I had maltreated him. His reason had gone astray, and I had sharpened his pain; for two days he was wandering on the mountain. He had forgotten his refuge, and I had not extended the hand of a friend to him. I had insulted his chagrins and rejected him harshly . . .

How frightful it is to be culpable toward someone that one loves, and how oppressive that memory is!

He has forgiven me since, but I shall never forgive myself. Lovely, this tear is still a tear of repentance.

He was absent for a long time; every evening I called to him, but he did not respond; I went back alone, and I hid my anxiety from his mother.

Chapter XII

The Evening Prayer

It was a beautiful evening at the beginning of September; three months had gone by since the evening when I saw Stella for the first time at the bottom of Brigitte's little field. I stopped where I had seen her; I sat down where she had sat down; I recalled the first words she had addressed to me; I repeated them aloud; I perceived the eglantine bush; I turned my eyes away; I got up and I went to the cottage. It was dark, but there was no one there, and I had never found the cottage deserted, unless Brigitte and Stella were in the little field. I was quite sure that they were not there, but I returned to it, and I was afflicted, as if I had expected to see them.

There was no danger that my imagination did not foresee and exaggerate. Sometimes I dreaded that her persecutors had discovered her retreat, and that idea reanimated my hatred for them. Sometimes I trembled that she might have been attacked by a ferocious animal or surprised by a brigand; they were rare, but what if Stella had encountered one?

I was walking, preoccupied by a thousand dreads, when I distinguished a light in the foliage a short distance away; I advanced and I heard a slight movement. I had heard a similar noise many times, but the sound had never resounded like that in my heart; it was the rustle of Stella's dress.

The lamp was suspended from a yew; it cast a dying light over Stella, whom it surrounded with a pale aureole, descending along her dress in tremulous reflections and dying out behind her.

Stella was on her knees, motionless, her head bowed, her hands joined, in an attitude of resignation and prayer; occasionally, she addressed a gaze, a sigh and a tear to the heavens.

Brigitte was by her side, her eyes fixed on her ebony rosary, and a radiance from the lamp illuminated her white hair.

Stella heard me; she turned toward me, and made a sign of the hand to bid me to be silent; I knelt down.

It was a long time since I had prayed, and I felt that it would soothe me; that meek communication with God penetrated my senses, elevated my soul, purified my thoughts and applied a consoling balm to my dolors.

I am far from professing the exclusive and poorly understood devotion that rejects the mistaken man and condemns error as crime. I sense that I could see an atheist without horror . . . but I could not see him without pity; he is to be mourned, the unfortunate! He does not know the charm of prayer.

"God has heard us," I said to Stella, when the evening prayer was finished. "That was not a spectacle unworthy of him, that homage consecrated by the double solemnity of misfortune and the darkness, and offered by two outlaws to an outlawed religion; he has heard us and his benediction has fallen upon us . . ."

Stella pointed at a grave covered in moss.

"She too has heard us," she said, "and her benediction had fallen upon us."

The light became brighter, and then went out entirely.

We returned to the cottage without articulating a single word. When we had arrived, Stella sat down and looked at me. She had conserved something of the divinity with whom she had just been communing. I lowered my eyes and listened to her respectfully.

"My friend," said Stella, "I have not always been alone in

these mountains. I had a mother,"

She was about to weep; she gazed at the heavens.

"She had accompanied me in this sad exile," Stella continued, "and we took the place of society. She died. A year ago we dug that grave and I remained alone."

"Alone!" I exclaimed, in a passionate tone of voice. "What about Brigitte," I said, blushing.

"Yes, amity," said Stella. "Amity is pleasant; but who can render me the kisses of a mother? She's dead."

"Do not doubt it, Stella, she lives. She can see you, she still watches over Stella, over her cottage; she collects the tears of filial love, and contemplates with pride the regrets she has left. When time has worn away the springs of your life, Stella, her soul will descend to your final couch, will be united with your soul and will escort you to the foot of the throne of God. Have no doubt of it, Stella, you will see your mother again."

And my thought reposes proudly on that sublime hope of a better life. Say what you will, grim materialist, you will not steal my immortality; my conviction is stronger than your sophisms. I shall live!

What mortal would feel capable of supporting the disdain of the great, the humiliations of poverty and the torments of outraged amour if he could not take refuge in his soul without finding it empty? With what gaze would he follow the coffin of a friend if he believed that he was descending entirely into the tomb? Crushed by the success of crime, sickened by persecutions and widowed of all the illusions of society, what would remain of him if not the profound need to exist beyond death and to witness eternity: the sentiment that smiles at him, which magnifies him, and consoles him for the past by taking possession of the future?

Why had Stella not deposited that secret in my heart sooner? *You still have a mother*, Stella said, *and the secrets of dolor importune the fortunate.*

Fortunate! And Stella was not!

XIII

The Esplanade

Some time later, Stella was coming back with me from Brigitte's little field, and we stopped on a verdant esplanade from which the view extended into a little valley.

The sun was setting, and its chariot of fire was already tracing a crimson band in the occident; its rays, rising to the tips of rocks, painted them with brilliant colors, which they reflected over the landscape, and which tinted all the objects rose pink.

I looked tenderly at Stella; her soul was associated with the vast concert of amour that saluted the dusk, and I did not know whether it was that ravishing scene that embellished her further in my eyes, or whether it was her that embellished nature.

I put my arm around her, and she laid her head on my breast; a mild languor closed her eyelids; a gentle warmth animated her complexion; her heart was beating rapidly. I was hot; I had a fever; my lips were desiccated as if by an ardent thirst; I united them with her lips, and I tottered, I shuddered, I could no longer see . . .

We descended from the esplanade, and Stella did not look at me or speak to me; I was so emotional that I did not perceive that we had quit the path to the cottage. We arrived at the boscage of the prayer; the sun had set; the lamp was suspended from the yew, and we fell to our knees,

The next day, we passed close to the esplanade; Stella smiled at me, and took a winding path.

Chapter XIV

The Garland

I was walking beside her; I perceived clumps of columbines on the rock; I picked them and brought them to her. She wove them into a garland, wrapped them in a crown around her blonde hair and let them fall in festoons over her shoulders, in the manner in which victims are ornamented. That funeral ornament reminded her of her sacrificed friends, and she strewed the flowers in her path, like an expiatory tribute to the manes of the innocent.

"Yes, Stella," I cried, "they have frightened the fatherland with their audacity and their crimes; they have devastated the temples, they have killed peace, they have outlawed virtue; they have cut the throats of daughters in their fathers' arms, husbands on the bosom of their beloved wives; they have made our native land the patrimony of executioners, and they have fertilized it with the cadavers of our parents; they have banished you, Stella, and I can never seal a kiss of pardon on their bloody lips. Never! *Vengeance and malediction to the tyrants!*

"When justice is no more than a word, vengeance becomes a right, and as soon as the laws contemplate, in a cowardly silence, the proud impunity of crime, it requires the dagger of the oppressed to take the place of judge and friend!"

I have said that; for there are times when I would have liked to be armed with the sword of the exterminator, in order to fell all those around me who have infringed my liberty and hindered my affections; but it is an aberration that outrages nature and degrades humanity.

"May the clemency of God descend upon them," said Stella; and I repeated it with her.

A great expression of piety shone in her gaze; one might have taken her then for an angelic benefactor summoning upon humans the indulgence of the Almighty; and she held the place of the invisible ring that unites Heaven and earth, the author and the creature.

I bent a knee in order to adore her; but her eyes, veiled by a cloud of amour, encountered mine, and I forgot the prayer that was already wandering over my mouth.

Stella was no longer only a mortal.

Chapter XV

The Fault

The sky was preparing a storm.

A hot wind was rolling whirlwinds of sand in the atmosphere and curbing the crowns of the forests, which ceded, groaning; thick clouds veiled the sun; vast darkness accumulated over the horizon, and wood-pigeons uttered dolorous cries from time to time.

I think that if amour did not exist, that disorder of the elements would make the need for it felt.

When we had arrived at the cottage, I sat down next to Stella, and Stella drew closer. I was at the peak of happiness, but I wanted something more. There was a tempest in my bosom, as in nature.

I sought all her gazes; I kept watch on all her movements. If I had found in her eyes a thought that was not for me I would have been jealous.

A flash of lightning descended over the cottage. It seemed to me that it established a more perfect communication between us; I wrapped my arms around her, and hers were already hugging me involuntarily.

The thunder rumbled; lightning could have struck me in that minute of ecstasy and the fortunate of the earth would have envied my tomb.

However, a confused desire ran through my veins, and my blood flowed back toward the heart. I lifted Stella up and held her tightly against me, and my inflamed mouth encountered her mouth . . .

At first, Stella trembled . . . soon she was deprived of life; her entire soul was united with mine in the intoxication of the kiss . . .

I no longer know what I experienced . . . it was a vague but delectable dream, which robbed me even of the sentiment of my being . . .

I had been culpable, since happiness can be a crime.

Chapter XVI

The Wedding Ring

My hand was fixed in Stella's hand, which was repelling it feebly.

As I disengaged my interlaced fingers, I caused a ring to fall, which divided in two at my feet.

"Wretch!" she cried, in a tone of despair. "I'm married . . ."

Married!

If the world had collapsed under its own weight, and I had remained standing in the middle of its rubble, all my faculties would have been crumpled in a less painful manner.

I tried to reject that idea, but it had attained the depths of my heart.

Chapter XVII

Sophisms

I went down the road to the cottage rapidly; Brigitte passed close to me.

"God have pity on us!" she said. "I thought that storm would overturn the mountain on its foundations. I was sitting up there under the rock that curves over like a vault, and I saw the whole sky on fire. Three times a long flame launched forth from the bell-tower of Sainte-Marie, and the bird of death was moaning in the fir trees. God have pity on those who have a good conscience!"

I shivered.

"But see, Monsieur," Brigitte said, "the storm is recommencing; you'd be better in the cottage."

"Better, Brigitte! Oh, no . . ."

The storm was indeed recommencing; a sudden light sometimes flashed over the precipice; an impetuous wind was blowing through the heather and making my hair float; a cold rain was steaming over my face and traversing my garments; but that did me good. My imagination reposed from its tempests in those of the mountain, and my disturbance was soothed in being thus shared by nature.

Oh well! I said, suddenly. *Married! What does that word signify, and does it have magic to force me to terror? Does that vain word affect my ears differently than other modifications of the voice? And furthermore, what is marriage itself if not an institution funded by human caprice, sanctified by prejudice and maintained by habitude? By what right does that despotic link subjugate the future to the present? What is the nature of the bizarre oath that submits all the inclinations of life to the will of one day? And what individual is audacious enough to be able to say, in the verity of his heart: "Now I swear not to love any longer."*

But it is not sufficient to enchain them to one another for eternity, and make them a long torture of that union, which would be happiness if it were only formed by amour, if it were only constrained by sentiment! As often as not they have united without interrogating their hearts, without consulting their rapports; they have immolated the peace of an entire generation to frivolous interests, to coldly calculated conventions; they have sold, for a price of gold, favors that wither as soon as one succeeds in paying for them; and the modest virgin who inspires tenderness and desire around her has been obliged to share her nuptial couch with hideous decrepitude, like a nascent rose that has been transplanted on a tomb.

That was not the intention of Providence; it wanted, in its protective designs, everything that respires to be happy; it had matched all characters with a beneficent care; it had prepared secret sympathies that were the signal and the guarantee of amour.

Am I culpable because the passions of men have violated the law of nature and destroyed the work of God?

And if I have conserved myself pure in the midst of corruption, if I have kept my soul new amid the disorders of society, do I not have the right to free myself from the yoke that it has invented for vice?

My soul rose up against that paradox, and folded back upon itself with fright.

The lightning fell.

Chapter XVIII

The Last Adieu

As soon as dawn illuminated the interior of the cottage I got ready to return to Stella. I desired and dreaded to see her, and the mysterious word pursued me with the relentlessness of an enemy.

I arrived in the little field; I recognized the eglantine bush; it had suffered from the storm and its leafless branches were inclined over the soil.

The fire from the sky had passed through the broom.

I went into Stella's room. She was lying on a camp bed covered by a rush mat; her body was enveloped in a shroud of an obscure color, which she had folded over her breast, and her hair was scattered around her; she was pale, but when I was there, an ardent fever, which rose from her breast, gradually tinted her cheeks deep red.

I stopped at a distance and remained immobile, waiting for her to speak to me.

"I was waiting for you," Stella said, with a bitter smile. "I have many things to tell you."

I sat down.

"An hour comes when one can be judged," she said, "and that hour has come for me, fortunate if divine justice does not condemn me like my heart!

"I have been culpable since I saw you for the first time. Since I saw you for the first time I have loved you. The edict of my destiny was cruel; it has weighed with all its force upon my head. Do you believe that an adulterous woman can find grace before God?"

She remained silent for a time, and continued: "I was born of a noble family, which honored its titles by its virtues; it was outlawed. I had lost my father in my early years, and I have forgotten his memory. My mother has died here, and I have soiled her bed of dolor! They had given me a husband of my choice, and I have betrayed him.

"When he was snatched from my arms in order to rally to the flag of a disastrous cause, he said to me as he gave me the last kiss: 'Stella, keep your heart for me'—and I have not kept my heart. He is wandering as a deserter, miserable and rejected, in unknown lands; he is wandering, overwhelmed by fatigue and by need, suffering from hunger and thirst; but he is thinking of me; he is consoling himself in my amour, and my amour has deceived him!

"Why have I hidden that fatal secret from you? A hundred times it approached my lips, my heart was constricted and I trembled to see you divine what I ought to have told you. Why have I met you? I would still be tranquil; I could still think about my husband without shuddering with shame, and I could implore my mother's shade without terror. I have lost everything; I no longer dare think either about my mother or my husband!

"Do you believe," she repeated, in an altered voice, "that an adulterous woman can find grace before God?"

She opened the Bible, searched for the page of the adulterous woman, attached her gaze to it, and moistened it with tears.

I pleased myself in believing that the recording angel who was floating over the cottage would allow himself to be flexed by her repentance, and would wipe away the sin with those tears.

I was close to her then; she took my hand and raised it toward the sky. "You," she said, "are not culpable; you will not follow me into eternal reprobation; it is me alone who has broken the knot; it is on me alone that all vengeances ought to fall, and I absolve you before the one who judges the actions of men, for your heart is unstained . . .

"But go away," Stella added. "Go away forever; that is Stella's final prayer, your lover's last wish. Leave me with my regrets; I need to prepare my soul to submit to its judgment."

"Stella!" I cried, throwing myself down at her knees; and I covered her hand with kisses.

"Leave me," she said. "Your tears burn me like your kisses. Go away."

And her pulse weakened, her inflamed respiration became slower, the movement of her heart remained suspended.

I ran to the door; I wanted to see her again, and her livid lips stammered an adieu.

Chapter XIX

The Village Bell

During that time, I did not return to the cottage.

I wandered around her dwelling with no other nourishment than the wild fruits of the autumn and no other bed than the damp earth, and I roamed the deserted countryside like a shade in pain that the angels of the night had exiled from its coffin.

On the fifth evening I came to sit down under the rock that had served Brigitte as a refuge during the storm.

While considering that obscure dome and the uninhabited grotto, parading my eyes over the solitude that surrounded it, searching that vast area in vain for something that respired, I convinced myself that I had plunged into eternal silence; that God had relegated me so far from his sight that what I could see was no more than an uncertain reminiscence of what I had seen.

The day ended; my senses became torpid, but my dolor was still awake.

I dreamed that I was surrounded by images of death, and that I was walking with difficulty through piles of bones. A funereal torch, carried before me by an invisible power, illuminated the horrors of my passage with its flame. At the end of that mortuary path I perceived Stella clad in the diaphanous robe of phantoms; I extended my arm toward her, but I only grasped a cloud.

Then I tore from my breast a cry of terror that was prolonged in the coverts of the mountain, and I stood up on my rock.

It was still there, the fatal torch, as I had seen it in my sleep; it was coming down the slope of the hill slowly, and my avid gaze never ceased to fix upon it, until its blue-tinted light was effaced in the darkness.

I was trying to reassure my reason against that frightening presage when the bell of Sainte-Marie suddenly began to toll. Its vibrations were interrupted by a frightful calm that filled the interval. Between that dream, that torch and that distressing harmony, there was a mysterious liaison of ideas that squeezed my heart.

I had moved forward, without any purpose in the difficult avenues of the grotto . . . and that light, that memory . . . I was in the boscage of the prayer . . . my blood froze . . .

Chapter XX

One More Grave

One more grave . . . a newly dug grave! Murderers! What have you done to Stella?

Yes, repeat, repeat again, Brigitte! Crush me with all the burden of my dolor. Yes, it's me who is the cause . . .

And my reason was alienated. I launched myself into the woods; I filled the air with my cries, I tore out my hair, I tore my garments, I rolled on the sharp points of rocks, and, broken, bruised and bloody, covered in dust and wounds, I lost consciousness.

Chapter XXI

No More Happiness

That night seemed as long as eternity to me, for I had conserved the faculty of feeling in order to exercise it on frightful chimeras.

The scene of Stella's death pursued my fatigued imagination. I saw her, in her funereal sheet, advance a desiccated foot over the grave and fall against the earth, which resounded with her fall. Sometimes it seemed to me that a cruel dream had deceived us, and that Stella was not dead. I heard her knocking against the planks of the bier, and uttering a muffled plaint. I lifted the stone that weighed upon her. I broke her hideous prison and I enveloped her in my arms in order to warm her heart, already cold, on my heart. Then the violent breath of storms lifted us up, thus united, into the air, pushed us, shivering, over glacial seas, held us suspended over the seething craters of volcanoes in the midst of burning lava, and precipitated us from tempest to tempest in the depths of the abyss.

When I came round I was beside Lovely; he had staunched my blood, washed my face and dripped cold water over my temples and on my bosom. That was beside the spring where I had encountered him on arriving in the mountains. The connection was terrible.

"Alas," I cried, "no more repose, no more happiness!" And I got up, vomiting frightful imprecations against destiny. Then I recounted my misfortunes to Lovely. He wept, but I could not weep.

"Listen," Lovely said to me, when the narration had finished, "now that you also have experience of great dolors, I believe that we are better suited, and my amity will calm your pain. One day, when your heart has healed, I shall tell you mine, and in seeing how misfortune can be reproduced in different forms, you'll admit that no man has the right to say that he is the most unfortunate. You're revolting against that idea," Lovely continued, "but if you knew . . ."

"Oh, tell me, Lovely, why didn't you die?"

"Oh," said Lovely, "I had a mother. It would have devastated her."

"Me too, I have a mother,"

"And then," he added, "I ought to render thanks to Providence for having disputed my days with despair. If I were dead, who would have consoled you?"

That is true. Has one the right to dispose of one's life, while unfortunates still remain?

I have suffered all that, and I have lived.

Chapter XXII

She is Immortal

My pains took a long time to soften. For a long time I sought deserts, solitude and nocturnal scenes, which seemed to give my dolor something calmer and more imposing. Every time the majestic disk of the moon rose in the sky and advanced over the horizon in its melancholy beauty, I roamed, pensively, the summits of the mountains, and when I allowed my gaze to fall toward the place where I had encountered Stella, I asked of Stella again all that we had seen together, and I groaned.

Often I believed that I distinguished in the shadows vague forms wandering around me, and I interrogated those phantoms, vain illusions of the darkness, regarding the problems of eternity.

"What has become of Stella?" I said. "Is she lost like you in the clouds, or is she still asleep, immobile in the grave that has been dug for her? Does the sound of the waters of the torrent sometimes trouble her slumber? Is she sensitive to the cold of winter? When long icicles are suspended from the branches of the yews and the rain penetrates the earth that envelops her, does she say: 'I'm cold'? Tell me; tell me, above all whether her soul is despoiled in its new life of all the memories of her past life, whether she still thinks about me, and whether, when I pronounce the name Stella, my lament reaches her heart?"

No, Stella no longer hears the storms of the mountain, and the north wind that groans in the fir trees respects the silence of her tomb.

Stella will sleep until the elements are confounded and time finishes. When the day comes, she will sit down beside her mother amid the radiance of an immortal light, and she will respire an eternity of delights in an eternity of repose.

When the day comes, and Stella approaches her judge, he will not arm his forehead with menacing lightning; and since there is a common law for everything that respires and loves, it is virtue, which is the wellbeing of every beloved being; God will not reject from his bosom those who have loved a great deal. What is divinity itself if not the need to love that fills all of creation, and which is the source of good, the motive of nature and the soul of the universe? Amour is the virtue of humanity; there are only punishments in the other life for those who have hated.

Sleep in peace, my Stella; your immortality will be mild. The poison of regrets is not mingled with the nectar of the blissful. Sleep in peace, my Stella; you were born to love, and you have accomplished your destiny on the earth.

One day, I shall return to you . . .

Stella, one day . . . one day . . .

When the angel of the last judgment awakens the dust of human beings on the dust of worlds, I shall get up without terror, for I have not ceased to be pure; I shall appear with confidence before the justice of God. At that time, I shall return to you, you will smile at me and we shall be reunited forever. Then, Stella, nothing will any longer be able to separate us; neither death, nor men, nor tyrants, nor nature; the times of proscription will be effaced; the innocents will have found their avenger and their recompense; the oppressors will be subjected to their punishment; evil will be forgotten and even destruction will be no more.

Thus, my soul, overwhelmed by so many perplexities, will be released from them in the peace of the future.

Chapter XXIII, and Last

Conclusion

A year went by and I was able to see the cottage again.

For some time I have been living there with Brigitte, Lovely and his mother. We cultivate the little field. Lovely and I; every evening, we say a prayer in the boscage of the tombs, and I have planted a cypress here, which is beginning to shade Stella's grave.

We have changed nothing in the furniture of her room; it is as it was then. Stella is missing, but sometimes I think that I still see her there.

And I believe that I will see her again.

THE END OF *THE OUTLAWS*

Letter

From a Curé in the Vosges to the Editor

Monsieur, I remember very clearly having seen you during one of your botanical expeditions in the Vosges, and having conversed with you about the unfortunate young man in whom you were so keenly interested; but although I have had, since then, more intimate relations with him than previously, I can only give you uncertain information regarding his present fate.

Some time after your departure, I was summoned to the cottage in order to administer spiritual aid to him during a slow illness, by which he had been attained since the death of his friend. He recounted his dolors to me and showed me his memoirs, which you have read, and of which you desired me to try to procure the fragments for you. I will confess to you that that touching expression of a suffering soul, which reigns therein from the beginning to the end, caused me a profound emotion, and that on seeing his tears I could not retain mine.

However, I had often remarked in that writing very bold propositions on several points of religion and morality, and surges of despair that seemed to depart from a heart accustomed to mistrusting providence. I observed to him that those passages were unworthy of an honest man, and that they had escaped from an imagination too strongly affected by his chagrins. He responded that he repented of having written that, and he burned everything that I had specifically condemned; after which he gave me the rest, telling me that he had initially had the project of publishing those fatal details, but that he believed that it might be best to leave them in eternal forgetfulness.

After his reestablishment I encountered him at the bottom of a small field that belongs to old Brigitte, and he hugged me affectionately to his heart. He told me that he was a little calmer, that his health was beginning to stabilize, and that he hoped to be entirely well before long. He added that he left me the master of the papers he had confided to me, and that I could dispose of them as I thought good, with the result that in transferring the property of that sad heritage of misfortune to you, I am not running the risk of violating his last will.

A few days after that conversation, the young man disappeared, without anyone being able to discover precisely what had become of him. Many conjectures, more or less plausible, were hazarded regarding that event, but they did not appease my anxiety.

I made the decision to go to the cottage, where I found the unfortunate man's friends in tears; it was a heart-rending scene that made me feel very ill. I tried to give them consolation, but it was impossible for the moment; they were suffering too much. I quit them, and confided their cure to time, which alone has the power to scar over the wounds of the soul.

I passed through the boscage where Stella and her mother are buried, and where Lovely's mortal remains had recently been deposited. The small cypress that had grown over the lover's grave had been uprooted by a gust of wind; I ordered that it be replaced with some ceremony, and the next day I said prayers in the same place, in the presence of several mountain-dwellers, for the repose of those souls, which had been so cruelly agitated by passions, and which were so worthy to remain without affliction in the world.

Afterwards, I pursued my enquires regarding the fate of our friend, and everything that was reported to me made me tremble.

One day, the rumor spread in the village that his body had been recognized floating in the torrent, and that the flooding waters had deposited it on a little island that you might have perceived in the valley, where it is enclosed by the detours of the stream. I went there in a boat, but the cadaver was so disfigured that it was impossible for me to recover any indication that could justify the presumptions of the people. I had it given a sepulcher, and I swear to you that the circumstances left me in such doubt regarding the future life of the unfortunate that I could only sleep after having assured myself that it was not him by an inspection of the suicide's garments, which were discovered in the sand a week later.

A short time afterwards, and, so far as I can recall, toward the end of that year, the public newssheets reported than an émigré had been arrested on the mountain, and that the unfortunate man was dead.

In my ignorance regarding his veritable name, I could not enlighten myself regarding the frightful relation that there was between that news and the date of his absence, but a man from the town, who had witnessed the death of the émigré, depicted him to us with features so similar to that of the unfortunate fellow that we dared not fail to recognize him, and we all cried: "It's him!"

It is, however, still possible that we have been misled by one of those striking resemblances that are sometimes observed in the world, and I like to believe that our friend is not lost forever, that Heaven did not want the experience of his misfortunes to be fruitless and that it will have conserved his life in order to render its example to another generation.

As for the intention you have to give the public the memoirs that I am addressing to you, I believe, in fact, that the depiction of the woes that followed an illegitimate passion would not be without utility in these days of corruption; but your enterprise will not be devoid of inconvenience; and merely considering the jurisdiction of taste, it has always seemed to me that writings of this nature are a poor gift to make to letters. You felt that yourself when you read it on the mountain, and you tried to destroy that obstacle by means that it is too facile to combat.

I agree that an uneven style ought to be tolerated in a book that is only a rapid effusion of sensibility, and in which words come to represent sensations without the author being occupied greatly in arranging them with order and nuancing the transitions.

I confess that it was impossible not to let escape many repetitions and similar turns of phrase in a work in which all the ideas are born of a single sentiment in almost identical circumstances.

I know that there are many things that appear to us to be bizarre, extravagant and gigantic, which would perhaps have come to us in the same situation, and that it is not astonishing that there is a derangement in the expression every time there is disorder in the thought.

As soon as a production in which these faults are remarked falls into the hands of a man of taste, however, do you not think that it would be better to allow it to circulate among a small number of persons than to deliver it to the crowd, which will only extract harmful or exaggerated ideas from it, and to the critics, who will tear it apart for want of having been able to feel it?

Permit me also to make the observation that the leaves that our friend has sacrificed to my representations contained, if I might express myself in that way, a kind of suture thread that links all the incidents of the story, and the absence of which has left, between the fragments such as they are today, a void that is injurious to the progress and interest of the work.

Will people attempt to fill in those intervals? I do not think that the cry of nature is easy to imitate, and I confess that I fear that those lacunae will only be substituted by an insipid marquetry.

However, I am addressing the fragments to you, and I shall rely, with regard to their employment, as much on your opinion as that of the respectable men that you propose to consult.

If you hope that this monument might be useful, if you believe that the misfortunes of a twenty-year-old outlaw might make a few tears flow, that his virtues might find a few enthusiasts, that the image of his remorse might prevent a few aberrations, do not hesitate.

In any case, all things considered, honest hearts are so rare that it is just and laudable to consecrate their memory.

The Painter of Salzburg;
or,
A Journal of the Emotions of a Heart in Pain

25 August

Yes, all the events of life are in proportion to human strength, since my heart has not broken.

I still wonder whether it is not some bad dream that has brought me to this blasphemy—Eulalie marrying someone else!—and I look around to assure myself that I am awake; and I am desperate when I find nature in the same order as before. It would be better if my reason had gone astray. Sometimes, too, I would like to repose in my courage, but suddenly, that incredible news has just resounded in my ear, and gripped me with mortal anguish.

I expected misfortunes, but that misfortune is too bitter! Banished from Bavaria as a wretched troublemaker,[1] outlawed and fugitive, wandering for two years from the banks of the Danube to the mountains of Scotland, I had been robbed of everything, homeland and honor. I still had Eulalie, however: that ineffable memory enchanted my poverty and populated my solitude. I was glad of the future and of her . . .

Yesterday, still, palpitating with desire, impatience and amour, I came . . . I believed . . . and today . . . !

---

1 Salzburg was not in Bavaria at the time when this story was written, and it is difficult to determine in what year it is set, why the narrator might have been banished, or how he was able to return. In December 1801, when French troops commanded by Napoléon were drawing nearer to the city, its ruler, the Prince-Archbishop Hieronymus von Colloredo, fled, never to return, but contemporary readers are unlikely have assumed that the story is set in the months leading up to that upheaval or its aftermath, and might well have made the judgment that it is set in the distant past.

26 August

There is an idea that constricts my heart, a dolorous and mortal idea.

How is it that our most profound expressions have something so vague and so uncertain that the revolution of a few months, a few days, or an almost indivisible instant can efface them? What is the nature of that sentiment, so violent in its intoxication, so rapid in its duration, that aspires to embrace the future, but that a year devours? Is it true that human affections are only an inverted hourglass, which is gradually allowing to escape everything that it has been given to contain? And is it necessary that we die everywhere that we have lived—even where one would find so much sweetness in immortalizing oneself, in the hearts of those who love us?

Oh, how wise Providence was when it assigned such a brief career to the travelers of life. If it had been more prodigal with days, and time had brought the hours of our destruction more slowly, how many men would have been able to flatter themselves with dragging with them a few memories of their youth? After having wandered in an endless circle of ever-new sensations, a man would arrive alone at the monument, and having cast an extinct gaze over the obscure and confused stage of the past, he would search it in vain for one of the emotions of his first age; he would have forgotten everything. Everything, from the first kiss of his beloved to his father's white hair!

But if the vulgar use up their days in miserable irresolution, it seemed to me, at least, that it was given to certain souls to eternalize their sentiments. Once, I thought that I had found it, that soul proximal to my own soul, and I confided my happiness to it. Who could describe all that charm that they had, those hours of intoxication when, leaning over Eulalie's bosom, respiring her breath, attentive to her slightest heartbeat, all my faculties sinking into one of her gazes? It is, however, her who deceived me, and when, pressing her with the sad embrace of a long farewell, I asked her for the title of husband, she promised me before the father of all amour. By what right has she stolen it from me? Why has she reduced me to this void?

They have all forgotten me, then! For I think that if some friendly voice had made my name vibrate in the midst of the solemn perjury . . .

But they have all forgotten me, and no one said to her: "Tremble, Eulalie, God sees you!" They have all forgotten me, and that treason was consummated.

28 August

This evening I was wandering at hazard; and, I don't know how it happened, I felt a weight oppressing me, a cloud troubling my sight, a fire running through my blood, and I sat down. A moment later I raised my eyes and I recognized the house opposite as Eulalie's dwelling. Her room was illuminated. Eulalie came and stopped behind the window, in a silent contemplation. She was suffering, because she was looking at the sky. Her bosom seemed inflated, her hair was scattered; she put her hand to her forehead; it was doubtless burning. Then she retired without having perceived me, and I saw her shadow grow on the wall and become confounded with all the other shadows. I wanted to speak, but I could not find a voice, and I was mute with shock, like a nocturnal traveler who encounters an apparition.

After that I approached the window, and I plunged myself into the light that descended from it. But I was unable to support those agitations for long; I resumed my route sadly, and when I arrived home my legs gave way; I let myself fall to the floor and I dissolved in tears.

29 August

Everything is conspiring to crush me. While wandering in the countryside I saw, outside a pretty farmhouse, a neatly-dressed woman, and, before I could distinguish her features, she threw herself into my arms and moistened my cheeks with tears. As I hesitated, she said: "Don't you recognize me? It's me, I'm the young woman whom despair had driven to suicide, whom you saved at the risk of your own life; it's me, whom you heaped with so many benefits, whom you extracted from poverty, whom you rendered to wellbeing; it's to you that I owe the life I enjoy, and my dear husband, and my beloved children; and I want . . ."

She wanted me to see her children.

"Stop, stop," I said to her, pressing her hand against my heart, "you don't know whether I'm strong enough for all this."

"And that young lady?" she added, mysteriously. "May Heaven be propitious to both of you! So beautiful, and such a great soul! Oh, with how many joys must she now be embellishing your existence!"

At those words I turned my face away, shivering with indignation and dolor. And the woman thought . . .

"Yes, killed, dead, lost forever!" I cried, and I abandoned her to the error of her regrets.

On returning here I learned that Eulalie had left today for the country. Left! Did she know? Oh, I shall leave, I shall leave too; and, a thousand times already I have turned the knife against my breast, and a thousand times I have asked God for death and annihilation—annihilation, for to be resurrected, and to remember what one has lived . . . I would rather not go. But perhaps I would not come back as I am . . . and the change . . . and then, in any case, it would require some time to adjust to a new way of lie . . .

Those are important considerations . . .

2 September

The day has been calm, the sky pure and placid; but at the moment when the sun descended in its occidental pomp, the horizon was suddenly enveloped by clouds, like a girdle, and gradually, a great darkness devoured the twilight.

Thus, I said, *I commenced in a mild and bright dawn, and I am going to finish, like this day, in the trouble of a nebulous dusk.* At that idea, I represented to myself, with a great deal of force, the new and superb sensations of the beautiful age, and I searched in my memory for the youthful desires and naïve hopes of a virgin soul, and I cradled myself in those memories.

Meanwhile, frequent lightning flashes traversed the atmosphere, and opened bright avenues and vast fiery porticos in the torn clouds. The thunderbolts slid beneath the vaults of night like a flamboyant sword, but by their transient light sinister shadows could sometimes be seen hovering over the valley, similar to those vengeful spirits that are sent on the wings of the tempest to frighten the children of men. The winds quivered in the forests or groaned in the abysms, and their impetuous voices were confused in the depths of the mountains with the grave sounds of the tocsin, the tumult of the waterfall and the rumbles of the thunder; and even in the sad and terrible silence that succeeded those imposing harmonies, strange noises and mysterious concerts could be distinguished, like those that must rise up in the solemnities of Heaven.

In these upheavals that desolate creation there is a balm for the heart's wounds, because our afflictions are absorbed by such august afflictions, and our compassion is obliged to spread out over a world. Just now, for example, I identified with that suffering nature and I embraced it entire with my pity.

I tried to maintain myself in that state, but since I am suffering alone, it was necessary for my pity only to react on myself.

3 September

I had often desired to see the abandoned monastery again, where I once collected touching impressions in the silence of cloisters. I remembered walking with Eulalie among its confused ruins and dilapidated buildings; and on perceiving at the summit of the hill the long steeple of the church, boldly launched into the air, I shivered with joy, as if at the approach of a friend. But I observed, not without dolor, that the breaches in the wall had been repaired, and the hedges had been pruned.

The disaster of demolished enclosures and the energy of a free and wild vegetation had imprinted sensations of a very different grandeur on me. But how they had laid siege to my thoughts, when, having arrived in the vestibule, I heard the sound of my footsteps resounding in the echoes of the chapels and the sanctuary; and how the trembling doors creaked as they rotated with difficulty on their hinges! With what lurches of the heart and what sensuality of tears I traversed the resonant corridors and devastated courtyards, to reach the foot of the great stairway of the terrace! There escaped, in the middle of the broken steps, the velvety cylinders of mullein, the blue bells of campanulas, clumps of thale-cress and tufts of gilded celandine; henbane grew there too, with its ashen colors and bruised flowers.

I leaned against a column, the only one that remained standing, like some noble orphan of an unfortunate family;

and nearby, there was also a large elm, which scarcely appeared above the old debris, but whose summit had already been burned by celestial fire.

I said: *Why is my genius no longer anything but a ruin? Why has the nature that I found so beautiful been discolored before its time? Why do I not still have the creative power, the exquisite delicacy and the flower of sentiment that inspired my first works? Now my pencils are cold, my canvases inanimate, and my soul is extinguished by dolors. If a powerful and magnificent idea appears to me sometimes, I struggle in vain to fix it. Soon my blood ferments and I no longer find anything but bizarre hues and gigantic forms, or I become weary of feeling, and then it degrades and pales under my brushes. Perhaps it's because the image of Eulalie reposes with too much empire in the forefront of my memory, and distracts me.*

In the meantime, I approached the ancient cemetery of the monks, and I saw a woman outlined there, sitting on a tomb. She cast her eyes upon me, and when mine encountered them I was dazzled, as if a meteor had passed before my sight, and I fell to my knees. Then Eulalie—it was her—advanced, lifted my trembling hand, and addressed words of consolation to me.

When I came round, and I was able to take account of that events; when I had reflected on the sinister hazard that had prepared that sepulchral rendezvous; when I had foreseen what our conversation would have of the painful and what new impressions were about to torment my heart . . . I desired that an abyss might open beneath our feet and bury both of us.

"You, here," I said, finally.

"Here," she replied. "It's in these places full of you, in the midst of my happy memories, that I wanted to be, and even that thought would be culpable today . . . culpable!" she added, ardently, "may Heaven have pity on us!" But she pronounced those words with a tone of voice, a sigh and a gaze that were no longer made for me.

However, I sat down beside her and abandoned myself to all my regrets; I expanded myself in imprecations against destiny and against her; I reminded her of the day of my banishment, the fatal hour of our separation, and the oaths that she had violated, oaths sealed by so many kisses and tears. I wept again with a great deal of bitterness, and the sobs that suffocated me prevented me from continuing.

"May the will of God be done," said Eulalie, "but let it not permit you to condemn me without having heard me. Do you know what I have suffered? Were you walking beside me when I watched the last traces of your passage, and my eyes, troubled by tears, could no longer distinguish the place from which you had departed? Did you witness the long evenings that I spent groaning, occupying myself with you? Did you see me, finally—and I why did I not die that day? I believed that I would, and hoped to die, because I didn't think that the feeble heart of a woman could contain so much dolor—tell me, did you see me, ready to expire of despair at the news of your death?"

At that word, which struck me for the first time, I sighed, so much charm did the mere thought offer me and inspire me with the desire that I might have died in that way, carrying away her amour and regretted by her! She went on:

"Monsieur Spronck arrived in Salzburg from Carinthia; he was introduced to us. I saw him. He pleased my mother. As for me . . . I don't know—but I found, as she did, that he had something of your air and your manner of feeling, and, above all, that imprint of melancholy, the touching character of a soul nourished on hidden troubles, something that imposed upon us before we had attempted to define it. He had, moreover, experienced great chagrins. The interest he inspired in me, he had obtained from you. Is it not true that there is a tender pity that one cannot refuse to misfortune?

"You know, Charles, that during your absence I lost my mother. When she saw the fatal moment coming, she summoned us to her—him too. At first she looked at me, and a cloud of anxiety seemed to tarnish the gleam that had begun to shine in her visage. Then she looked at us both together; she placed Spronck's hand in mine, and an expression of irresistible determination settled on her dying lips; then she passed so gently from this life into eternity that one might have thought she was asleep if our dolor had not testified that she was no more. That is how, a deplorable heritage of misfortune and death, I became the wife of another; it is thus that I betrayed your memory in order to obey the voice of nature and the tomb; thus, what all the powers of the earth could not have constrained me to do, my mother's last gaze obtained from me . . ."

Having said that, Eulalie turned to me with a mild compassion. "Charles," she said, "we are like two voyagers in the desert who had dreamed of repose and the homeland, and who resumed a laborious path through the sand. Everything has vanished—but arm yourself with courage, and be sure, Charles, that my amity will follow you . . ."

As she pronounced those words she slipped away, disappearing by favor of the darkness that descended over the monastery. I followed her; I wanted to find her and see her once more; but the sound I heard was that of the weeping willow, which was shivering in its scattered branches and it melancholy tresses.

Suddenly, I repeated these words: *her amity will follow me*; and with what sweetness I am repeating them now. That idea soothed my senses, embalmed the air and cast over all nature an indefinable charm that held enchantment. I was happier—why not? I was avid for affection; and God knows with what chimeras I sometimes filled the void of my heart!

4 September

Her amity! Up to what point can that sentiment be sufficient for me, that is the question? What can there be in common between a cold and austere society which only has serious joys and compassed pleasures, and the union full of intoxication and sensuality in which two individuals predestined to cherish one another confound their entire existence; between that aliment of a few impoverished souls and the pure and regenerative fire that devours life and reproduces it? Amity? A toy to ward off dolor thrown to a stubborn child who asks for the return of the object that has been taken from him.

At twenty-three, I am cruelly disillusioned with all the things of the earth, and I have entered into a great disdain for society and myself, for I have seen that there is only affliction in nature, and that the heart of a man only hosts bitterness. He arrives, he cast an inexperienced gaze over what surrounds him, and his immense affection avidly embraces all creatures. He believes that, by himself, he can animate another world while he is marching, alas, thorough a dead one, and he squanders his fleeting days and his inconsiderate amour in vain. Soon, he observes, he learns, he judges; already, his imagination is being extinguished, his illusions withering, his sphere is shrinking, all his relationships are contracting around him, until the moment when a dolorous experience shines in his eyes, like a torch ignited over a tomb, and completes the illumination of his void. In sum, he only finds dull and refractory souls; amity neglects him, amour betrays him, society rejects him; he senses that all bonds are about to be broken. They do, indeed, break, and he is fortunate if he cedes himself to the great laceration. After that epoch, I no longer see anything but egotists who have succeeded in desiccating their hearts and enthusiasts who exhaust themselves upon chimeras.

Drifting in an ocean of anxieties and dolors, when one is released with so much difficulty from so many violent emotions, when exaggerated appreciations have scarcely begun to be rectified, death comes along, rapid and unexpected, to grip you in its inflexible arms and put you to sleep entirely in the silence of the tomb . . .

6 September

Another dolorous memory! This evening, I found myself again on the river bank the corner of a semi-demolished bastion, at the foot of which we reposed during our walks on beautiful summer evenings. The carpet of moss where we so often sat has conserved its freshness; the menacing ruin that looms over it is still standing. I sometimes thought that it might bury us in its fall; now, it has survived the immortal love that Eulalie had sworn to me, and the immortal felicity that she promised me. There, a few days before my departure, following the movement of the water with my eyes and transporting myself in thought into the midst of those distant seas to which I was about to follow it, penetrated by dolor at the idea of a separation that might be irreparable, I seized Eulalie's hand and inundated it with tears. As troubled as me, she tried to distract me from an excessively painful sentiment by singing one of the ballads that had charmed my evenings so many times. It was—can I ever forget it? Oh, there is not a note of her voice that does not still resound in my heart!

Claire and Paulin with simplicity
  Spent their days,
Seeing their youth flourish
  And their amour.
Nothing in appearance

Could disunite them;
The time dear to their hope
Was about to come.

They only dreamed of hymen and joy,
Happy leisures
That a consoling God sends
To lovers.
But Paulin's father comes:
". . . It's necessary to leave.
And from the love of your Claire
. . .To depart."

He went toward his future
. . . In great emotion,
"Deplorable misdaventure
Has done for me!
My father wants me to follow him
This evening!
But let us swear, whatever happens
To meet again.

If someone with culpable love
Wants to bind you,
You'll reply: 'Am I capable
Of forgetting him?
Soon my friend will come to say:
'Are you awake?
The hour has finally come to smile
At your husband.'

But if one of us, while waiting
Has passed away

Let the soul remain constant
    To the absentee
That with soft gazes and expressions
    And soft words
She might come in a black cloud
    To console him."

Paulin left. A novice heart
    Is so light!
A trivial desire or caprice
    Can change it.
Claire is far away; Rose is pretty;
    A dart attains him
Time flies; the oath is forgotten
    The amour extinct.

Claire, learning by renown
    Of his new flame,
Summons him. "Another beloved
    Obtains your vows;
The one who occupied me
    Has betrayed me."
Claire forgives him, weeps
    And goes to die.

At first, to great alarms
    He yields;
But Rose, full of charms
    Reassures him:
"Why do you believe the news
    Of that death?
One laments, one quarrels
    One does not die.

Joy is so quickly stolen
From our desires
Is it necessary to consummate our lives
In displeasures?
Come to the fête in preparation
To end the day
And you'll receive from your Rose
Amorous thanks."

He goes to the ball and cleaves a path
In search of her;
It seems to him that everyone hastens
To hide her;
He believes he hears her in the crowd
In every sound,
And sees his hope disappearing
With the night

But there is his lover
The domino,
Her lily-white neck, her charming hand
And her ring.
"Rose, a happy project calls you
You remember!
You will soon say to me, cruelly
Day is coming."

"Disappear, borrowed form,
Envious mask!"
He says, and Claire all bloody
Offers to his eyes
Her hand, armed with a humid blade,
Her eyes wild
Her face bruised, her breast livid
And torn,

Without yielding him to that shade
    Day has him;
She casts a somber gaze
    Around her
As soon as his wearied senses
    Fall asleep
She murmurs in his ear
    A long sigh.

But when his pain was full
    Mercy came
And rendered his crushed soul
    To blackness
May likewise every perjurer
    To his oath,
Submit his cowardly imposture
    To punishment.

In remembering that, I surprised myself repeating that imprecation in a loud voice, in an angry tone, and I fled, full of terror, for I feared that Heaven might have heard me.

8 September

A short distance from Salzburg there is a small village cut out in a light and rustic fashion in the side of a mountain. Several streams descending from rocks come together beneath the enclosure of the presbytery to form a channel that winds across the plain like a broad silver furrow and flows into the river. The murmur of little ripples, the distant roar of waves and the rustle of poplars stirred by the wind harmonize with an inexpressible sweetness, and bring to the soul I know not what languor, a delectable disturbance that one loves to entertain. But that scene never has a charm more inexpressible than when the sky, ornamented by the colors of the dawn, smiles at the approach of day, when a damp white mist floats over the valley and the first fires of the sun begin to gild the lead of the bell-tower.

This morning, I was strolling in that direction, prey to reveries more pleasant than usual, when the lugubrious, distant and prolonged sounds of a mortuary bell came to distract me from all the dreams of the past. I turned toward the city and I saw, at the corner of the road, a procession that was advancing slowly, reciting prayers in low voices. Four men were carrying a bier covered with a large shroud opened the dour cortege. Next to them marched as many young women dressed in white, their hair scattered, their eyes reddened by tears, their breasts heaving with sighs, and with one hand they were lifting the extremities of the funeral sheet. Then came, pell-mell, women, children and old men who all seemed penetrated by grief, but a mute and resigned grief, which made me think that the unfortunate individual who was about to be deposited in her final dwelling was not accompanied by her parents, for regrets of that nature have another character. I forgot to say that the shroud was white, and that a small wreath of flowers had been attached to it, similar to those with which the foreheads of virgins are ornamented.

When the crowd had passed by, I addressed myself to an almost-octogenarian woman who was following at a belated pace because of her great age, and I asked her the name of the person who was being carried in the bier.

"Alas, Monsieur," she replied, sobbing, "you can't have failed to hear mention of the good Cordelia. Still so young, she was already the mother of the poor and the edification of the wise. She died yesterday."

When I testified to the good woman that the name of Cordelia was unknown to me and that I had been away from Salzburg for some years, she told me the following while I took her arm in order to reduce the fatigues of the journey for her.

"Cordelia was born of an opulent family, but she was so humble and so sympathetic to poverty, that no one ever perceived any evidence of her fortune except her liberalities. Cordelia's mother gloried in her daughter; fathers gave her as a model to their children; her friends named her with pride; the poor blessed her; and even envy fell silent when people spoke about her, for everyone loved poor Cordelia, she was so mild and good. The angels must have been jealous of her, in order for God to have tested her to this extent. A long time ago her mother perceived that she was devouring a hidden chagrin, and she strove to penetrate the mystery of her heart. 'What's wrong with you, my Cordelia?' she said, but Cordelia only leaned over her mother's bosom and groaned. 'Are you in love?' her mother added, one day, but Cordelia made no reply. That is because that was her secret, and she dared not either deny it or confess it.

"However, she had no reason to blush over the choice she had made, for Guillaume is a worthy follow; but she believed that they would not consent to her marrying him because he was poor. That is why she hid the knowledge of her sadness, even though it was increasing every day. Finally, she was afflicted by an alarming malady, and in the fits of delirium that seized her she often pronounced Guillaume's name. When the fever began to come down and Cordelia recovered her senses, her mother sat down beside her and interrogated her again. Once she had admitted everything, because she was told how she had given herself away, her parents discussed it, and after mature reflection, they resolved to marry her to Guillaume, since she had given him her amour.

"They took advantage of one of the peaceful moments when Cordelia allowed some hope of convalescence to give her the news, and as it was thought that her complete cure might depend on that desired union, they hastened to set a day for it in a chapel neighboring the house. That was yesterday, at the same hour as now, precisely as she would attain her seventeenth year. She got up, got dressed, and went to the chapel between her mother, who was quite unsettled, and Guillaume, who was not joyful. The friends who are surrounding her walked by her side. As she passed by people said: 'Look at Cordelia; she's paler, but at least as beautiful.' In fact, her appearance was full of nobility, grace and serenity, except that, at the foot of the altar, she said in a whisper, while leaning on Guillaume: 'I feel ill.' She was taken away, but the blow had fallen and had destroyed all the resources of life. A few minutes after midday, her eyes seemed to tarnish and become extinct. She looked tenderly at her husband and her mother, sighed and smiled. Then she turned her head away and remained motionless. Frightened, Guillaume took her hand; it was cold. Cordelia had just died."

We were already walking through the village that Cordelia had selected, during the course of her illness, as the place of her sepulcher, and I asked again, with a sad curiosity, about the details of that event. I loved to hear how that sensitive and generous soul had made herself known to the unfortunate during her brief sojourn on earth. I felt sorry, above all, for Guillaume, for to survive the person one loves . . . what am I saying? He will doubtless die of it.

Meanwhile, we have arrived at the church. The door opens, the corpse is deposited on the threshold, and the priest, standing with his eyes raised to the heavens, his brow calm and his arms extended, sprinkler in hand, lets a few drops of holy water fall on the narrow and mysterious prison that contains Cordelia. Then the coffin is taken in; the procession accompanies it, silently, under the antique nave and divides into two ranks next to the railings of the choir; the people kneel down and the sacrifice commences.

What a spectacle it offered to my eyes, and what ideas it brought to assail my heart, the touching pomp that religion has placed as a point of repose between death and eternity! The sanctity of the place, the grandeur of the ceremonies; the imposing melody that resounded in the sacred enclosure; the vapors of the incense that mingled with the smoke of the funerary candles; an august priest who brings the prayers of the multitude to the Almighty; a pious crowd that summons the inexhaustible mercy of the Creator to the tomb of the creature; God himself, descended as an expiatory victim for the redemption of humans, and bringing back the faithful to the steps of his father's throne; and next to me, in that bier, under the sad livery of the dead, a young woman who had only dreamed of the embraces of a husband, and who exchanged her roses for cypresses so quickly, the delights of her spring for the secrets of the future, and her nuptial bed for a grave! A virgin who had not yet taken off her wedding dress, and who was about to be thrown forever into the damp and profound earth, at the mercy of all the vagaries of the seasons and all the ravages of time! That innocent Cordelia, yesterday, alas, so ravishing in the perfection of her beauty, today a cadaver!

While I was delivering myself to those reflections, the procession had made its way to the cemetery, where it was to leave Cordelia, and the regrets she inspired had burst forth with more bitterness. Then one might have thought that everyone was mourning in her a cherished sister, so much had the idea of being separated from her forever, and soon losing sight of the little of her that remained augmented the development of all the grief.

At that very moment a stranger approached, and what a man he must have been. He appeared to be approaching mature age, but some great dolor had already engraved on his forehead the imprints of an anticipated old age. His mild and proud gaze, tender and yet slightly somber, commanded respect, admiration and amour; and something celestial and dazzling floated over his face with an incomparable majesty.

He came to me and interrogated me in an emotional voice. I repeated to him briefly what I had been told about Cordelia and her death, but when I reached the end of the narration he had ceased to interrogate me, and perhaps to see me. His cheeks were inflamed, his limbs were stiff, and his entire body was trembling with a sudden convulsion. He launched himself toward the grave and attached an avid gaze to it, and when the coffin was lowered into it and the boards creaked as they slid along the ropes, his arms, which were seeking a support, enlaced around me.

"Oh, you don't know," he cried. "You'll never know what this morning brings back to me of torments. You don't know that once I once saw die and fall into the earth like this the person who was, alone, all my joy and all my amour, my adoptive sister, the friend of my youth, the wife that I was to be given . . ."

And he lost consciousness.

As soon as our urgent cares had revived his heart, I drew him away from that scene of affliction, and, marching in great haste in the direction of the city, we stopped at a bend in the road from which I had seen the procession descend, from which the village is hidden behind the foot of a wooded hill, as if behind a curtain.

There we separated, but before quitting me, pressing me to his bosom with a fervor of amity of which I was proud, lavishing on me testimonies of grateful affection for such a simple action, he named himself; and that stranger, toward whom my heart had immediately flown—is Eulalie's husband!

When I remember, after that, that Eulalie thought she had discovered some rapport between us; and when I represent him with his physiognomy of a demigod, it seems to me that it is a faculty that has been accorded to tender souls, in compensation for the vicissitude of our affections, to be able to find everywhere images of that which one has loved.

9 September

This is another mark of the weakness of our spirit and the futility of the efforts that we employ in combating our penchants. It has been demonstrated to me that our life has been foreseen and ordered with all its harmonies, that all the habits and relationships that we contract in the commerce of society are necessary consequences of our organization, and that it does not belong to us either to explain or to vanquish the sympathies by which we sometimes find ourselves bound. By virtue of what other ascendancy than that of an omnipotent fatality could that ravisher, who had dispossessed me of my dearest hopes, have come to subjugate me, when everything about him was odious to me, and I would have liked to be able to put a world between us? Is he not Eulalie's husband, and do I no longer love Eulalie?

What, however, prevents me from passing my life with them? An idea so rich in delights that my feeble imagination is astonished by it! What prevents me from becoming her spouse, like him, and her from dividing her tenderness between us? Might not a soul of a sensitivity so keen and so tender confound us easily in her heart? Is it necessary that the happiness of another should only be enriched by my loss and dolor?

It is necessary to admit that mine is a condition well worthy of pity, for all those maltreated by fate, who are the majority of men, can at least, as I have seen, be compensated for the severity of their fortune in a few consoling sentiments. I alone, on this miserable earth, unite all the miseries of humankind, and all the charms or soothes them is cruelly forbidden to me. My sweetest affections become insupportable torments, and on my lips the very air that I breathe has become poison since God has disinherited me from his providence.

10 September

However, he has loved, he loves, and he regrets another. He cannot love her as I love her. He does not report back to her alone all his memories, all his thoughts, all his life; and on Eulalie's bosom he dreams of another amour and another felicity. Disabuse yourself of your happiness, tender and confident soul! That husband was not destined for you. His transports, his sighs and his tears are not for you. It is not you that he desires, whom he seeks on awakening, but the one that the illusions of the night have shown him, and who enchanted his adulterous slumber. Unfortunate! It is not you that he loves, and by what right does he demand from you the affection that he can no longer give you? Is not an engagement null that violates all the engagements of the heart, and which has betrayed nature?

I could, therefore . . . never! That idea can ferment in my bosom in vain . . . never! Chimera! Illusions of darkness! Who am I, alas? A captive whose imagination reposed momentarily in voluptuous dreams; who believed that he was marching on verdant paths under rose-buses, who was only occupied with facile hopes and cheerful thoughts, but who suddenly finds his chains and his cell around him.

When I see myself separated thus from all happiness by a shoreless ocean; when I feel myself crushed and annihilated by despair; when I observe how my faculties are degraded and irritated by turns in that state of convulsion and despair;

when I try to calculate to what point slight modifications of circumstances or temperament might influence my gravest resolutions, and I reflect on how many wretches Heaven has thrown, with a burning sensibility, into the midst of the constraints and struggles of life . . . I am less astonished to count such a great number of reputations written in blood, and I am indignant at the insensate judgments of the crowd. Interrogate the proud, those blind dispensers of glory and punishments; they have evaluated everything, measured everything, foreseen everything. There is no crime, no thought, that escapes their laws, their inquisitions and their executioners; and yet they do not know, and will never know, how short, narrow and imperceptible the distance is that separates a rebel from his emperor and the torture of an outlaw from the apotheosis of a demigod.

11 September

For the second time I have seen him. I went into a strange house; I am announced and Monsieur Spronck flies toward me with the marks of the keenest affection. "Charles Munster!" he said. "Alas, it's you then . . . !" And he did not finish; but even his silence speaks to my heart. It seems to feel sorry for me and to justify him; it wants to defend itself from my hatred. And in the meantime, shuddering, nonplussed, my eyes moist with tears. I have been tempted twenty times to throw myself at his knees, or into his arms.

12 September

There are pleasures that we have savored with so much delight that we would gladly believe that the memory that remains to us of them ought to be sufficient to nourish our heart with cheerful and happy ideas throughout the course of life; and when we find ourselves in the same circumstances after a long time, it happens nevertheless that those emotions, so agreeable and so regretted, have lost almost all the intoxication that they had. We lament then the instability of earthly things; and because we are no longer able to enjoy the beauties that transported us, we foolishly criticize nature for having changed.

Is there anything sweeter, I said, than being able, after great traverses and years of exile and dolor, than reporting back in thought to the pure days of happy childhood; than to see again the places that were the theater of our first games, our first endeavors and our first successes; the perspectives that exercised our first drawings; the natal roof and the hereditary domains; than recognizing the field that our father cultivated, the tree whose shade he loved, his plow, his rustic hearth and the bed of peace from which he blessed us? One recalls that time, rich in ignorance and simplicity, so desirously, in which a laborious mediocrity limited our desires, and a narrow horizon our world. So many times we have wished to reassemble around us all those with whom we served the apprenticeship of life and in whose conversation we experienced so many delights.

I have quit Salzburg to come and refresh my heart at this hearth of innocent sensualities, and instead of the consolations that I sought here, everything I have seen has only served to redouble my chagrins. Pleasures painfully bought are those that have such returns! Past happiness can, therefore, be only one torment more!

I imagine myself as one of those reproved angels who are consuming their eternity in futile repentance. Sometimes he rises up pensively as far as the confines of his first homeland; he contemplates, with a profound sadness, the Heaven from which he has been banished and the wealth that his rebellion has cost him; his misfortune is augmented by it, and roaring with despair, he plunges back into the abyss.

14 September

How many people complain about the monotony of nature, who only see sterile and tedious scenes, who think that they can perceive everything and embrace everything with a single glance, and who ought to attribute the imperfection of their enjoyments solely to the poverty of their imagination and their organs, while the artist bemoans the impotence of his resources and curses his canvases and his palette when he remarks so many inimitable nuances, so many mobile aspects so many varied expressions in the great tableaux of the superb creation. And what a subject of uncertainty for the man who sees a single point of the horizon modified by all the influences of the seasons, by all the accidents of the light and all the emotions of his own heart!

I stopped this morning under an old elm around which, on certain feast days, the young people, assembled by the simple concerts of a fiddler, cause their strength and agility to shine, while the old people of the village, stirred by delightful memories, recall between them some notable event of their youth arrived at such an anniversary. That happy tradition has doubtless been preserved, for I saw, on the trampled grass all around, scattered flowers and shredded daisies. Fortunate are those, at least, who are still faithful to their first pleasures and their primal mores.

From that place, the view extends over an immense valley hollowed out and deployed with grace between forested slopes, the calm and cheerful aspect of which enchants the heart. A few streams bordered by willows distributed in the plain, not too distant from one another, divide it into elegant compartments, seeking one another and fleeing one another by turns, and soon coming back, all together, to embrace the boscage with their indecisive contours. To the right, among the peasants' huts, the turrets of a Gothic château can be distinguished, the ruined wings of which extend heavily over a broad platform; and, lower down, the river that suddenly emerges from behind the hill as if it had obtained its source there, and then goes to disappear a long way away in the blue depths of the sky. The bridge that traverses it in the distance resembles a little black crescent applied to a field of azure.

When the orient commences to be colored by the first tints of day, everything is dubious, vague and indefinite. The landscape, scarcely sketched, offers uncertain hues, confused lines and capricious forms. As the daylight rises, the mountains are born, the perspectives recoil, the planes are detached and characterized; flocks of birds of every color travel the air with all kinds of flight and song. Soon the hour of labor populates the roads and the fields. The agriculturalist descends from the hamlet, the muleteer follows his beasts of burden and the pastor his ewes. Every approaching hour brings other scenes. Sometimes a single gust of wind suffices to change everything. All the forests incline, all the willows are blanched, all the streams are rippled, and all the echoes sigh.

When the sun descends, on the contrary, toward the occident, the valley darkens, the shadows extend. A few higher points still stand out, with their golden reflections, among the crimson clouds; but those dying lights do not shine anywhere with more brightness than the surface of the river, which precipitates, sparkling, and envelops all of the west with a vast fiery scarf.

The moon finally opens a passage in the spaces of the sky; whether its light, as tender and timid as a virgin's gaze, reposes dormant on the plain, whether it trembles under transient shades, or whether it unfurls in sheaves or in silver nets over agitated waves, it is then that one thinks that one finds an inexplicable charm and an infinite softness in all objects; it is then that all the woods have religious sounds, pomps and secrets. All the aspects of the sky and the earth take on something ideal. The air is charged with pure emanations and agreeable perfumes. The sound of a hunting-horn, the ringing of a distant bell, the barking of an attentive dog watching before a human habitation, something trivial, disturbs you and penetrates you; it seems that the night is casting something imposing over all your sensations.

What am I saying? Superstitious inspirations and credulous reveries are daughters of solitude and darkness. What prevents me from giving that château inhabitants and mysteries, bemoaning the fate of an oppressed wife who is dying in its subterrains, and evoking over those towers the old shades of their ancient possessors?

Might not those cottages hide a couple of true lovers who have preferred the simple roof of their fathers, a little field cultivated by their hands and pleasures without regrets to all the seductions of the city?

Let us dream, let us dream of that felicity in what surrounds us, since it will never become our share.

17 September

This village is only separated from the one where I saw Eulalie for the first time by a hill planted with various trees, between which a thousand little paths have been placed. Whether out of predilection or hazard, my solitary reveries always brought me back to a pretty esplanade carpeted by a soft verdure, which large maples covered with their cool and shady vaults. On the slope of the hill a belfry, blackened by a recent fire, raised its smoky tower in the midst of a few buildings crudely grouped in an amphitheater, and on the edge of the plain a few farm-houses could be counted with their fields and a few pleasure houses with their gardens.

In one enclosure of an agreeable shape and a fortunate exposure, I had often seen Eulalie wandering pensively through the orchards, allowing the folds of her white dress and the tresses or her hair to float at the whim of the wind, or coming at dusk to sprinkle pure water on the flowers of her garden when they were inclining, wilted by the ardors of the sun, like touching symbols of a tender soul consumed by its languor; and every time, an unquiet desire, a sentiment mingled with trouble and sensuality, slid through my veins and made my blood seethe. My soul burned to be allied, across space, with the soul of the unknown woman; if she drew away I followed her with my gaze until she escaped me; I waited until she came back, and as soon as she reappeared I sought to take possession of her image, to appropriate it entirely, and to identify it with me in order never to lose it. Standing still, not breathing, not moving, her presence was a mystery that I hesitated to trouble.

Sometimes, too, black presentiments extended over my future like a veil of dolors, and then I experienced a heartache, a general malaise. Bloody clouds floated before my eyes and obfuscated the sky; tears, as warm and heavy as the first raindrops of a storm, rolled from my eyelids, and the earth fled beneath me. Did I want to leave? I had forgotten everything: my paper, my pencils and my Ossian.

Then I went into the woods at random and frayed new paths for myself, parting the wet branches and the thorn-bushes with my hands. I took pleasure in roaming in places which people were not accustomed to penetrate, so jealous was I of the sentiment that filled my soul, and so painful was it for me to be distracted from it. I talked about her under a thousand imaginary names; I engraved them in the bark of trees or in the sand, and often I combined them with mine. If I passed the same spot some time afterwards and recognized the initials I quivered with joy, as if I were able to believe that they had interlaced of their own accord. Often I bent young trees in order to make domes of verdure, or I rounded them into porticos, wove their branches together and suspended fresh garlands of creepers there with their spear-head leaves and their ivory cymbals brilliant with dew.

Perhaps one day, I said, then, *I'll bring her to my bowers and make her pass under my flowery vaults, and crown her with my creepers.* They were the pleasant chimeras and presumptuous illusions of inexperienced amour.

Today I wanted to see all that again, but the magic of the beautiful days is no longer there. The house is abandoned to new owners, and, devoid of respect, they have ravaged the flower-beds and torn up the honeysuckle. They have spared nothing of what she loved. What she loved! Did these strangers even know?

However, I ceded to the illusion of my memories with so much confidence and abandon that before quitting the esplanade I turned round mechanically to see whether Eulalie was there—after which, reflecting on that error, I started to weep; but how much more bitterly I wept when I perceived my arbors desolated and destroyed by the wind, my little trees felled by the woodcutter's ax and the ground littered with their branches. At that final loss, slight as it seems, I recalled everything that I had lost, and I contemplated myself fearfully in my solitude and my misery: devoid of friends, family and fatherland; devoid of support and hope; betrayed by the past, crushed by the present and dispossessed of the future; abandoned by Eulalie and by Heaven.

There, I had once resolved to consecrate to my dear Werther a grave covered with undulating grass, as he had often desired; and today I felt a secret desire soon to dig my own there. It is such a cruel destiny to die far from what is dear to us and to leave the cares of one's sepulcher to the pity of a passer-by.

24 September

Yes, at the fire that is running through my veins I sense that there is nothing good for me on earth except in that other half of myself from which unjust fate has separated me. Who can render to me those days of delights and glory? What god can enable me to relive the jealous past that has devoured my future? The time, alas, when my heart was inundated with such happy affections; when all my faculties enjoyed such a powerful activity; when, merely at her approach, at the sound of her voice, at the slightest rustle of her dress, I felt life ready to fail me everywhere and my soul to turn upside-down in all my nerves; when I lamented not having sufficient strength for my happiness or enough amour to succumb to it. How sweet it would have been to finish thus, and to exhale my last sigh in that bliss!

Why did I not dare to go wrap my arms around her, carry her away like a prey, drag her out of the sight of men and proclaim her my wife before heaven? Or, if that very desire is a crime, why is it so narrowly united with the sentiment of my own existence that I can no longer exile it without dying? A crime, did I say? In the days of barbarity, the memory of which is linked to all ideas of ignorance and servitude, the vulgar individual took it into his head to write his prejudices, and he said: this is the law! Strange blindness of humanity, spectacle worthy of scorn, that of so many generations governed by the caprices of an extinct generation, and of so many centuries determined by a single obscure century!

After having groaned for a long time over those odious constraints, who would not want to abridge the painful trial of life, if that joy at least remained in our power? But Heaven and humans are in accord in forbidding it to us, and we only free ourselves from our days in order to recommence dolor. It lies in wait at the door of the tomb like those monsters which nourish themselves on cadavers; it disenchants us from the sleep of death and takes possession of our eternity like a heritage.

Whatever that terrible future might be, however, the future of blood and tears that you keep for your reproved, suffer, suffer, O God, that Eulalie be returned to me for a moment, that for a single moment my heart might palpitate against her heart, that my feeble existence might vanish in the intoxication of her gaze and her kisses, that I might die in her amour. And Hell, at that price!

8 October

It is an admirable thing and full of charm to follow a great genius in its course, to be in some way associated with its discoveries, and to reach distance with it that one would never have been able to attain without a guide, like a ship accustomed to short-haul voyages when a skillful pilot suddenly sets a course for the milieu of unknown seas, toward unknown ports. Thus our imagination is drawn into the sublime flight of your Muse, divine Klopstock, and, traveling in her wake the spaces that you have populated, is astonished by the miracles that surround it, and stops, gripped by fear.

With what magnificence you assemble before our eyes all that poetry has of marvels, whether you introduce us into the councils of the Almighty when the first-born of the angels is celebrating the mysteries of the heavens, and the cherubim, penetrated by a religious fear, veil themselves with their golden wings; or you pierce before us the tenebrous vaults of infernos, to invoke with an incredible authority the fallen powers that an eternal vengeance pursues with eternal torments, and show them to us quaking under the weight of their burning chains and their shattered rocks; or you transport us to the great sacrifice of Golgotha, when the creator of the world devotes himself to the anguish of death in order to redeem his executioners!

But the reading of the Bible offers me even more delectable enjoyments. There is no circumstance in human life with which it does not mingle some mildness, no disaster that it does not solemnize, no prosperity that it does not embellish; that is the character that a book emanated from Heaven ought to have.

Often, when nature, in all the splendor of its autumnal adornment, with all its forests variegated with gold and crimson, smiles at the setting sun, I sit down on the slope of a hill, under some old oak, and I reread the ingenuous bucolics of early times, the naïve story of Ruth and the love songs of Solomon. At other times, under the Gothic arches of a ruined church that raises its solitary towers in the valley, I listen; and in the moaning of the winds that rumble through its walls like brazen voices I believe that I grasp the prophetic speech of a Daniel or a Jeremiah. From time to time, on my father's grave, in the melancholy shade of trees that I have planted there, I recall, with abundant tears, the story of Joseph and his brothers, for I too saw brothers in all men, I have been sold by them and they have sent me into a distant exile. But more often, when night, veiled by obscure crepes, advances in its silent paths, standing on a rock covered with moss, I repeat with Job in all the effusion of my dolor the profound cry of the disabused soul:

"Wherefore is light given to him that is in misery, and life unto the bitter in soul?"[1]

---

1 *Job* 3:20.

16 October

I would willingly break my brushes with chagrin when I think of the extent to which the nature of this sad Occident is paltry and disgraced; when I dream of the favored climates, pure skies and cloudless suns of the magnificent Orient; and I wander, in idea, among the nomadic and patriarchal huts of pastoral oases, or the august monuments of ancient Egypt; when the magnanimous inhabitant of those fortunate regions rises up before my eyes in all the energy of his primal grandeur and his original forms; whereas I observe here how all forces are compressed and all faculties restricted; when I seem to see that Arab, alone with his charger, which respires, like him, all the liberty of solitude; when I seem, as I say, to see him crossing the torrid sands, or reposing in the reparative shade of palm trees; in reassembling his features before my thought. I sometimes lament the Providence that has exiled me to a cold zone, in the midst of a timid creation, so far from the superb gaze of the inspiring sun; and I cry: *Why have men made me their captive, and why have they taken me prisoner in their cities, when you might have seen this lion, in the desert, throwing himself upon the thirsty earth, forgetting that it burns, and savoring it at length between his teeth?*

In the desert, I said; for in the iron shackles of society, under the weight of its ignominious institutions, poor slaves that we are, our weary organs could not support for long the glare of that exuberant nature. Its rich prodigalities could not belong to humans who have allowed themselves to be degraded of the dignity of their species and have trafficked their independence in cowardly fashion. And as it senses its profound humiliation, the generous soul that has engaged all its strength in that contract, when it comes to realize at what price, and for what pitiful advantages, it has made the sacrifice; when it finds itself subjugated by the audacious ascendancy of its insolent dominators, it takes itself back to those fortunate ages of the youth of the world, when societies circumscribed within the narrow enclosure of families recognized no other powers than those conferred by the divinity and no other chief than the one obtained from nature.

It is then that one feels the need to choose among the harmonies of the earth those that have a more particular affinity with our wretched condition; it is then—and I have often experienced it—that one prefers to the radiant pomp of the sun the dubious clarities of the moon and the mysteries of the night; to the apparel of summers, the graces of springs and the opulent favors of autumn the sad nudities, cold wings and black frosts of winter.

Thus, when my soul has detached itself from its youthful illusions, and it finds nothing that can fix it among humans, it seeks the secrets of darkness and the silent joys of solitude; it wanders among the dwellings of the dead and under the moans of the north wind; it loves ruins, obscurity, abysms: all that nature has of terrors; and that it how it has studied in itself some of the characteristics of misfortune.

Yes, I repeat, winter in all its indigence, with its pale stars and its disastrous phenomena, promises me more delight than the proud profusion of beautiful days. I love to see the earth stripped of its fecund adornment, gloating in its misty horizons as if in a sea of clouds. In the midst of those vanished grandeurs and that repressed vegetation, everything seems to take on moaning voices and funereal aspects, everything becomes severe and terrible.

Through the gray veils and the formidable clouds by which it is enveloped, one might take the sun for a meteor in the process of extinction. The rivers have no more ripples; the forests have no more shade or murmurs. One only hears the creak of dead branches breaking and the sound of the wind whistling over the dry heaths. No more verdure than that of ivy, which deploys its broad drapes under the sides of rocks, attaching them to rustic walls or rolling them over old oaks, and that of holly, with its armed foliage, which groups its thorny bouquets on the edge of woods.

Only a few fir-trees stand out here and there against the snow of the mountains like dark obelisks, as many monuments to the memory of the dead. And you see from time to time, in the distance, voyagers traversing the plain precipitately, or pilgrims praying over a tomb.

17 October

After abundant rain, a broad and rapid torrent, swollen by all the streams and all the ravines, descends from the heights of our mountains, falls with a thunderous din, launches forth furiously into the plain, fills it with fear and disasters, breaks, invades and devours everything that obstructs its passage and, charged with uprooted trees, rocks and rubble, it flows and precipitates, rumbling, into the Salza.

If, by chance, you find on its bank a grove of poplars that opposes its mild and tranquil majesty to the vehement agitation of the water, your soul opens to grave and religious thoughts, and you meditate sadly on those vain grandeurs of the world, which suddenly appear, like the torrent, without one being aware of their source; which likewise flow with a great deal of noise and ravages, and are similarly lost without leaving a name.

For myself, I smile with pity at the puerile cares that humans give themselves while time carries away into the still-nascent future the brief present that they enjoy; and I sense my troubles becoming less burdensome in considering that life is only a fleeting moment in the milieu of immense eternity.

19 October

Last night I found myself in the indefinable situation that has almost nothing of the activity of life but which is not entirely slumber. I thought I could hear a melodious music, of a suave and touching expression, the sounds of which were modulated with so much softness that even a harp does not have such a tender and seductive tone. You might have thought it an angelic concert, but its inconstant and capricious harmony only multiplied my fugitive joys in order to multiply my regrets, and I had scarcely grasped it than, wandering at the whim of all the currents of the air, it escaped me again. Finally, with a lamenting cadence that resonated profoundly in my soul, it ceased and I no longer heard anything but a muted sound similar to that of a distant river. Then a cold weighed forcefully upon my heart; a phantom bent over me and named me in its shrill voice, and I felt that the breath of its mouth had chilled me. I turned round, and I thought I saw my father, not as he had once appeared to me, but a vague and somber form, pale, disfigured, his eyes sunken and bloodshot and his hair scattered like a little cloud; then he drew away, becoming less distinct at every step and decreasing in the obscurity like a lantern about to go out. I wanted to run forward in order to follow him, but at the same instant, the light, the voice and the phantom all vanished with my dream, and I only embraced darkness.

23 October

As it is true that, since the commencement of this short passage of life, everything that we have seen around us only leaves us with regret, fortunate is the sage who wraps himself in his mantle, abandons himself to his skiff, and no longer turns his eyes toward the shore. But that difficult courage has not been given to me.

I am astonished myself by the irresolution of my heart and the blind facility with which it embraces new chimeras every day. Everything that has an appearance of novelty seduces it, because it knows nothing more than its ordinary state, and trusts in change. It wants uneven and distracted emotions, a diverse and fortuitous way of being, because it has observed that it gains more from what it leaves to chance than what it gives to foresight. Such is its anxiety, however, that in the midst of the agitations it seeks it still desires repose, perhaps uniquely because repose is something other than what it experiences habitually; but it does not take long to weary even of repose. It only sees wellbeing far away, and as soon as it thinks it has glimpsed it somewhere, in order to attain that point, it breaks the knots that attach it elsewhere—happier, at least, if it can break them all! What happens, however? Before the route that leads us to the desired goal has been traveled half way, the illusion ceases and the phantom flies away, toying with our hopes. God preserve me from existing in that manner for long!

To be closer to Eulalie, I said this morning, *to live near to her, to live where she is living, to respire the air that she is respiring!* And since then, everything that I see here importunes me.

30 October

The other day I had been walking, almost involuntarily, toward Salzburg, but as soon as I perceived the fortress on the mountain, the spires of the churches and the domes of the palaces, and as soon as I was able to recover the sensation that I experience with all my memories, I found myself drawn so powerfully that I would not have changed direction at any price. However, night was approaching and the thick and rainy mists of the season had hastened the darkness. I had need, in any case, of meditation and liberty, and I did not want to go into the city until I had exercised my soul in supporting the agitations that menaced it. I took possession sensually of that long and rigorous night in which nothing any longer limited the independence of my thought. All the scenes that daylight animates and colors, everything that reminded me of life, crumples and constrains me. If there is any omnipotent activity within me; if I sometimes feel a superhuman force, it is in the isolation of the night and in the contemplation of tombs. All sublime ideas are born in the heart, and the human heart is somber and suffering.

As I passed into the village where I had seen Cordelia buried and encountered Eulalie's husband I penetrated into the cemetery through a breach in the wall. The obscurity was profound. The owls of the old church were weeping or whistling on the ledges. The bell, slowly vibrated by the wind, rendered plaintive sounds, and I know not what lugubrious accents rose up around me. Then a man launched himself into my passage; suddenly stopping, and, letting his head repose on his breast, he named Cordelia sadly. It was Guillaume, and Heaven permitted me to give him a few consolations, for the voice of the unhappy sometimes reaches the hearts of the unhappy easily; and it has been said that those who have suffered a great deal know words to charm dolor.

We conversed for a long time.

"If I had wanted to," he told me, "life is easy to quit, and the days of a man can be shed like a garment. But what can I tell you? It was midnight; I was sitting on these stones, and, ready to break the fragile talisman of existence, I went astray in the contemplation of times; I embraced them in my thought. Already, all the events gone by had succeeded one another before my memory, like the reminiscences of a dream, but I still aspired to the future, and that uncertain future I was populating with my chimeras when, suddenly, a horrible idea struck me.

"Listen to what Heaven inspired in me. 'The future!' I cried. 'And by what right, wretched suicide, dare you count on a future? You have wanted to cease to be before your hour, and who knows whether your punishment will not last forever? You can open an issue in order to escape the dolors of life, but who knows whether you are not closing eternity? Cordelia, meanwhile, the purest of the daughters of the earth, is waiting for you among the righteous and, with an ineffable joy, preparing to initiate you into the delights of Heaven. But the man who has destroyed the image of God can no longer live; he has sown death, and he will reap annihilation.'

"Since then, I have reflected a great deal," Guillaume continued, after a moment of silence. "I believe that the man who gives himself death has thwarted the intention of the divinity; and, reflecting on the host of relationships that attach a man to all the objects down here, I considered him as the center of a multitude of harmonies that are born and perish with him, with the consequence that he cannot fall without dragging an entire creation down with him, and the last sigh he exhales puts all nature in mourning. Meditating on those things, I recognized that the supreme virtue is to love one's fellows, and the supreme wisdom to support one's destiny.

"I know, however, that human reason is a reed that cedes to many storms; alas, I have learned painfully how difficult it is to struggle with dolor when one cannot oppose absence to it, and above all religion. That is why I have resolved to exile myself from here and to seek a tomb elsewhere. Near Donnawert there is an ancient monastery whose walls are bathed by the Danube, and at which one arrives through a fir-wood of sad and formidable aspect. That place is full of mysteries and solemnity, and the soul abandons itself there to sentiments of an order so sublime that they absorb, it's said, by a miraculous privilege, all the former sentiments of life. That monastery will be my refuge."

Daylight surprised us in that conversation. The sun rose behind the tower of the church and crowned it with its rays like a pale aureole; the air was charged with moist vapors, and through the mist by which we were enveloped, we might have been taken for shades wandering, with their robes of cloud, in the midst of sepulchers. I understood that it was time to separate; I embraced Guillaume tenderly and I climbed over the wall of the cemetery.

On entering Salzburg, however, I know not what frightful presentiment gripped my heart; my eyes were obscured, and the sentiment of my life has remained suspended.

Conclusion

Charles Munster's journal finishes at this point. It appears that he had experienced agitations so violent that he did not even retain the strength to take account of them, and we only recovered of them notes on his multiplied relations with Guillaume, until the departure of the latter for the convent of Donnawert. What we are about to add to those memoirs is written in another hand in the original.

For a long time the melancholy of Monsieur Spronck had only been augmenting; he had heard mention of Charles Munster before his marriage; he had believed him to be dead when he married Eulalie and at the news of his return he sensed all that those unfortunates would have to suffer. The event that represented to him in such a sharp manner the loss that he had suffered a few years before and put before his eyes again the funeral pomp of his beloved bore the final blow to his heart; pursued by the sentiment of his own dolors and those of which he was the occasion, his character contracted something sinister and alarming. Even Eulalie's cares envenomed his chagrins, and when she approached him with a gaze full of tenderness and mildness, he turned his eyes away sadly and pushed her away, groaning.

At that time, hazard informed him that Charles, whom he thought had departed again for distant lands, had returned to Salzburg after having spent a few weeks in his natal village.

That news seemed at first to bring him considerable consolation, but the same evening his condition suddenly worsened; his complexion became leaden, his eyes strayed, all his strength abandoned him, and those surrounding him expected to see him expire at any moment, when Charles arrived at the monastery, to which a letter from Eulalie's unfortunate husband had summoned him.

Monsieur Spronck was lying down, unconscious and almost devoid of life. Eulalie, kneeling beside his bed, was bathing his hands with tears; only a lamp that was about to go out cast some light on that scene of dolor. At the noise of the door opening, the dying man gave signs of life; his eyes fixed and his physiognomy immobile, he was in the situation of a man emerging from a painful dream, who is searching to reconcile his senses with the objects that surround him. Finally, he appeared to be struck by a powerful memory. And he pronounced, in a loud and urgent voice, the name of Charles Munster. Scarcely had he named him than he recognized him a few paces away; immediately, he saluted him with a smile so tender and so paternal that Charles, softened by emotion, let himself fall to his knees before him.

Then Monsieur Spronck imposed his hands on his friend and on his wife, and after having assembled all the force of his soul, he depicted for them in a touching manner the adversities that had poisoned his youth, the magnitude of his losses, the dolor of his ordeals, and above all the stubbornness of the deadly fatality that had enveloped them both in the horrors of his own destiny. He asked them to forgive him for the involuntary harm that he had done them; he spoke to them about his imminent end; and, enlacing them in his arms, he spoke to them in these terms:

"Be happy," he said, "now that my miserable life can no longer pose an obstacle to it. Be happy, now that I am going to render to the earth this heart broken by despair. Be happy, and have no regret for the days that fate might perhaps have reserved for me; for I cannot hope for any sweeter than this one, when it is permitted to me to bequeath you a future without alarms, and to compensate you for the pain that I have caused you. In permitting my death to be a benefit for those I love, Heaven has placed in my death the sole joy that I ought to savor down here. It will doubtless pardon me for having hastened the hour, and will not condemn me—unlike men! Love me, at least, and forgive me."

With those words, his breast rose with a great effort, his body stiffened, and speech expired on his lips. Eulalie escaped from the room uttering frightful cries, and Charles lost consciousness.

A short time later, the latter recovered his senses, but the lamp was no longer shining, and nothing remained to him of all that had happened but vague ideas as uncertain as nocturnal illusions. He extended his arms, groping, and encountered a cold and immobile body. The men who came to fetch that body for the tomb conducted him back to Salzburg.

The profound impressions that he had received were not of a nature to be promptly effaced. An entire month passed before his soul had recovered from those violent emotions. In the meantime, a letter from Eulalie was brought to him; at the mere sight of that handwriting, so dear, he immediately changed countenance and color; his cheeks were inflamed; all his life was fixed in his eyes, and by the anxiety that agitated him, it could easily be seen that he was suspended between the dread of learning his fate and the torment of not knowing it. Finally, he gradually recovered his calm and self-assurance.

He was ready for anything; and a resolution that occupied him secretly deflected him from his dolor.

Eulalie declared to him, as he had foreseen, that she could not envisage without horror the idea of passing on to a new engagement after the voluntary death of her first husband; that she augured as well as him the certainty that he would never want a happiness that had cost so dear, if it were even possible to call happiness a union that depended on such a cause, and which entertained such thoughts; that to profit from Monsieur Spronck's generous crime would be to render it personal and to invite its punishment upon themselves; that it befit them, on the contrary, to spend their life expiating it, and placing themselves, like just holocausts, between the wrath of God and the devoted shade that was about to be delivered to its punishments. She finished by telling him that on the day that the letter reached him she would already be separated from society by a barrier that it was impossible to cross once it had closed behind her, and that she was entering into religion.

Charles recommenced that reading several times with the same resignation; then he closed the letter, imprinted an ardent kiss thereon and attached it to his heart with a ribbon that he had once obtained from Eulalie. Then he wrote to Guillaume to make him party to the project he had formed to retire among the monks of Donnawert; and he disposed of his patrimony in favor of a few poor families of Salzburg, because he no longer had any relatives.

He set forth on his journey in the early days of January. When he arrived at Eulalie's convent, which is a league from the city, he sat down outside the wall of the cloister and stopped there for several hours, but he did not see or hear anything. A few persons of his acquaintance passed before him without him perceiving them. His hair was unkempt, his beard long, his complexion pale and his eyes wild; in spite of the rigor of the season he was not wearing any garment except a kind of coarse tunic closed over his breast with a woolen belt. The snow, swept by the wind, swirled around his head, and an icy north wind whistled through the folds of his garment. Finally, at sunset, he got up and drew away at a precipitate pace. The sky had become purer, the moon rising without clouds; the night was calm.

A few days later, the temperature changed again and it began to rain; the molten snow and ice descending from the mountains swelled all the rivers. All labor was halted and all the roads were deserted. In that epoch, however, Charles was seen in a village not far from Donnawert; he was encountered by a rustic wedding party, His face was partly veiled by his hair; his feet were bare and his attire had fallen into rags. He had occasion to talk to someone; his voice, his gestures and his gaze announced a profound mental alienation. It is probable that solitude had allowed more activity to dolor, and that his reason, which had not recovered from the afflictions that he had recently endured, had finally given way. It was added that a few sympathetic souls had endeavored to retain him, making the observation that the environs of the village were impracticable, and that it would be dangerous for him to continue his journey, but he was obstinate in his resolution.

The next day, the Danube flooded.

Meanwhile, Guillaume was astonished that Charles had not arrived, and he counted the days impatiently that had elapsed since his friend was expected. His regret increased further, however, when saw that the flood, which had reached the foot of the monastery, must have covered the entire countryside and broken all communication. Sometimes he gazed with anxious eyes at that almost motionless sea; sometimes he followed its decreases and flattered himself that there was only a short distance to cover in order to return within its limits. As the land began to elevate little islets here and there, his heart was reborn to hope. Once, among the debris with which the river was charged, he thought he perceived something pale and shapeless, which the waves brought to collide with strands and reefs, and which, engulfed and rejected by turns, ended up running aground on a sandbank, to which the waves abandoned it completely.

Impelled by a vague but invincible curiosity, he descended from the cloister, traversed the church and, having arrived under the walls, recognized the object that had struck him. He approached it, shuddering with horror.

An almost naked cadaver, pale and torn, covered with bruises and mud, the limbs contracted, the head dangling, the hair stiff and bloody, and through the disorder of its distraught and soiled features, an aspect still full of nobility and mildness: thus it was that Charles Munster was offered to his sight.

Then Guillaume, without uttering a plaint or shedding a tear, extended his black robe over the body devoid of life, wrapped it up, loaded it on to his shoulders, and went back into the monastery. He stopped on the parvis of the main staircase, and, after having deposited his sad burden, he summoned the monks of the convent by ringing the bell. When they had assembled around him and he saw them disposed to listen to him, he removed the veil with which Charles was covered abruptly, and in a pained and dolorous voice he said: "This is Charles Munster." But the words expired on his lips; he felt his strength failing, and he fell on the cadaver.

When he opened his eyes again he only perceived a brother who told him that the community had not felt obliged to accord the stranger a Catholic sepulcher, and that, in the doubt that remained regarding the nature of his death, it feared transgressing its duties by surrounding the coffin of the unfortunate with the pomp of religion.

At those words, he took his friend in his arms again and returned silently to the river bank, where he dug a grave. Above it he placed a block of stone and he had a brief inscription engraved thereon; but the first gust of wind covered the inscription with sand and dust, and the first Danube flood dragged away the stone, the grave and everything.

Guillaume died the following year.

Eulalie is still alive; she is now twenty-eight years old.

The Last Chapter of my Romance

Preface

The Publisher: What are you bringing me there?

The Author: The fruit of a year of meditations; a sheaf of masterpieces.

The Publisher: The public might judge otherwise. Let's see.

The Author: *New Views of Politics.*

The Publisher: Let's pass on. People are weary of searching for the philosopher's stone, and alchemy is no longer fashionable.

The Author: *The Wit of the Latest Works.*

The Publisher: The work is too thin.

The Author: *Translation of the first Six Books of the Aeneid.*

The Publisher: No one has read the one that is promised, but it's irrevocably decided that it will be the best.

The Author: *Manual for Honest Men.*

The Publisher: I fear that those who would appreciate your book are not in a state to purchase it.

The Author: *A Romance in Imitation of the English.*

The Publisher: Six dramas have been made of it.

The Author: *A Drama Translated from the German.*

The Publisher: Ten Romances have been made of it.

The Author: *A Choice of Plays that Have Never Appeared.*

The Publisher: They risk never appearing

The Author: That is, however, the extent of my portfolio.

The Publisher: Too bad.

The Author: What do you need, then?

The Publisher: Something that pleases me. Publishing is subject to the vicissitudes of fashion. Don't you have some subject of devotion?

The Author: No.

The Publisher: Some orthodox poem?

The Author: No.

The Publisher: Some mystical, ascetic, liturgical or canonical historiette?

The Author: No.

The Publisher: In that case, I can retrench in the licentious genre.

The Author: But I can't resolve to soil my pen with it.

The Publisher: Who is telling you to do so? Be voluptuous without licentiousness and humorous without coarseness.

The Author: I hear you. You want one of those books that your wife finds too "brisk" and your mistress finds too "airy."

The Publisher: Precisely.

The Author: I have what you need at home.

The Publisher: Tell me the title.

The Author: *The Last Chapter of my Romance.*

The Publisher: It's singular.

The Author: I've always found it as well to take Romances by the tail.

The Publisher: I'll take that one.

The Author: It only lacks a preface,

The Publisher: I'll have our conversation printed.

The Author: Get away! What interest can the public have in what happens between us?

The Publisher: None, doubtless; but it's fashionable.

The Author: As you please. Don't forget to insert an advertisement in the newspapers.

The Publisher: Don't worry; I have a eulogistic formula here that has only been used twice.

The Last Chapter of My Romance

Yes, my dear, here I am, married, and very married. What do you expect? Pleasure is worn out, youth is past, debts are accumulating. One is disillusioned with the pomp of society; one senses the necessity of putting an end to it; a brilliant fortune attracts friends and a pretty wife retains them. Do you count for nothing the pleasures of a well-matched union, in which decency defrays the expenses of amour? Do you give no credit to the joys of paternity, with which amour sometimes defrays the expenses of hymen? For myself, I hold marriage in the highest esteem . . . and you'll come to it yourself, I wager, bad lot as I know you to be. You're twenty-five years old and you owe twenty-five thousand francs. Marry, damn it, even if it's a dowager. Marriage is the talisman of fortune, the garlic of libertines.

You're going to expose your terrors to me . . . Get away! How can a great man like you lower himself to such puerilities? It only belongs to common souls to revolt against destiny. A generous heart braves its rigors. What do you see that's so fatal, anyway, in a risk that so many honest men have run? Do you know that one could cite enough to fill a hundred volumes, in the Atlantic format. I've even written one; I was going to offer the work by subscription, and I only renounced it by virtue of my respect for the ladies.

Oh, I ask their forgiveness, for the thousandth time, for such a surly enterprise; for, all things considered, even their faults are charming, and I believe that if they were more perfect they wouldn't be so lovable. They make fools of us, persecute us, and betray us; there's no perfidy that a kiss doesn't redeem, no chagrin of which a sweet reconciliation doesn't embellish the memory! A curse upon the ill-advised mud-slinger who dips his pen in the poison of the furies to paint a portrait of the graces. Don't confound me with him, enchanting sex. I know full well that you are the masterpiece of creation, the ornament and the treasure of life; I love your delicate wit, your heart, endowed with such a vivid sensibility, and, from time to time, your pretty caprices; I adore you in good faith and cheer myself up a little on your account—for, forgive me this impertinent remark, the wits of society love to exercise themselves on the piteous expression and the gauche manners of a new bridegroom; he is assailed by gibes; malevolence unearths a hundred forgotten anecdotes, calumny invents a thousand more, and that chain becomes insupportable if one doesn't affect to play along with it. It's a tribute that I'm paying to the mores of the century.

In fact, my friend, and you were right to wager, my marriage is another romance. Since I've known myself, all my adventures have had that cachet, and one can find chapters of my life everywhere, I think, except in Grandisson.[1] Reassure yourself, however, I am forbidden the tenebrous genre today. I shall not take you into the subterrains of Ann Radcliffe, through dungeons and cemeteries, and I shall not enrich my story with the sublime conceptions of our dramaturges of the boulevards. You will not see here any bandits, specters or towers of the North, and you will be grateful to me for having spared, as best I could, the unnecessary effusion of blood. Finally, you will easily perceive that the marriage and the dowry have gilded my imagination, and on that account, my readers have gained as much as my creditors.

1 The intended reference is presumably *The History of Sir Charles Grandison* (1770) by Samuel Richardson, whose eponymous hero is a model of virtue, a calculated counterpart to the infamous Lovelace of *Clarissa* (1748).

But you might perhaps believe that I am only going from one extreme to another, and that I have exchanged the obscure colors of anglomania for the gritty pencils of cynicism. Undeceive yourself once more. A young man of twenty can perpetrate follies on occasion, recommence them out of habit, love them by virtue of temperament and recount them by virtue of stupidity, but sensuality wears a veil and amour a blindfold. I only married the other day, and if my juvenile robe is not exempt from impurity, I shall at least make efforts to be more chaste in the choice of my expressions than that of my subject; I hasten to inform my reader of that, in order that my ideas should not be accused of resembling the debauches of base origin that mingle with good company by virtue of a decent garment.

Now, I am sure of not being condemned by scrupulous people who would not have finished reading me, and journalists who would not have commenced. May God reward them! I am very much of their opinion and I am thinking seriously about everything; I even have the hope that my books will be employed one day in the education of young women and a subject of meditation in pious families. I will only make an exception for this one; you will read it anyway, beautiful Myrté, but instead of forgetting it in the dust of your oratory you will hide it with precaution under your pillow and you will take care to lower your eyes if anyone ever mentions it in your mother's boudoir.

I do not know whether you remember Mademoiselle Aglaë de la Reinerie. At eleven years of age she already offered the expectation of so many qualities and charms that no one doubted that she would become the flower of the fair sex of Strasbourg. Unfortunately, she was stolen from us by her father, a determined speculator, who went to seek his fortune in India. The young woman remained in Paris under the guard of her aunt and her older brother. The father embarked, voyaged fortunately, succeeded in all his enterprises, and died last year. It was not worth the trouble of enriching himself, you might say, but it would be poorly reasoned: I shall inherit.

Monsieur de la Reinerie still possessed a few domains in Alsace, and he had interests in several houses of commerce. Mademoiselle de la Reinerie decided to make the voyage to Strasbourg, where she arrived with her aunt, in the course of the month of October last, after eight long years of absence. Since the passage of the man with the big nose of whom there is mention in *Tristram Shandy*, no one had paid any particular attention to our good capital. There was no talk of anything but Mademoiselle de la Reinerie; no one but her was cited, no one but her was sought at the Cathedral, at the theater, on the Breuil . . .

But I, my friend, I alone . . . pity my destiny! While that beautiful star was illuminating Strasbourg, I was absent from the horizon, and I was spinning perfect amour at the window of a petty bourgeoise of Hagenau.

I arrived too late and I was doubly unfortunate, because I no longer saw Mademoiselle de Reinerie, but I still heard all the bad verses that had been written in her praise. My regrets were augmented when my mother told me that there had been question of uniting me with her, and that it would have had the consent of the aunt, who is not without influence in the family, but I was desperate when I was told about the dowry that had just escaped me irredeemably. It was added that the brother had other views and that, the opportunity having been missed, it was necessary not to think about it any longer; the sensibility of my heart could not withstand that final blow.

My mother knew what the passions of a young soul like mine can do. She perceived the change that was taking placed in me, the decline that was undermining me, the emaciation to which I was about to succumb, and she divined the cause.

"My dear Alphonse," she said to me one day, "you're thinking of marrying; it's a sage project, which proves a precocious maturity of which I did not believe you capable; your resolution charms me. Go to Paris; Mademoiselle de la Reinerie must have arrived there; I don't know her exact address, but I'll send it to you when I can, and I hope that your efforts will turn out for the best."

She added a few instructions to that speech, which I received with an entirely filial deference. I had horses brought, and I departed from Paris the same evening, accompanied by Labrie and my amour.

Now, my friend, take the trouble to follow me across country and roll with my post-chaise if my adventures interest you, for I am determined not to spare you a single circumstance, in order to conform to the routine of our modern storytellers. Refrain, however, from censuring the abundance of my episodes and the prolixity of my details. There is nothing but the essential in my narrative, and my incidents are woven with so much artistry as I make my Iliad and my Odyssey move forward.

First of all, in order not to leave any doubt as to my exactitude, you should know that I was on the road from Strasbourg to Chaumont for twenty-eight hours. As I had been unable to sleep throughout that time and the cold was intense, I decided to spend the night there. Those, I am sure, are circumstances that you hardly care about, but don't protest too much about their dryness, for, once again, I am saying nothing that is not useful, and you are approaching great events. There is even an art in hiding grave and important combinations under trivial details. The result is more piquant, the denouement more unexpected, the surprise more vivid; that is called the skillful management of interest.

It was ten o'clock, and I was finishing an impromptu supper, while dreaming about my adorable intended, when the hostess extracted me from my meditation by entering the dining room with an anxious expression.

"Is Monsieur thinking of sleeping here?" she asked.

"Undoubtedly, Madame," I replied, more astonished by her disturbance than the singularity of the question.

"I am in despair, Monsieur, but that isn't possible."

"Not possible . . . that's strange. Why not, if you please?"

"For a very powerful reason, Monsieur. I have no bed."

While she was saying that I scanned her with my eyes in order to know to what extent an honest man could compromise himself by sharing hers, and I repeated: *not possible*.

The good woman believed that I was putting her assertion in doubt, and she hastened to justify herself with a loquacious speech that might have diverted me in any other circumstance. After half an hour she finally arrived at the end of her peroration and notified me, in the most demonstrative manner, that it was necessary for me to resolve to share a wretched campbed with my valet de chambre, unless I would prefer to spend a poetic night under the stars.

The proposal appeared to me to be unpleasant, and I did not know what to decide when the hostess dispensed me of reflection by crying, as if by inspiration: "There's the yellow bed in number eight!" But she continued, with a solemn prudishness: "But no, that can't be done."

"For what reason, if you please?"

"Because the green bed . . ."

"What about the green bed? What is there in common between the green bed and the yellow bed?"

"Monsieur, the green bed is occupied."

"I have it! Madame sleeps in number eight!"

"No, Monsieur, but it's the same thing. There is a young woman there, so pretty, so interesting . . ."

"The same thing? No, by all the devils."

"Eighteen years old at the most."

"I'm all ears."

"And as sweet as an angel."

"You can see how that inflames me."

"She arrived a week ago with a very respectable lady who fell dangerously ill here and who has scarcely recovered. If you knew what cares she has lavished upon her, how attentive she is to the slightest desires, with what patience she had stayed with her constantly, without permitting that anyone but her should share that employment . . ."

Here, while the hostess paraphrased her thoughts and strung out punctuation marks, the order of my ideas was completely overturned; my nascent amour gave way to an almost tender sentiment, and much more respectful. The story of a touching action restrained the most lustful impetuosities of my imagination, and my transports vanished at the aspect of virtue, like farfadets before the holy water sprinkler of an exorcist. Believe me, I hold in low esteem a woman who has attractions enough to excite desires but not sufficient ascendancy to repress them. That suffers few exceptions.

Those reflections succeeded one another in my mind with lightning rapidity, and the expression of my features was modified with them. I conjecture, at least, that that fortuitous disposition of my physiognomy contributed to ensuring the success of a speech that I could cite somewhere as a model of insinuating eloquence and oratory precaution. In truth, I delivered it in such a honeyed tone, with an expression so composed and with such a transcendent hypocrisy that Lavater[1] would have been fooled by it. I concluded by referring myself entirely to

1 The Swiss philosopher and theologian Johann Kaspar Lavater (1741-1801), the most influential popularizer of the pseudoscience of physiognomy. A poet himself, he had a considerable influence on Romanticism in Germany via his friendship with Goethe, although the two eventually fell out, and in England because his aphorisms were annotated in translation by William Blake.

the opinion of the beautiful stranger, and protesting that I only intended to sleep in number eight with her consent.

The hostess, shaken, accepted the preliminary conditions and immediately took them for ratification to my judge of last resort. She did not take long, for I saw her come back in after five minutes, her brow as radiant as that of a general who has just won his first battle and the assured step of a plenipotentiary about to open a congress.

Scarcely had she made me party to the success of her embassy than I got ready to retire, but she retained me in order to explain the articles of the treaty to me. By the first, it was demanded that I sleep without a light; by the second, that I depart before daybreak; and by the third, that I did not embark upon any conversation; without which, any species of admission was refused to the proposed condition. Although that arrangement irritated me, I was obliged to subscribe to it.

The hostess indicated to me very precisely the bed destined for me; I went up without candles; Labrie undressed me blindly, and I lay down in order to sleep. But what angel could sleep so close to temptation? The perfections of the adorable unknown came in a host to retrace themselves in my memory; I invented new ones, and if you want precious style. Amour occupied so much space in my alcove that Morpheus had been forced out of it.

I divine you, are you going to say?

I defy you to do it; it ill befits you to claim to divine me! Life is so abundant in events, seduction so fertile in means, the hearts of women so weak, and the nights of winter so long! One could bring a conspiracy to a conclusion in less time. How do you know, anyway, whether I would have difficulty in meditating and enterprising, and whether fortune, faithful to its favorites might have contrived a facile victory for me? Would I be this first, in your opinion, to obtain the honors of a triumph without having run the dangers of a battle?

Midnight chimed; I heard a slight movement, and a high-pitched voice addressed me with a timidly-pronounced "Monsieur," to which I riposted in the same tone.

"Monsieur," my charming interlocutress went on, "I've forgotten to warn you that I'm a somniloquist, and it sometimes happens that I say the most bizarre things during the night. I make up tales . . ."

"I'm charmed," I replied, "and if they're piquant, I'll employ them in my romances."

That was scarcely worth mentioning, but of one's children, as you know, it is the most disgraced that one prefers, and it is thus that paternal tenderness is ingenious in avenging them on nature. At any rate, either because that idea had something soporific about it, or for some other reason, our conversation came to an end; my neighbor in the green bed contented herself with adding that she would be very sorry to disturb my slumber, and I contented myself with thinking that I would hang myself rather than interrupt hers.

In fact, after an hour, she was profoundly asleep, and the monologue was underway, but in a voice so low that I was unable to grasp a word of it. Curiosity gripped me, however; I listened carefully, I held my breath, I leaned out of bed; I got out of it; I took a step, and then two; finally, I found the curtain, and I raised it; then I encountered the covers and I slipped underneath.

Until then I had been impelled by a laudable desire to instruct myself and my conduct was entirely innocent. I guarantee, however, that you are about to poison my intentions. Calumny! You know it. Fortunate is he who, like me, can oppose to it the sentiment of a pure conscience and the courage of virtue!

"Great gods! What are you doing?"

"I'm listening."

"Our conventions . . ."

"Are intact."

"There is fraud . . ."

"See rather."

"I warned you that I am a somniloquist . . ."

"But I forgot to warn you that I am a somnambulist."

"You're a monster . . ."

"That's better than being impertinent."

"Ah . . . !"

Exert yourself, my friend; this is the moment of the lacuna.

Labrie came to wake me at four o'clock in the morning.

"That's strange," he said. "Monsieur is lying to the right, but I can hear him to the left."

"That's because there's an echo," I replied, "and Robertson will explain that to you in his acoustic illusions."[1]

I took my leave of my beauty, and as it is necessary to compensate you for the length of my story by the rapidity of my transitions, here I am half a league from Troyes and four paces from my post-chaise, which has just broken down: an incident that might not appear to you to be very new, but which you will permit me to find indispensable.

I know all the advantage that an industrious intelligence could extract from such a fecund resource. For instance, it is only up to me to injure myself slightly and have myself transported to some nearby château, which would be inhabited by

1 "Robertson" was the stage name of the showman and mechanician Étienne-Gaspard Robert (1763-1837), famous for his invention of phantasmagoria. He was in Paris during the 1790s, working as a painter and attending lectures at the Collége de France, where he formed a friendship with the balloonist Jacques Charles. He approached the French government with a proposal for employing balloons and a version of Archimedes' legendary mirror to burn the fleet of the English navy, but they turned him down. His development in 1799 of the Fantoscope, a "magic lantern on wheels," took his horrific phantasmagorias to a new level; his show also employed actors and ventriloquists to imitate ghosts, and was sufficiently terrifying to be briefly banned in Paris, although it subsequently achieved enormous success and toured Europe and America.

the prettiest woman in all Champagne; on that foundation, slight though it seems, I can construct at my ease the most laboriously complicated intrigue, which will reach its denouement at the end of three or four volumes with a marriage that everyone would have divined on the first page; and if that canvas appears too simple to me, I am the master of embroidering it with episodes well or badly conducted, which would not fail to produce a marvelous effect and turn the heads of all the dressmakers of the capital.

But I have made it a law to tell nothing but the truth, and instead of drawing you into the long corridors of the romantic habitation of my chatelaine, it is necessary to persuade you to follow me into a city that will not give such beautiful impetus to your imagination, where I shall stay for a week.

However, I do not have a soul malicious enough to take pleasure in retaining you there for such a long time, and I attach too much value to your good humor to compromise it in that Gothic city, where one would have something to regret if a charming woman whom everyone could name did not embellish it with her presence. In seeing her adored by everyone surrounding her, one would recall that the most barbaric peoples raised temples to Venus, and I believe that antiquity would have been less wonderstruck by Psyche's voyage to the underworld if it had been able to foresee that the Graces would settle one day in Troyes.

Between Tartarus and the chief place of the département of the Aube the comparison is less bizarre than you think. I do not know, at least, whether the bloodhounds of the police of Rhadamanthus have a more implacable and more suspicious humor. One accused my passport of irregularity; another swore that he had seen my description posted somewhere; one mistook the list of characters in a vaudeville in my notebook for a list of conspirators; and some other, to whom I showed, in order to reveal my value, my bouquets to Chloris and my diplomas from the Lycée, responded to me with a humorously magisterial gravity that men of letters were unknown in Troyes, but that there was an Academy there.

As soon as I had escaped from that labyrinth of jurisdiction, I ordered that my carriage be prepared, and as that required some time, I went to divert myself in the meantime at a performance of *Mahomet*[1] in a hall of such comfortable construction that one could easily transport oneself, with a single step, from the forestage to the amphitheater. The legislator of Arabia had a right hand truncated by an entire carpal, which is of no small importance in exclamation; Zopir was paralytic, Séïde affected a vocal extinction and Palmire, eight months pregnant, could not dissimulate the evidence of her incestuous amour. But what was most enjoyable in that parade was the delight of the audience, whose members stamped their feet and howled long acclamations every time the Rosciuses of the boards suspended their bombastic speeches to command the hubbub.

I was in such a hurry to quit Troyes and arrive in Paris that I would not have put off my voyage to the next day at any price. Nine o'clock was chiming when I leapt into my post-chaise, where Labrie was already profoundly asleep, and I was pulling the door shut behind me when a veiled woman appealed to me softly, and begged me to lend her a hand in order to enable her to accompany me.

Astonishing as that proposition appeared to me, I acceded to it without proffering a word. I wrapped my arms around a charming waist and I deposited my pretty burden in the back of the carriage, of which I took the front beside my valet de chambre.

---

1 Voltaire's tragedy *Le Fanaticisme, ou Mahomet le Prophète*, was first performed in 1741. Napoléon was said by his biographer the Comte de Las Cases to have thought it very unjust to the prophet and his followers, representing them as murderous thugs and not giving them enough credit for changing the world; Nodier had no way of knowing, in 1803, the full extent to which Napoléon would change the world.

An entire quarter of an hour passed in thanks on the part of my traveling companion and compliments on mine, and we were far beyond the barrière when that mystery, which is probably disquieting you, was explained to me. It was with regard to a very pronounced snore on the part of Labrie that the young woman, believing that her aunt was already asleep, demonstrated to me quite clearly that she was not where she thought she was, and that she had simply mistaken my carriage for a public vehicle. I recalled having seen one at the door a few paces from mine; I presumed that the aunt had preceded the niece thereinto, and that the latter had only addressed herself to me by virtue of a misapprehension easy to comprehend.

I laughed so loudly and wholeheartedly that I could not dispense with explaining why, and you will easily divine that the scene took on a new aspect. The tearful beauty overflowed in the most pathetically touching laments, and in imprecations regarding her stupidity. I had a great deal of difficulty reassuring her and convincing her that there was nothing desperate in her adventure. Fortunately, her aunt, like us, was following the road to Paris and we were able to wait for her at the first relay, where she might perhaps catch up with us without having perceived her absence. I concluded with protestations so ardent and respectful that her regrets appeared to me to be considerably soothed, and she thought it appropriate to assure me of her gratitude.

I seized the opportunity to speak to her in a penetrating tone about the affectionate sentiments that she inspired in me, the tender attachment that I felt the need to consecrate to her as soon as daybreak, and I even had the rascality to add timidly that I had never experienced anything in my life similar to what was passing through my heart.

She sighed. I took her hands in mine; she made a slight effort to withdraw them, but I pressed them more energetically, and the movement that I made to retain them drew her toward me. A stupidity would have cut things short, but I had another three hours of good war, and preliminaries have their price. I only gained from that skirmish, therefore, a few inches of terrain and an advantageous position.

Our hands were united, our legs crossed, our breath confounded. Labrie was asleep; it was dark; we did not speak, but that allows time for reflection and desire. I did not attempt anything, but that familiar communication gradually put decency to sleep and awakened lust. Add to that the fact that there is no woman who pardons respect in such circumstances, and by virtue of wanting the attack, one forgets to defend oneself against it. Here, everything favored me, and at that price, I would attempt a Penelope.

That had lasted for twenty minutes when a violent shock to the vehicle transported my traveling companion from her place to my knees. I abandoned her hands in order to pass mine behind her, and she was about to employ her liberty to oppose to me all the resistance of which she was capable when a second shock determined otherwise and forced her to seize me instead of repelling me. My mouth encountered hers and stuck a passionate kiss to it, for which she did not have the right to reproach me, since it was only up to me to attribute it to hazard; but I have reason to believe that it produced an effect other than anger, for she leaned her head tenderly on my shoulder, sighing with languor and sensuality.

Already things were in the best disposition in the world, but Providence, which favors me in such a striking fashion, did not want to leave me the honor of concluding that delightful adventure on my own, and a third shock even more fortunate than the other two spared me the expenses of the enterprise.

I savored my victory for a long time, to the sound of moans of vanquished modesty and murmurs on the part of Labrie, who, disturbed by the jolts, cursed while half-asleep highways, horses and postillions.

The vehicle carrying the aunt reached the relay immediately after mine. I embraced my unknown beauty, bid her a tender adieu, and left her the care of clarifying the matter, in which I did not think it prudent to involve myself.

At five o'clock in the evening I arrived in Paris and I took a room in my usual lodgings, the Hôtel de Hambourg, at numbers sixty-nine and seventy Rue de Grenelle-Saint-Honoré, opposite the Hôtel des Fermes.[1]

Although I already knew Paris, I was certain to experience new sensations in that immense theater, where ever-varied scenes succeeded one another infinitely, and where fashion, that indefatigable Proteus, multiplies its metamorphoses with so much activity. During a year of absence, everything must have changed form, and in fact, Paris was for me a new city, where I felt the need for a guide who could instruct me regarding the resolutions of taste and indicate good manners, for those frivolous notions are indispensable to being seen favorably in society, and even to being understood there. Conduct a stranger from circle to circle, from the Faubourg Saint-Germain to the Marais and the Chaussée-d'Antgin to the Cité, and that man would have the right to be persuaded that the nomenclature of clothing and jugglers was the whole foundation of the language; and that, except for a few conventional phrases that do not signify anything in any idiom, we have no other vocabulary than the *Journal des Modes* and the *Feuille des Spectacles*. He could at least guarantee that he had heard few conversations the day before that did not require translation into the style of tomorrow in order still to be understood; and that if all of France had decided to obey such an impulsion, the masterpieces of the previous century would have been as obsolete as our petticoats and furbelows.

1 This was the address at which Nodier stayed during his first sojourn in Paris in 1800-01; the house was managed by the wife of the driver of the diligence that traveled between Besançon and Paris.

As I knew that our friend Frantz was very prevalent in society, I resolved to consult him with regard to the employment of my time, the nature of my habitudes and the choice of my pleasures. After a few days I went to see him and I found him faithful to the taste you know him to have for sensualities more facile than delicate, in which the sentiment of peril always troubles that of success. Clara was disputing the door with Honorine, Pauline was swooning in the antechamber while reading a new romance, and Frantz, lying on a bed between Laurence and Virginie, like Compère Mathieu's Diego,[1] was distributing his vigorous amours left and right. My presence disconcerted the eloquent demonstration slightly, and I succeeded in extracting my Renaud from the arms of the half-dozen Armidas, who could not resolve to quit him yet. We spent the day together and went to conclude it at a tea, to which he was urgently pressed to go and where he obtained, without difficulty, the permission to introduce me, even though he was presenting himself there for the first time.

The gathering was numerous, and the women most elegantly adorned. I say nothing about their allure, for they were of a maturity so advanced that the most judicious eye would have had difficulty recovering vestiges of it, and I believed at first glance, that I had been transported to the court of Reine Berthe.[2] Would you believe it, though? Those sexagenarian nymphs, who owed their figures to their lingerie, their flowery breath to the perfumer, and the carmine of their dilapidated complexion to the colorist, were surrounded by a pressing swarm of admirers, who intoxicated them competitively with insipid compliments and incense. I would willingly have taken

1 In the libertine romance *Le Compère Mathieu, ou Les Bigarrures de l'esprit humain* (1766) by the defrocked monk Henri-Joseph Du Laurens.

2 Bertha of Swabia (907-966), Queen of Burgundy by her first marriage and of Italy by her second, was subsequently venerated in Switzerland as a model of virtue, accumulating various pious legends around her memory.

that extravagant worship for a sacrifice to the Fates or for the mysteries of the witches of Thessaly, if I had not remembered the king of fable who had the power to turn everything to gold. It is thanks to a similar faculty, in our country, that the most decrepit old age can still obtain homages, and one sees our elegant men practicing with so much zeal the most beautiful of the virtues of Lacedaemon.

Frantz and I remarked at the same moment a woman that it is necessary to except from those observations, whose piquant charms were further embellished by the effect of the contrast, as the splendor of a rose seems more vivid when spring has given birth to it among brambles. We took advantage of the movement that our arrival had occasioned to take possession rather abruptly of neighboring places in order to be able to observe her at close range.

"In general, the woman is not so much beautiful as pretty, but her features seem to gain in softness what they lack in regularity, and the expression of her physiognomy is enriched at the expense of its forms; cleverly contrived nudities, the sight of which she is able to dispense with all the art of an ingenious coquetry fix gazes for a time, but the favors it promises make those which it gives forgotten. Everything about her respires tenderness and sensuality; her head, tilted gently over an alabaster shoulder, expresses abandon; her lips, slightly parted with a slight quiver, appear to be stammering the tremulous and uncertain language of pleasure, and her eyes roll over their humid crystal a tear of desire, of which amour will one day make a tear of happiness . . ."

"Stop!" cried Frantz, to whom I said all that as we passed from the drawing room to the tea room. "Either you're abusing strangely your facility for description or we've seen that woman from very different points of view. She is pretty, in truth; the character of her figure has more boldness than grace, more finesse than suavity; what you call her coquetry could pass for cynicism, and I find that she accords too much to the eyes to leave something to be desired by the imagination. All her mannerisms have an air of affectation and symmetry that does not resemble abandon at all; and her gaze, where you have read such a touching expression, seems to me to have an indecent assurance; however, it's not her fault, and I don't believe that her dark eyes, crowned by ebony eyebrows, could ever interpret a mild and delicate sentiment."

"This time, you're not thinking," I replied, hotly. "Her eyes reflect the purest azure of the sky, and it isn't from ebony but from gold that her eyebrows have borrowed their color."

The dispute was becoming heated when the rest of the company gathered around us. Everyone took their places around the circular table, and for the second time, the woman who had just been the object of our discussion found herself seated between Frantz and me.

As soon as we were free and the teapot was about to be passed round, we flew toward one another in order to continue our argument, but with entirely different intentions. Frantz confessed that he had seen poorly at first, and that my description was the only one in conformity with the original, while, brought around to his ideas, I claimed the opposite. My timid blonde had become a provocative brunette, and his proud Juno a modest Hebe. Thus we had exchanged opinions without ending the quarrel, and the same cause still animated the same combatants.

Have you seen in Homer the two armies remaining motionless at the sight of Helen? The arrival of our Helen produced a similar effect on us. She smiled at me; I responded to that favor with a sign of intelligence, and she terminated the mute dialogue by slowly raising her arms, in such a manner that her hand described an angle of about ninety degrees, geometrically speaking. I followed it because in all countries, that energetic sign means *follow me* or *come here*, and it is particularly in use at windows on the entresol in many of the good quarters of our fine city of Paris.

As the drawing room had remained free, we stopped there, she sat down and . . . !

Imagine my surprise when I recognized that that strange woman was, in fact, brunette and blonde, and that nature had treated her very nearly like Janus in sticking to one side and the other two profiles very astonished to find themselves together. That singularity had absorbed all my thinking faculties when I was extracted from my stupefaction by a loud burst of laughter, which was followed by the following speech, in a tone whose inflections appeared to me to be as fickle as her features and her character.

"You see," she said to me, "that hazard has endowed me singularly; or rather, Providence has wanted to manifest, in a very bizarre manner, the versatility of my mind. Whatever the cause might be, I have noticed that the observation has struck you, and what would you think if you could perceive as easily everything that is disparate in my principles and my conduct, my ideas and my action? Grave or flighty, prudish or libertine, good or bad by caprice, I have rarely been the same for two days in succession, and I make no mystery of that for you, for I'm sometimes frank but always without further consequence. You pleased me at first sight and I wanted to warn you; tomorrow, you would have come here too late to be welcomed, and it is a hundred to one that in twenty-four hours you will appear detestable to me.

"Today I love you madly and it only depends on you to take advantage of it; furthermore, you will be grateful to me for that step, if I tell you that I have made it here and there, to Saint-Preux[1] and Werthers, and that among all the talents with which a prodigal heaven has endowed me, I have from time to time that of resistance, with the consequence that, during

1 The tutor in Rousseau's *La Nouvelle Héloïse* (1761).

a good part of my life, I have only passed from the role of Madame Lignolle to that of Pamela,[1] and from extravagance to prudery. My language seems extraordinary to you—good; it will be pleasant if you understand me; personally, I have never understood myself.

"Such as you see me, however, I am capable of solid resolutions. Two years ago the whim took me to marry a man I abhorred. People opposed it. I insisted. If everyone on earth had wanted it, I would never have ceded, but my project displeased everyone and I carried it out in a spirit of contradiction. My spouse was mortally tedious. He was a fool who took it into his head to believe himself noble as soon as titles were suppressed, and constituted a posthumous marquisate in spite of all Paris. All I gained from my marriage was the title and the *particule*. That was not sufficient for me and I yearned to change existence.

"I had myself abducted by hussar and entertained a *trente-un* banker.[2] The laws are convenient for infidels and I had had enough of marriage to be curious about widowhood. I presented a petition for divorce and obtained my definitive liberty by alleging an incompatibility of humor, which did not surprise anyone. Since that time I have had many lovers, but of all the men I have seen, none has inspired more interest in me that you. I'd like to promise you a passion, and I feel capable of rendering you happy for a week; that has happened to me three times, and yet I mistrust my frivolity so much that I'm firmly decided, as I told you, not to put you off until tomorrow.

"Very well," she continued, "I can see that your eagerness responds to my generosity, and I expected that, for you have an advantageous physiognomy; but I want to put your tender-

---

1 Madame de Lignolle in a character in *Les Amours du Chevalier de Faublas* (1787-90) by Jean-Baptise Louvet de Couvrai, whose adventures were continued in sequels by other hands; Pamela is the eponymous heroine of Samuel Richardson's 1740 novel *Pamela; or, Virtue Rewarded*,

2 *Trente-un* was a slang term for a gambling den.

ness to the proof, and prove to you that my possession is not something that one obtains without purchasing it. I require two hours of cares and a romantic denouement, firstly, because it's piquant and, secondly, because it's almost indispensable.

"You've seen that man with the suntanned complexion, the ignoble face and the trenchant tone, who talks about everything without knowing anything, and who prides himself on having manners; that's my current lover; it would take a great deal, in truth, for him to have the privilege of rendering me constant. If that were an easy thing, he'd still be an exception; but he suits me because he's liberal enough to merit holding on to, and gauche enough to suffer being deceived. I've never known a more maladroit dissipater and a more inept rich man. I'll add that I don't know of any jealous person more suspicious, and who's more suited to being. He possesses me for the sake of ostentation, not by virtue of taste; for the sake of fashion, not by virtue of temperament; but he has the fury of propriety, and he keeps me under lock and key, like his library, of which he makes no more use.

"You'll conceive that such a lover rarely obsesses me with his ardor, but on the other hand, he's as assiduous at the door of my apartment as a eunuch at the door of a seraglio. It's necessary, therefore, for you to resolve to penetrate into it by means of a rope ladder, which I'll throw down to you at midnight. This is my address. Be punctual, and spare me the insipid compliments that you're getting ready to spout. I divine that it would be sad to perish, and I have a nervous malady to think about. Adieu . . . I'll expect you."

That speech was reeled off with such volubility that I was unable to manifest the emotions of astonishment, pleasure, dread and uncertainty that occupied me, except by more or less significant gestures, which, in spite of the scrupulous exactitude with which I sought to conserve all their expressiveness, I dare not guarantee entirely.

As soon as I was alone I tried to reflect, which hardly ever happens to me, and I ended up doing the opposite of what I had resolved, which always happens to me—which is to say, that I went to my rendezvous, at the risk of suffering the fate of Psyche. In the boudoir of a courtesan, it is Venus who holds the scissors of the Fate.

The marquise lived in the vicinity of the Opéra, in one of those houses whose ground floor is surmounted by a rather wide ledge. At the precise hour, the first-floor window opened, the rope-ladder was thrown down to me, I climbed it, detached it, threw it into the room and was getting ready to follow it when a noise was audible at the opposite door.

"It's him!" cried the marquise. It was indeed; he appeared at the same moment, so that I could only be hidden from his gaze by slamming the casement shut on me.

I presume that it would have been rather amusing to see me elevated thus at a height of twenty feet on a ten-inch base, in the manner of the statues of Hermes with which the ancients decorated the front of their houses; but the season was so advanced, the weather so rigorous, and the issue so uncertain that I did not have the slightest desire to find my position diverting, and I was only thinking about getting out of it. I therefore made my way along the whole length of my ledge, measuring the height of the fall with a fearful eye; I retraced my steps, and then made further attempts, as impotent as the first, and I ended up stopping, shivering, paralyzed and faltering, from annoyance, dejection and lack of sleep, next to the window from which it seemed to me that I had departed.

I did not take long to open, at the sound of my nocturnal excursion; a naked woman appeared to me and I did not doubt that my rival had left the field free for our pleasures. All the more delighted by that fortunate event because it was unexpected, I passed into the room with an incalculable velocity; I took possession of my prey and carried her palpitating to the throne of amour.

Meanwhile, she mingled cries of fright with my cries of triumph, and heaped me with laments and pleas, which I interrupted with as many kisses. Never had a more formal resistance been opposed to me; but I remembered the conversation of the evening, and I was determined to vanquish the capricious spirit that was disputing with so much stubbornness a promised victory. I had, in any case, purchased it too dearly to cede it without a fight, and my impetuous ardor soon broke the barrier, although one obstacle that I had less right to expect than any other came to delay my success; but that incomprehensible obstacle rendered my adversary's defeat more precious and multiplied the audacity of my attack a hundredfold. In any case, if the defense was nullified, or at least became very light, abundant tears succeeded it, and I did not know what to think of that manner of acting in a rendezvous.

"In truth, Madame," I said to her, "it appears that all your actions reflect the bizarrerie of your mind, and that you have the habit of not doing anything like others. Who would have thought that you would weep on such an occasion?"

"Monsieur," someone said, in a sobbing and halting voice, "I suspected your error but you didn't want to hear anything."

"What are you saying?"

"That you mistook my window for that of my neighbor."

"You aren't the woman who was expecting me?"

"No, Monsieur.

"You haven't seen me this evening?"

"Never."

"You didn't close your window on me an hour ago, on the arrival of your jealous lover?"

"I have had the misfortune of opening up to you ten minutes ago, at the noise you were making."

"You're not brunette and blonde?"

"I have ashen hair."

"And it's against your consent . . . ?"

"Yes, Monsieur."

"And I'm perhaps the first . . . ?"
"Not entirely, but very nearly . . ."
"I suspected as much."
"I'm very unfortunate."
"You should have warned me."
"You should have listened to me."
"It's necessary to resolve yourself."
"That's sage."
"I'm not responsible for a misunderstanding."
"That's true."
"If necessary, I'll repair my fault."
"That's impossible."
"I'll come to see you."
"I'll change lodgings."
"I'll follow you anywhere."
"I'm soon going to marry."
"Good—there's no reply to that."

Her tears dried up, her regrets began to calm down; I consoled her completely and I left, after having engaged myself by oath not to make any effort to find her again.

I returned to my hotel and arrived there before daybreak, reflecting on the vicissitudes of life and the singular blows of fate. You can see that in my moral works.

Frantz had gone on campaign, and a week went by without me seeing him again. Finally, one day he came into my room while retiring from a play and invited me to accompany him to a masked ball at the Société Olympique, where he was going to spend the night. I consented gladly, for I like noisy and tumultuous pleasures that subjugate the attention without interesting the heart overmuch, and in which rapid and varied distractions even forbid the soul the leisure to fold in on itself.

Everything pleases me in a masked ball: it is a faithful image of the world, but life seems to accelerate there by reason of the multiplicity of events: in a fortunate imitation of Saturnalias, equality, banished from the rest of society, appears to have taken refuge there, and it can at least reclaim its rights there once a year. People are confounded, huddled together, conversing; the language of familiar amity flies there from all mouths; ugliness can make itself adored by favor of wit; verity can make itself heard under the protection of folly; and a severe lesson that would have alarmed self-esteem elsewhere is welcomed at a masked ball.

There alone it is possible to say anything; there alone frankness is something common, and the mask is the celebrated talisman that forces speech to become the interpreter of thought. The powerful man who has damaged your interests with an iniquitous judgment; the bad writer who has deceived your attention with a tedious pamphlet; the insolent journalist who fatigues you every morning with his defamatory articles; the superannuated prude with the wrinkled face who crushes you with her disdain; the rich parvenu who, from the height of his brilliant carriage, splashes you with the mud from which he has emerged . . . console yourself; hazard, in assembling them at a masked ball, promises you a vengeance that will be facile without being cowardly, and piquant without being cruel.

Reassure yourself also, you whose new and timid heart is smitten with a respectful ardor for some lady of high birth; this evening, Amour will work a miracle in your favor; he will smooth out all difficulties, stifle all prejudices, and conciliate the conventions of rank with the interests of happiness. Profit from that moment, which liberty has stolen from etiquette; at a masked ball, there is no longer any temerity in a confession, no longer any pride in a hope; fashion pays the expenses of the enterprise for you, and the advances of success. Although the majority of the affections of the world finish under a mask, it is not rare to see them commencing in the same manner, and the sweet intimacy that mystery favors has revealed more than one tender sympathy.

In a word—and I could prove it with good arguments—the masked ball is the masterpiece of all human institutions, and the last tradition of the Golden Age.

As Frantz's urgency did not leave me time to think about my costume, I substituted a flax-gray domino and hid my face under a Venetian mask. Either because I sensed in advance, as I went in, the pleasures that I was about to savor in that place of enchantment, or because there is, in fact, something rapturous that acts on all souls, the sight of the ballroom filled me with a delectable disturbance, and an unaccustomed emotion.

Forgive me that surge of puerile sensibility. I know how unworthy such movements are of us, but Achilles was able to hide among women until he was reminded of his valor by presenting him with weapons.

Frantz had frequented that gathering during the previous winter, and he had acquired notions so perfect of the bearing, mannerisms and disguises of all the habitués that he took responsibility for naming the masks to me and becoming as instructive a guide as the devil Asmodeus was for the student Cleofas.[1] In consequence, we sat down in one of the busiest places in the hearth and we commenced our inspection.

"It would be superfluous," he said to me, "to name for you all the individuals who will pass before us in succession. There are a great number who are attracted to the ball by curiosity, by the desire to be seen, or by the need to fill some hours of idleness that they cannot employ better. You've encountered those people everywhere, and they're equally unworthy of attention everywhere. To indicate one of them is to indicate them all, and nature has so neglected their character and their intelligence that one can say, without overmuch exaggeration, that those fashionable automata have emerged ready-made from the hands of Catel.[2]

---

1 In *Le Diable boiteux* (1707; tr. as *The Devil on Two Sticks*) by Alain-René Lesage.

2 The mechanician Peter Friedrich Catel (1747-1791), who owned a toy

"It would also be futile for me to extend myself on people that you can divine as soon as me, and whose characteristic physiognomy does not escape perspicacity. What would be the point of designating those eccentrics that everyone recognizes, and whose livery is already signaled to public attention? That man with the swollen face and woolly black hair, freshly trimmed, wearing fashionable attire gauchely, displaying half a dozen diamonds ostentatiously on each hand, who thinks it good form to provoke all the women with scandalous glances, have I any need to say that he is a supplier?

"When I have shown you that tall young man who is walking through the crowd with embarrassment, fearful of crumpling his new suit, who bumps into passers-by while gazing at the caryatids, is it necessary to add that he is a provincial on his first voyage? That woman with the thick corsage gravely promenading the remains of a beauty once dearly bought, deluding herself disdainfully in her ceremonial adornment, can you not see that she is a kept woman reformed by time, searching for bidders?

"You already know the greater number of those young men that we can see from here next to a table laden with punch and liqueurs, who are making the hall resound with their outbursts of noisy joy. But if you were distinguishing them for the first time, I have no doubt that by the dilapidation of their attire, the affectation of their manners and the ridiculously precious tone of their conversation you would recognize them for a few of those authors by the dozen who vegetate arrogantly in a prideful obscurity. They are, in fact, authors, and don't be astonished if the insipid quips in their frothy conversation cause such universal hilarity; they have the custom of laughing at everything they say, and they all talk at the same time.

---

shop in Berlin, attracted international attention in the 1780s with an orrery of his construction, and went on to manufacture ingenious magic lanterns.

"I make an exception of that one, who is listening to them modestly and admiring them with condescension. He's a petty provincial litterateur who has come to try himself in the capital and who is making his debut, so he has only as yet put thirty-two thousand three hundred and fifty sheets of paper in circulation.

"Among the men who remain for us to examine, you have doubtless remarked the one with his hat pulled down, his arms folded and a pensive expression, wandering sadly from one group to another without addressing a word to anyone. He is wearing yellow trousers and a sky blue coat in order to have one conformity more with Werther, who is his hero; but that mania has procured him adventures so pleasant that I have often envied him their collection and cannot dispense with talking to you about him for some time.

"That enthusiast, who is also endowed with amiable qualities, and who has more wit than is necessary to pass for originality, had arrived at the age of twenty without experiencing any violent sentiment. Welcome in all the circles that it pleased him to frequent, he had limited himself thus far to the ordinary routine of gallantry. It was in that epoch that the romance of which I spoke came into his hands and he conceived the project of making it the agenda of his conduct. From that moment on he occupied himself exclusively with all the studies that could bring him closer to his model. He bought a Westein Homer,[1] in expectation of being able to read it, and by dint of hard labor he succeeded in a short time in being able to sketch the landscape passably. The verity of an imitation Charlotte

1 In Goethe's romance Werther is greatly influenced by Homer, although his reading of the text is idiosyncratic, aided by the fact that the edition named is devoid of commentary and thus open to whimsical interpretation. For instance, Werther, infatuated with the married Charlotte, identifies with Penelope's suitors, whom he sees as romantically patient rather than brutally opportunistic, as in the conventional reading. In this sarcastic account, the young Wertherian's reading of Goethe seems to have been equally idiosyncratic, if not frankly perverse.

was already striking, but he was determined to complete the resemblance, and his splenetic imagination was increasingly familiarized day by day with the fatal denouement. Finally, it was no longer a matter of anything except discovering his heroine and fixing the duration of the attack. He studied all the editions of Werther in order to determine that essential point, but for want of finding anything precise, he settled on a month, as an average term, and precipitated himself with all the power of his will into that perilous enterprise.

"You know," Frantz continued, "that I received the name of Guillaume at the baptismal font, and it is by virtue of that fortunate coincident, which earned me his correspondence, that I am informed of the various incidents of his story.

"The first woman who obtained the bizarre honor of representing Werther's Lucrèce in his regard was a newlywed, infinitely sentimental, who had formed her mind and her heart reading English romances and had just been united, by inclination, with a charming man. She did not go out, did not dance and did not appear at spectacles without her husband. Present, she heaped him with her caresses, absent she was untiring in praising him; in brief, our philosopher was as delighted by such an encounter as he was impatient to take advantage of it, and after a week of assiduity he risked a declaration. It was received, as he expected, with all the anger that such an outrage can inspire in virtue, but she soon softened in consideration of his youth and inexperience. The boldness of his step was pardoned, out of regard for the violence of his passion, and she went so far as to promise him amity, if he could be content with that. He capitulated under that condition, and thus disguised his pursuit without interrupting it. Gradually, the meetings became more frequent, the relationship more affectionate and the confidence more intimate. After three weeks, an adroitly contrived reef caused the Penelope to fall, and she ceded to the lover, while still protesting her tenderness for the husband.

"That setback did not disconcert him. He knew that the character of the sex has strange inconsistencies, and that one can make a mistake initially when one is in quest of a faithful woman. He paid court to a devotee. *Now*, he said to himself, *I'm certain of being rejected, for the woman I love is both pious and constant, and Heaven is a third party in the interests of the hymen.* His hope deceived him as before, and the result demonstrated it. He chose the highest temple for his battlefield; he seduced the saint by means of grimaces, attacked her with homilies and addressed passionate ballads to her to the tune of plainsongs, and the mystical Charlotte succumbed to the tempter while sighing prayers.

"We have too many things to see for me to follow him with the same precision in all the skirmishes of his campaign; it will be sufficient for me to tell you that amour, obstinate in despairing him with what makes the happiness of others, had not ceased to lavish favors on him that he never ceased to curse, and that thus far, all his trials had reached the same denouement.

"Only three women have defeated him roundly. The first is a coquette who flirts openly with everyone but does not give herself to anyone; on the twenty-eighth day a caprice decided the matter. The second is a woman of principle who detests her husband but treasures her reputation because she values the right to be arrogant and malevolent. A favorable and mysterious opportunity caused her to succumb eventually. The third is the pretty wife of a farmer in the environs of Paris, who had always lived in a manner so irreproachable that she was generally thought to have some secret fault or negative dispositions of temperament. Those reasons were not of a nature to determine the death of our eccentric; he submitted them to me and was awaiting my response when vanity delivered her conquest to him an hour before the monthly revolution was completed. That was the thirty-sixth of his attempts, and in the chagrin that he experienced in not having found his phoenix in the village, he has come to seek her at the masked ball.

"Hazard has served us well," Frantz went on. "It has been kind enough to assemble here all that Paris has of the most amiable, and the Graces have arranged a rendezvous at the ball, where I have just seen them enter in rose-colored dominos. I cannot show you among them the celebrated beauty that all men adore and all women esteem, and who would still be the foremost by reason of her virtues, if she were not by reason of her charms. She is absent, and another land is lavishing on her the homages that she tried to avoid. Thus, the goddess of Amours inhabits by turns Gnide, Amathonte and Paphos, but her charms betray her and she has altars everywhere.

"You will have no difficulty in divining who the charming women are to whom I've just called your attention. They owe too universal a celebrity to the splendor of their attractions, their fortune and their wit for their names not to have reached you. What am I saying? Calumny will have informed you of them in default of renown, and a cowardly defamer has recently dragged them once again in the mud of his libel. But let us abandon to scorn that literary Erostratos [1] who thinks he is acquiring rights to glory by dint of burning temples and outraging divinities.

"That one combines all the qualities that can seduce the eyes, flatter the mind and fix the heart; sage without prudery, amiable without effort, never have more perfections been allied with more modesty. An enlightened patroness of the arts that she cultivates, the sight of her inspires talent, her liberalities favor them, and she is simultaneously the Muse and the

---

1 Erostratos, or Herostratus, was accused of setting fire to the temple of Artemis at Ephesus, one of the Seven Wonders of the World, in the fourth century B.C. He is alleged by legend to have confessed under torture to have done so in order to immortalize his name, so his judges decreed, as a posthumous punishment, that it should never be spoken, thus ensuring what they were supposedly trying to prevent.

Maecenas of our poets. Severe people reproach her for her fêtes and her prodigalities, but even her faults are those of a beautiful soul, and she has none, however slight, that is not redeemed by a virtue.

"She cannot be mistaken for the one who is following her. Her name is on all mouths, because everyone recognizes the vivacity of her stride and the beauty of her deportment. She is cheerful to the point of folly, but her enjoyments do not harm her sensibility, and her graces embellish her frivolity. Sometimes mild and reserved, sometimes impetuous and petulant, she has all the bad habits of a fashionable young man and all the charms of a lovable woman; in the morning she tames a charger and causes a phaeton to fly; in the evening she attracts all gazes by her enchanting dancing. Her varied tastes do not suit all characters, but all those who see her cannot dispense with loving her.

"Immediately after her you can see two phenomena of the sex. There is a pretty woman who has no coquetry and female author who has no pretention. The person accompanying her is a charming Swedish woman who combines judgment with imagination and finesse with sentiment. I do not know any woman who possesses more eminently the double talent of pleasing and touching, and gaining successively, either the heart via the mind or the mind via the heart.

"But let's pass on to another part of the hall," Frantz continued, "and we can't fail to find material there for further observations."

"No, if you please," I replied, "and all the esteem that I have for your learned conversation cannot determine me to leave here; I'm retained here by too powerful a bond, and to spare you a question, I'll inform you in a single word that the bond in question is amour.

"What, you have recognized . . . ?"

"I haven't recognized anyone."

"You must have seen . . ."
"No one at all."
"And you're impassioned . . . ?"
"For a mask."
"A joke!"
"As you wish; but I have never felt anything similar to what that woman in a black domino inspires in me who is sitting four paces away from us . . ."
"Good! An old woman!"
"That may be."
"An ugly one . . ."
"Who can tell?"
"Or a stupid one . . ."
"I can't answer for that."
"But you love her!"
"Madly."
"As you please."
"Good night."

I approached my beauty, and began the conversation with a madrigal. Her response completed inflaming me; her soft and timid voice produced on my heart the effect of a voice already known, and I loved her presence like that of an adored lover from whom one has been separated for a long time.

That idea emboldened me. I animated the dialogue, and I soon perceived that the young woman had a romantic imagination and an inflammable heart; that nuance of character is common to the majority of women, and that does not astonish me. Endowed with an ardent sensibility that seeks aliments everywhere; delivered to idleness by their weakness, and to seductions by the flattery of their vanity, avid for a happiness that they are only ever to calculate on the basis of false appreciations, because their education has deceived them regarding the world and themselves, they almost always bring to society exaggerated judgments that they only rectify at the price of a costly experience.

In similar circumstances—and they present themselves often—seduction is so facile that it has to need to be reduced to principles, and the triumph so infallible that it belongs to the first comer. Souls of that sort are expansive and confident; in a moment of conversation they are revealed to the least penetrating eye, and if necessary, a few well-prepared maneuvers constrain them to confess the rest of their secret. Then it is easy to calculate all the means, to foresee all the obstacles and to arrive at one's goal without contradiction; you know already what the weak side of that naïve heart is, and that is the direction from which it is necessary to attack it. Caress its errors, for you can take advantage of them; praise what is vicious, for women love their faults more than their qualities; mold all your thoughts, all your words and all your manners to those of the beloved object, taking care to remark continually on that sympathetic conformity.

Have you produced some emotion? Seek to make her believe it; pass from sadness to joy, from abandon to recklessness; play the trouble of passion; seize a hand that she will not dare refuse you; try a confession that she is yearning to hear; but let your language be hesitant, irreflective and halting; let all your notions be caught in the throat, and let your breast, inflated by the lungs, seem full of sighs. If you do not have the art of weeping at will, at least pretend to wipe away tears that are on the brink of escaping and to constrain your dolor. If you are consoled, become bolder; it's certain that you are loved, and that you will not be opposed by more than the customary resistance. But let your efforts be ardent without ceasing to be delicate; you might lose all the fruit of the enterprise by allowing yourself to be recognized before it is complete.

Remember that one abandons to seduction that which one disputes to force, and that an insinuating politics opens more cities than audacity conquers. Thus, mistrust too impatient an ambition, and make sure of your success without abruptness.

When you command intoxication, pretend to be yielding to it yourself, and to be obeying in spite of yourself the impulsion that you have provided. It is necessary that the first favors be filched and not plundered, but the moment that the emotion has progressed as far as disorder, do not delay; one poorly-employed minute might doom you, and you would only have reached the port in order to see it fleeing without return.

Interrogate all women; there is not one who does not have a moment marked to succumb, and our tactics are reduced to bringing it about and seizing it. I would conclude from that willingly that the class of sage women is composed of those who have enough sang-froid to disguise the shepherd's hour, and the class of unfortunate lovers of those who have insufficient penetration to divine it.

At any rate, I put into practice what I have just established in theory, and I produced all the effect for which I had reason to hope. There is something original in an amour born under the mask, and that excites the imagination. There is something disinterested in a sentiment that owes nothing to sight, and that reassures innocence. There is something flattering in a triumph that is owed to one's wit, and that awakens self-esteem. In sum, reason adopts the cause of the heart; one reflects, or, rather, one believes that one is reflective. One weighs everything, anticipates everything; one is sure of not being known; one is firmly decided not to allow oneself to be seen; one is risking neither one's repose nor one's reputation; one is not putting one's happiness at the mercy of an inconstancy, or one's honor at the mercy of an indiscretion; and one can savor the sweetest pleasures of amour without fearing the slightest chagrin. Do you know many women who would not attempt the adventure at that price?

In the heat of the conversation, I had adroitly changed position, and we had arrived, as if involuntarily, in the garden. That is because a crowd is a confusion, a tumult, is it not?

One is exposed to such insipid pleasantries; one is distracted by such importunate people. Talk to me about the pleasures of nature, the meditation of solitude, the expansion of two souls in harmony: that is delightful! It is cold, but that season pleases me; I like its nebulous days, its glacial nights, its piquant winds and its carpets of snow. Am I mistaken in that? Impossible! I would swear that you are melancholy . . .

Well, what idiot could be mistaken about it? Convene the entire sex, make an exact appeal; scrutinize, examine, interrogate, and tell me whether you have encountered an individual of the species who is not melancholy or does not pride herself on being? It's necessary; melancholy is, in this case, mistaken for amour, and amour is the sole occupation of women.

That young woman, who has only quit the toys she had at twelve a few days ago, and who is walking under the great trees of the park, dreaming about her cousin the officer . . . Melancholy!

That blonde with the dying gaze, who is looking at everyone anxiously, because she is trembling that someone might divine the man that she prefers . . . Melancholy!

That coquette who has lost one of her admirers and is thinking about replacing him; that alert brunette who has received a love letter and is preparing the response; that modest virgin who has resisted the opportunity and is yearning to see it reborn; that aged woman who regrets the past and is moaning over the present; that wife who is comparing her lover and her husband; that prude who is striving to conceal an intrigue; that Agnes who is striving to cover up a false step . . . Melancholy, my friend, melancholy! Say no more.

My digressions are not taking me away from my subject, or, at least, I am giving free rein to my imagination, which can easily fill with its conjectures the intervals left by my pen. Shall I say that two o'clock chimed while we were sitting in the hornbeam arbor? Shall I say that it is now five o'clock, and attempt to sketch . . . No; I've already told you; I intend to pass for a first-class libertine, and a bad lot who is rather good company.

We went back into the ball, very satisfied with one another. The crowd was beginning to flow away, and either by chance or by design, my unknown woman was lost in the affluence of masks. She had talked to me about a brutal and jealous lover who was obsessive in his pursuits, whom she detested to such a point that she was thinking of getting rid of him by means of a marriage of convenience. I attributed her sudden eclipse to the appearance of that unwelcome gallant, and after some futile research, I made the decision to retire.

It is necessary to admit, however, that I would have liked to see my Eurydice, at the risk of losing her forever, and I was beginning to weary of my occult good fortunes. Adventures of that sort certainly have an advantageous side, and there is certainly a charm in the vagueness of confused memories and conjectures; our active thought, the creator of illusions, assembles like an ancient painter the features of a hundred beauties in order to compose one; it combines those ideal perfections at will, and, proud of its chimera, it substitutes it for reality.

Thus, the mystery that had enveloped my conquests gave me the right to choose between all objects, and that has happened to me ten times in the boxes of the Opéra and Frascati's salons. But how disagreeable it is, on the other hand—and you will agree with me—only to be able to count as a windfall on anonymous enjoyments, regarding which our self-esteem might be abused, and which society does not credit to our account. God preserve me, however, from approving of those wretches who make a game of the honor of wives and the repose of families; who calculate the number of their pleasures by that of their perfidies, and who make of the reputation of the wives they have obtained as many trophies for as many victories.

The man who abuses confidence, who betrays amour in order to deliver a weak being to despair and tears is, in my opinion, nothing but a coward and a scoundrel; those gratuitous atrocities, the gross aliment of petty souls, are not made for us, and I do not want that barbaric glory, which devours its victims like the gods of Carthage. But the delicate art of deceiving women without dooming them, of subjugating them without oppressing them, and of showing one's triumph without declaring it; the ingenious combinations of circumstances that tell everyone the secret that you affect to hide; the marvelous logic by means of which one can demonstrate that which one refutes; the methodically-prepared distractions that let notions escape that are not yet perceived: all that is of more or less utility in those intrigues of display in which two parties are playing the game, and in which there're is a need to prepare in advance an honorable exit and a savant retreat.

In any other case I incline toward discretion; and be reassured, chaste bourgeoises, innocent provincials, naïve deities of early youth, you to whom I owed so many beautiful days and so many happy nights, be reassured; I shall not engrave your names on the altars that it pleased me to raise to you, and they will remain empty, like those the Romans erected to the unknown gods.

I can anticipate from here the grave reproaches that might be made to my book by my readers in all countries, my Aristarchuses of all times,[1] my century, finally, and posterity.

"No plan!" someone will cry.

"A masterpiece!"

"No interest!"

"It's only necessary to believe!"

"He's already forgotten his mistress!"

---

1 Not to be confused with the astronomer Aristarchus of Samos, Aristarchus of Samothrace was a severe grammarian of the second century B.C., whose name was applied in general to judgmental critics by Classical scholars.

"That happens to me every day."

"And his marriage!"

"That's something else. The merit of the dowry reminds me of the excellence of the sacrament."

Suspend your decision, then, severe censors, who condemn without having heard; know that of all the works I know, mine is the one that it is the most indispensable to finish, if one aspires to understand it, and that is the sole means that I have found to make people read me until the end. That reasoning appears to me to be so victorious that if I am ever reprinted I shall intercalate it in my preface, where it will fit better than here.

A short time after the masked ball I received a letter from my mother. She sent me the address of Mademoiselle de la Reinerie, who had just fixed her abode in the Rue Neuve-de-Berry in the Faubourg Saint-Honoré; but she did not reassure me regarding the fears that we had conceived before my departure; she even had reason to believe that the rumors of marriage then being put about were only too plausible, and it appeared that that fatal news was the absolute despair of my enterprise.

I commenced by yielding to discouragement and ended up exhaling my fury in invectives against destiny. After that unphilosophical transport, I tried to reason; my ideas were rectified, my forces were returned to equilibrium along with my fortune, and I glimpsed consolations. Soon, presumption mingled with it; a certain sentiment of myself which is very favorable to me and very familiar, heightened my audacity again and reestablished my hope; pride smoothed out the difficulties, the horizon was embellished and I engaged myself with more assurance than before in the projects that I had been ready to abandon.

However, I felt the necessity of hastening my visits and giving great activity to my solicitations. While reflecting, I had emerged from the Rue de Grenelle; I had followed the Rue Saint-Honoré as far as the Rue Saint-Florentin; I had traversed the Place Louis XV and was advancing into the Champs-Élysées; it was ten o'clock in the evening, but time was precious to me, the urgency legitimate, the meeting indispensable, and I increased my pace in the direction of the Rue de Berry.

I was only a short distance away when a man who had been following me for a few minutes, and whom I had scarcely noticed, seized me abruptly by the arm. I turned round at that impolite gesture, and recognized, to the extent that the obscurity permitted, that I was dealing with an officer of the hussars, whose hostile and surly physiognomy did not presage anything agreeable.

"Where are you going?" he said, making his sword vibrate melodiously above my head.

"The question is singular."

"I have my reasons for asking it."

"As I have for not replying to it."

"You're going to the Rue de Berry?"

"So be it, since you know."

"And it's a matter of marriage."

"Very well, since you're up to date."

"No one deceives me. *En garde!*"

"You forbid entry to the Rue de Berry, then?"

"No procrastination. *En garde!*"

"And you have something against people who marry?"

"I'll prove it to you. *En garde!*"

"But I have no weapon."

"A second without a weapon! *En garde!*"

"I'm not a second and I have no weapon; it's a mistake . . ."

"It's all the same to me. *En garde!*"

A braver man would have recoiled; the accursed man attacked me, cut and thrust, and deafened me so much with his furious provocations that there was no means of getting in a word of clarification. I had already retreated five or six toises when my foot collided with something sonorous and I picked up a sword. At that unexpected encounter, I gathered all my strength in order to justify the favor of providence and I opposed a stubborn defense to a vigorous attack.

Our clashing blades pressed one another, struck one another in all directions, and to see us so stubborn in that homicidal struggle, one would have taken it for the consequence of an ancient enmity envenomed by further insults; but my star serves me in an equally bizarre manner in all genres of combats, and after having delivered me pleasures that I could not have foreseen, it created adversaries for me that I could not hate; I therefore limited myself, as much as possible, to preserving myself from the soldier's assaults and deflecting his attempts by means of parries more fortunate than cleverly orchestrated.

I did not lose any of my sang-froid, but the heat of the action seemed to augment the wrath of my antagonist; he launched himself forward like a lion, coiled up like a snake, and multiplied himself around me by the rapidity of his movements and the variety of his positions. I was about to succumb to fatigue when, breathless, exhausted and still furious, he precipitated himself on to my sword of his own accord and was run through.

I withdrew my blade, all bloody; I tore up my garments and hastened to prepare a dressing, unfortunately futile. He had just rendered his last sigh.

I sat down in order to get my breath back and to meditate upon that strange event, but the sight of the unfortunate fellow inspired such a strong emotion in me that I was obliged to turn my gaze away from the place where he was lying.

Imagine my astonishment when I discovered, in another direction, the spectacle that I was fleeing, and the terror that gripped my senses when I saw that I was placed between two cadavers. That circumstance explained to me the fortuitous encounter with the sword that I had picked up a few paces away, but it doubled my uncertainty and the danger of my situation. I had done nothing that was not irreproachable, and yet, that unexpected concurrence of extraordinary incidents compromised my safety all the more gravely because no one could testify to my conduct and disculpate me from the double murder, if anyone decided to attribute it to me. I made the sole decision that prudence suggested to me and ran away, with all the velocity of which I was capable, from the theater of the misadventure.

Fear ran with me, however, and my bravery, which an unexpected brawl had not found lacking, could not stand up to the idea of the pursuits of the law. The slightest noise, the most uncertain appearance, caused me to dread an accuser, and I saw commissaires and prévôts everywhere. Having reached a ditch of meager width, which I was getting ready to cross, I thought I perceived more distinctly the form of a man, upright but motionless, who seemed to be waiting for me to pass and staring at me.

After a moment of perplexity, I composed myself as best I could and marched to meet the enemy. Fortunately, that new peril was not of a nature to justify my fear, and I could not prevent myself from smiling when I had convinced myself, by means of a rapid inspection, that the object that had stirred me so much was nothing but a black coat surmounted by a ceremonial wig, symmetrically fixed to the top of a pole, like the coat of arms of some noble knight.

I did not try to take account of the motives that had necessitated the erection of that singular mannequin and to explain why someone had displayed the apparel of an appeal judge in the middle of the Champs-Élysées, but I thought I could appropriate it innocently and that there was no better means of sheltering myself from the suspicions that I trembled to excite. It would have been too extravagant to seek a hired killer under that pedantic accoutrement. I took possession of it unceremoniously, rendering thanks to Heaven for my discovery.

I continued my journey with security and I thought myself certain of not being recognized in my fortunate disguise, when a man ran toward me with the most vivid demonstrations of joy, and embraced me in a manner to stifle me.

"It was up to you" he cried, "to rebuke severely an impertinent, and you have expeditive methods."

"What are you saying?"

"I was a few paces away and I would not have been found wanting if necessary, but you can take over."

"What has happened?"

"Moreover, this catastrophe ought not to give you the slightest anxiety, and the aggression is well proven."

"Explain."

"Sixty people will depose, like me."

"Sixty people?"

"Very distinguished bankers and women of the highest consideration."

"Bankers and women?"

"Undoubtedly, and nothing henceforth will raise an obstacle to your pleasures."

"Ah!"

"You're awaited with impatience."

"Good."

"Don't worry, and come as quickly as possible."

"But where, by all the devils?"

"Good question. Come and sleep with my sister!"

"With your sister?"

"You're hesitating . . ."

"You're joking!"

"No, truly, you can't think so. However, I realize that you don't have your head straight on your wedding day."

At that remark, which had the appearance of an epigram, I darted a glance at my impromptu costume; I suspected the mistake and the enigma was explained to me.

You could bet, in case of need, that my penetration got away with a slight effort. In fact, you might say, it was clearly demonstrated that the man in the wig had got married that day, that he had deposited his university apparel in order to fight a duel, and that it was him whose death you had avenged, without knowing it, by killing the officer of hussars outside the Rue de Berry. It is quite natural that the fellow in question had been deceived by your responses, and had mistaken you for his adversary's second. It is even more natural that the newcomer, who had only seen the duel from a distance, had been deceived by your disguise and had mistaken you for his brother-in-law. Thus far, it leapt to the eyes . . .

I agree; but it is also well demonstrated, in my opinion, that on such an occasion, ideas are difficult to categorize in the head, and it is not easy to put order to one's judgments when one has just killed a man, when one is representing another, when one is being harassed by a third, and it is a matter of nothing less than violating a sacrament!

What is certain is that I was still reflecting on that interminable complication of events when my introducer pushed me abruptly into a drawing room furnished with elegance and closed the door on me, shouting: "Good night, Doctor, there's the bride's bed . . ."

From that moment on, irresolution was no longer permissible for me, and it only remained for me to consummate courageously the marriage that was the windfall that Heaven had reserved for me. However, I was not without anxiety on that point, and the curiosity that was clawing me had already taken me as far as the nuptial bed.

Finally, the soft cadence of an even respiration reassured me. The bride was asleep, or feigning sleep, which made me think that either she had not been informed of the risk that her husband had run, or that she did not care. As it scarcely mattered to me, however, what species of sentiment she had consecrated to him, I passed promptly from that idea to the execution of my design, and after having masked myself almost entirely with the doctor's voluminous wig, I lifted the curtain gently, trembling that I might only receive, as the prize of my indiscretion, a disagreeable certainty.

My destiny had served me better, and although the position of my adorable spouse did not reveal the tenth part of her attractions, I know that the bursts of my enthusiasm did not betray the lover and did not cause him to lose the rights of the husband.

Her head, lying on one arm and covered by the other, only allowed the appearance of a chin molded by the graces and half of a rosy mouth. Over her ivory shoulder floated ashen tresses in large ringlets, and their undulating curls followed meekly the gentle movement of her breast, which was half-hidden from me by jealous linen. My eyes fixed on that voluptuous globe, delicately nuanced with azure, I was spying ardently on the amorous palpitations when my quivering and ill-assured hand quit the curtain, the fall of which was accompanied by a long rustle, and the moment of awakening was announced to me by a sigh.

I did not have a moment to lose, but in less than a minute I had extinguished all the lights, I had rid myself of my grotesque outfit and I was disposed, burning with impatience and amour, to fulfill the duties of the deceased and to conquer his heritage.

Although I had not expected to enjoy such a delectable night, I had reason to think, at least, that the enchantress to whom I owed its pleasures had not conceived more favorable hopes; I had scarcely succeeded in familiarizing her modesty to my caresses than she was already crying, in a tone of astonishment: "Dear doctor!"

"Dear doctor!" she repeated, every time I guaranteed my ardor by means of an eloquent homage, and when slumber had weighed down her eyelids, her arms enlaced around me, her breast heaving and her mouth burning, still dreaming about the sensuality that she was no longer savoring, she was still stammering: "Dear doctor!"

Those charming hours went by too quickly, and when the first rays of daylight, illuminating the apartment with a faint light, came to dissipate the illusion of my happiness the intoxication of amour gave way to the anguish of dread, and I only remembered my transports as a vanished dream.

I escaped silently from the alcove; I approached the window, which was fortunately only at a low elevation, from which the fall could not be perilous, and after having recognized by feel my borrowed garments and swiftly put them on, I opened the casement and threw myself from the first floor into the street.

Either because I had misjudged the distance, however, or because my uncomfortable apparel had hindered my movements, I fell face down on the ground and only got up after some time, covered in mud and contusions.

I was in the Champs-Elysées. I saw again in the distance the bloody theater of my nocturnal altercations and I drew away from it by means of a long detour. The dolor that I felt in all parts, which my recent accident had aggravated, slowed my pace even more, and when I arrived in the center of Paris my watch marked nine o'clock. However, I observed with a fright of which I was not the master that all gazes were fixed upon me and that everyone stopped as I went by.

Soon, the crowd was augmented and opened in front of my route in two parallel ranks, from which a thousand confused cries rose up, which seemed to me to be as many threats and imprecations. Finally, chilled by fear and without hope of salvation, I tried nevertheless to hasten my flight, elbowing aside the insolent populace that was harassing me with its barbaric curiosity, and I reached my hotel, pursued by the affluence that had swelled in my wake.

For a long time Labrie did not know what to think about the state in which he saw me, but as soon as I had pointed out to him the numerous cortege that had gathered behind me, and which I had attributed to that cause the mortal terror by which I was gripped, he cried: "Damn it, in such a grotesque get-up, Monsieur ought to have expected to gather all the rabble of the quarter." Gravely, he added: "You've doubtless come from Paphos, or a late night!"

"Insolent fellow!"

"And the masquerade is so new that it must have produced a great effect . . ."

"Scoundrel!"

"What! It isn't in honor of Mardi Gras . . . ?"

"That's today, you say?"

"Precisely, and upon my soul, everyone might have made the same mistake."

As he spoke, Labrie had conducted me to my mirror, and, my eyes staring, my mouth open, my respiration suspended, I tried to study the disparate pieces of my strange attire.

My deerskin trousers and my black velvet coat, largely spattered with mud, which increased the singularity of the contrast, were the least extraordinary part of that monstrous decoration. In the trouble in which I was plunged and the still-uncertain morning light, I had mistaken a poppy-red scarf for my cravat, put on a sand-colored spencer as if it were a waistcoat and forced on a pair of nacarat gloves; but what rendered the motley more complete was the bride's blonde wig, with which I had coiffed myself instead of the doctor's, and the tresses of which, artistically distributed, escaped in golden waves from a lace turban.

As soon as I was reassured with regard to the most pressing dangers, I communicated to Labrie my anxieties regarding the future and told him an exact story of all my catastrophes. He found the affair so grave and the inconveniences so awkward that he did not believe that I could reasonably subordinate interests of such importance to a doubtful project of marriage.

My opinion was in conformity with his; I paid my bill, ordered horses, and departed for Strasbourg, to which I shall perhaps bring you back without digressions, although with would be easy for me to lard my story with fifty topographical notices in the example of a certain writer who, for want of material to nourish his volumes, amplifies them at the expense of the Vosgien.

"Without digressions," Labrie interjected, who heard me reading back that passage. "I believe that Monsieur's work would not lose by it if he had my adventures printed here."

"What, rogue, you have taken it into your head to have adventures?"

"Listen," he said; "do you remember the old baron who held you in particular esteem, whom you went to visit in the little house in Brumpt when you were sure that he was not there and that you would only find Madame?"

"Young Baronne Valdeuil."

"Exactly. The other day, while traversing the terrace of Feuillans, I perceived ten paces away from me a pretty face that I had seen before. I looked; the pretty face smiled. I approached; the pretty face stopped, and I recognized . . ."

"Madame de Vaudeuil?"

"Not exactly, but Adèle, her former chambermaid, a piquant sprig of a girl, an alluring brunette, nicely turned out, with whom I once spent time in the servants' parlor while Monsieur was spending it with Madame in the bedroom. I learn that my beauty has been the chambermaid of the wife of a parvenu for some months and that she is consequently on the sidewalk of consideration. I walk her to her hotel; I recognize the locality, and I have a rendezvous for midnight. Would you like me to make an invocation to the night, Monsieur?"

"I dispense you of that."

"I have, however, made a great error; but love is blind and stupid. The house has four floors and I have not asked Adèle which one she inhabits."

"Very embarrassing."

"Judge by your own example!"

"You won't go."

"I'll go.

"And where will you look for her?"

"Everywhere. Here I am on the first floor; I knock; the door cedes. I go in; it's dark; I hear a noise; I stop. Someone sighs; I name Adèle; there's a response."

"You're very fortunate."

"Not very. I encounter a fleshless hand that wants to be caressing; I hear a cracked voice that wants to be honeyed. I fall on to the bed, and I measure with all my length a skeleton over sixty years old."

"You recoil!"

"I advance, and I hoist the flag of triumph over that dismantled fortress."

"A fine victory!"

"I'll give it to you ten times over. 'Alas!' someone says to me, with a passionate sigh. 'How well inspired I was when I took you for my nephew's tutor.'"

"You've passed for an abbé."

"I've done everything necessary to confirm the mistake. 'Take good care of that dear child. He has a mild and timid nature, which doesn't suspect anything. One can take advantage of that, I confess to you ingenuously; I prefer him to my daughters. And then, my dear fellow, be discreet; no one must know anything of our amour, not even Adèle; she's an intelligent girl, but so young . . .'"

"Oh! A bad night!"

"Oh, a good night!"

"You're joking."

"I'm speaking seriously," said Labrie.

"You're no longer on the first floor, then?"

"No, I'm on the second."

"Bon voyage."

"*Is that you, my little cousin?*"

"Who said that?"

"The little cousine."

"Very good."

"*You're an infidel, a traitor, a perfidious . . .*"

"The little cousine is changing her tone."

"*You make love to the whole house.*"

"The little cousin isn't so timid."

"*You're rendering me the unhappiest of women.*"

"What does the little cousin reply?"

"He justifies himself and runs away," said Labrie.

"Where does he go?"

"To the third floor."

"And on the third floor . . . ?"

"He finds the third Heaven."

"The little cousin is awaited there?"

"He's awaited everywhere."

"That's a little cousin who has a lot of work to do."

"I can answer to you for that. As for this one, she's blonde."

"This time, I've caught you out. There's no light . . ."

"There's plenty of the light in question. Fine and undone hair; soft and delicate skin; fresh and moist mouth; slow respiration; sweet breath; soft and tender voice; supple movements, but a little lazy. What do you say to that?"

"What happened on the third floor?"

"Marvels upon marvels."

"And what did the little cousine say?"

"She said that I no longer loved her as I had loved her before, and that I changed my disadvantages every day."

"It appears that the little cousine is demanding . . ."

"And that the ardent little cousin has the devil in his body."

"You're right, Labrie, that's a good enough night."

"You don't know the *tu autem*."[1]

"The *tu autem*?"

"That's Adèle, whom I've just encountered."

"The rogue wouldn't miss a floor, even in the Tower of Babel."

Labrie sighed. "Ahie! Ahie!"

"What happened to you?"

"Alas, Monsieur, nothing happened to me."

"What did Adèle say?"

"Adèle curses, and I, in a piteous tone and in a nonplussed manner, ask her if she also knows the little cousin; I would wager that she does."

"That is, indeed, a funny story."

"Adèle says no."

"The old lady says yes."

"The little cousines don't know what to say."

"And the public will decide. This evening I'll alert my publisher; tomorrow I'll write, and the day after, it will be in print. Whip, coachman, we're in Strasbourg."

I learned on descending from the carriage that I would have gained nothing by postponing my departure, and that Mademoiselle Aglaë de la Reinerie had recently been united in legitimate marriage with the physician Raffour, one of the most illustrious members of the Faculté.

At that news I smiled upon the bizarrerie of my star, which had so humorously appropriated my vengeance to my insult, and which, while delivering my mistress to one of the henchmen of Aesculapius, had reserved for me the right of compen-

1 "*Tu autem*" is an abbreviation of "*To autem Domine, miserere nobis*" [But thou, O lord, have mercy upon us], a formula once used at the end of Biblical readings in the Catholic Church.

sating me with the wife of one of his colleagues. In any case, I supported with a philosophical resignation the reverse that had ruined my hopes and my creditors; and the innumerable distractions that ordinarily assail someone newly arrived from the capital suspended the sentiment of my sadness, including the memory of my amour.

Since I had seen Paris again I held a distinguished rank in all circles; I was invited into all societies, and not a single difference arose in good form of which I was not the arbiter. People hastened to hear me and to interrogate me; all my remarks were cited, all my mannerisms copied, and it was unanimously agreed that I had profited greatly from seeing the world.

An old coquette asked me whether the color amaranth had not diminished in vogue; a figurante at the Opéra-Comique whether it was true that Pamela hats were passé in the class of young women; a courtier whether two-thirds bonds would lose another three-quarters, whether Martin was making fewer roulades and Brunet more puns;[1] everyone at the same time whether the cocks had been gilded, whether the bridges had been finished, whether the column had been erected, whether anyone was thinking of perfecting elastic cravats, repairing the carillon of the Samaritane, and whether the *Journal des Modes* and enigmas still occupied the first place among the productions of modern literature. More wonderstruck by my progress than all the others put together, however, my little widow in the Rue de Mésange cried effusively, five or six times a day, that voyages were a marvelous thing, and that they formed the minds and hearts of young men prodigiously.

Three months had gone by since my return when my mother came into my room one day, her eyes gleaming, her brow radiant and her physiognomy splendid with gaiety. She sat down some distance from my table and threw me a letter

---

1 Martin and Brunet were the names of two vaudeville actors famous in the early days of the Consulate.

addressed to her, postmarked Paris and signed by Léopold de la Reinerie. He let her know by that important missive that he had received the news of my pretentions too late, and the signal recommendation with which she had supported my request; that at that time, his sister's marriage had been newly concluded and that it was no longer possible for him to dispose of her hand otherwise. He added, however, that the death of the husband, which had occurred the day after the union, having rendered his sister her liberty and the power to make a new choice, he had without an effort determined her will in my favor; so that if I persisted in my first intentions, and the alliance I had projected had not ceased to be agreeable to my family, nothing opposed henceforth that I might contract it.

That unforeseen event filled me with joy. I convinced my mother easily to hasten all the necessary steps, and a month later my marriage was definitively arranged, Monsieur Léopold de la Reinerie and Mademoiselle Aglaë, his sister, made the journey to Strasbourg, where I was to enter into possession of my future. I found her charming; she deigned to find me amiable. The families were invited, the contract was drawn up, my debts were paid, I married, and everyone appeared delighted, from my creditors, who gained a great deal by it, to my mistresses, who lost nothing.

The first hours of the first night of our marriage passed as usual. Finally, I indicated the time of repose, executing a quarter-turn and wishing my wife the good night that I was no longer in a state to give her.

"My dear friend," she said, as if on reflection, "perhaps I've forgotten to warn you that I am a somniloquist, and that I have the bad habit of dreaming aloud."

"Madame," I replied to her, "it's a fault that you have in common with the majority of our philosophers and makers of projects. But," I continued, "it reminds me of an adventure that I might recount to you one day."

"An adventure!"

At that word, she fell asleep profoundly; but, whether because it produced an irritation of the fibers of her brain that slumber could not calm, or for some other reason, which I refer to the decision of our ideologues, she repeated it for a long time in a low voice, with interrogative inflexions that seemed to mark the design of memory.

"An adventure," she exclaimed, suddenly, "two, three, four . . ." while spreading the fingers of her hand, which reposed on my breast and closing it again promptly, with the exception of the thumb; "that's the sixth time that it has happened to me to savor the pleasures of amour."

"May Heaven curse the day when I took a somniloquistic wife," I murmured, completing the half-turn and burying my head my pillow. "I could gladly have done without knowing that.

"The first time," she said, raising her voice, "I was in Chaumont, and an enraged somnambulist was allowed to sleep in my room."

"Good, at least for that time, I know what it is; but who the devil could have guessed it?"

"The second time, I was passing through Troyes; I mistook the carriage, and God knows what happened."

"I know that too," I said breathing a little more freely and turning toward her, "but who would have believed it?"

She did not say any more; my heart was hammering, my blood boiling; I listened, I calculated, I lost myself in my calculations, and at the end of it all, it was demonstrated arithmetically that, taking away two from six leaves four . . .

An hour later I was extracted from my reflections by a loud burst of laughter.

"That time," said my wife, "I was violated."

"That's truly pleasant,

"I wept hot tears."

"A fine despair!"
"But I ended up appeasing myself."
"A fine character!"
"There was no reason to be annoyed . . ."
"Indeed."
"Because he'd mistaken the window."
"That was me again . . ."
"Oh, the fourth time, my weakness was excusable."
"How do you get there?"
"He was so amiable."
"I'm greatly obliged to him."
"And so interesting!"
"Damn, what sensibility!"
"I was at a masked ball."
"Aha!"
"In a black domino."
"Aha!"
"And he was . . ."
"Well?"
"In a flax-gray domino."
"Hurrah!"
"As for the dear doctor," she continued, drawing closer to me.
"No!"
"If he hadn't been killed in a duel . . ."
"Good!"
"In the Champs-Élysées . . ."
"Precisely."
"By that brutal officer . . ."
"Here I come."
"On the morning of Mardi Gras."
"No, it was the night before . . ."
"Perhaps I would have accustomed myself to his ugliness."
"I believe so."

"For he had qualities!"

"I flatter myself on that."

"He had a heart."

"Just so."

You will understand that I had not been able to contain the outbursts of my joy, and they had been all the more vivid because I had scarcely expected to get out of it so cheaply. I leapt out of bed. My wife woke up suddenly.

"What are you doing?"

"I'm listening."

"I warned you that I'm a somniloquist,"

"But I forgot to warn you that I'm a somnambulist."

"I'm doomed . . ."

"You'll find your aunt at the first relay."

"Believe that you've mistaken . . ."

"The window."

"And that it's hazard . . ."

"That made you cede to a mask in a flax-gray domino."

"You're making me despair."

"Reassure yourself."

"Can you forgive me . . . ?"

"My happiness!"

"The faults I've committed."

"They were for me."

"What, you were . . ."

"The enraged somnambulist, the traveler in Troyes, the climber, the lover in flax-gray and, what is more, the substitute for Doctor Raffour."

"You'll have to explain . . ."

"Gladly."

What says that prude with hoarse voice, the bloodshot eye, the methodical stance and the compassed stride, who is playing with her fan and biting her lips?

She says that your Aglaë has committed one folly after another, and that she is, at least, a woman devoid of principles.

Perhaps she is right, but I want her to agree with me that one would discover many others if all women were somniloquists. Fortunate is the husband who is only deceived in the bud.

What says the Lady with the sentimental jargon, who believes herself to be an honest woman because she is not entirely lost, and who pretends to rule her sex because she only has two lovers?

She says that your Aglaë is a scatterbrain who has no respect for decency and who yields herself to the first comer.

That is not without foundation, but I want her to agree that I do not have the right to complain about weaknesses that I have caused to be committed.

Fortunate is the husband who has only sacrificed his rights to himself!

What does that fop say who is balancing on his hamstrings and caressing his chin with "a capable air"?

He says that your fate frightens him and that the last chapter of your Romance might well not be the last chapter of Aglaë's Romance.

That is not common sense, and he will permit me to remind him that my wife has the custom of recounting every night what she has done during the day. Where will he find a better guarantee of the fidelity of his own?

Fortunate is the husband whose wife is a somniloquist!

The Napoleonad; an Ode

Let the vulgar bow down
On the gilded parvis of Sulla's palace,
Before the chariots of Julius
Under the scepter of Claudius and Caligula.
They reign as gods over the tremulous crowd,
Their bloody domination
Overwhelms the debased world;
But the centuries curse their memory,
And it is only by bequeathing sins to history
That their reign escapes forgetfulness.

Let a pusillanimous crowd
Burn its odious incense at the feet of tyrants
Exempt by the favor of crime,
I walk without constraint, only fearing the gods.
I shall not be seen begging slavery
And repaying with a culpable homage
An infamous celebrity.
When the people groan under their new chain,
Mastery makes me indignant, and my fickle soul
Still respires liberty.

This perfidious stranger has come
Insolently to sit down above our laws;

The cowardly heir of the parricide,
He disputes with the executioners the spoil of kings.
A sycophant vomited from the walls of Alexandria
For the opprobrium of the fatherland,
And the mourning of the world,
Our vessels and our ports welcome the turncoat,
From abused France he received a refuge
And France has received his irons.

Why do you destroy your work,
You who fixed honor to the French flag?
The people adored your courage.
Liberty is exiled weeping for your success.
By a hope too proud your soul is rocked.
Descend from the insensate pomp,
Return among your warriors.
Do you think that your grandeur will absolve you?
Do you think to shield your head from lightning
By hiding it under laurels?

When your ambitious delirium
Imprinted such shame on our lowered brows,
In the intoxication of your empire
Did you sometimes dream of Brutus' dagger?
Did you see the hour of vengeance rise,
Which is coming to dissipate your power
And the illusions of your fate?
The Tarpeian rock is near the Capitol,
The abyss is near the throne, and the palm of Arcole[1]
Is united with the cypress of death.

---

1 In the battle of Arcole, in November 1796, during the siege of Mantua, Napoléon Bonaparte's French army outflanked an Austrian army to win an expensive but highly significant victory, which helped pave the way for the capture of Venice.

In vain the dread and baseness
Of an adoring cult have cradled your pride.
The tyrant dies, the charm ceases,
Truth stops at the foot of his coffin.
Standing in the future, Justice calls you;
Your life appears before her
Widowed of its illusions.
The cries of the oppressed thunder in the dust
And your name is avowed by nature entire
To the hatred of nations.

In vain to the laws of victory
Your triumphant arm has submitted destiny.
Time is flying away with your glory.
And devouring in fleeing your reign of a morning.
Yesterday I saw the cedar; it is lying in the grass
Before a superb idol.
The world is weary of being enchained.
Before your equals become your slaves,
It is necessary, Napoléon, that the elite of the brave
Mount the scaffold of Sidney.[1]

1 The previously-mentioned English parliamentarian Algernon Sidney, author of the republican tract *Discourses Concerning Government*, executed for plotting against Charles II.

Sorrows;
or,
Miscellanies
taken from the Notebooks
of a Suicide,
published by
Charles Nodier

Publisher's Preface

I expect the protests that the mere title of this work cannot fail to excite. They have been repeated to me a hundred times over, and I am still astonished to have heard them; do not trouble them any more with your plaints and sobs, they say; the sound of moans is importunate to them. Is a pensive and suffering soul soothing itself by communicating something of its suffering to its surroundings, or, is a bold and tender pen engraving in more profound strokes the tableau of the human miseries and vague anxieties of a sensitive and passionate heart? They will call it a conspiracy against taste, and hasten to cite a thousand fine spirits who have not followed the same path, as if the aspects of thought were not susceptible to incessant modification, and a new order of ideas did not demand a new order of expressions.

Yes, that illustrious family of poets born under a superb sky and nourished by the most favorable inspirations, then, still flourishing in its last offspring in the beautiful centuries of Leo X and Louis XIV, is prepared not to recognize itself in its nascent posterity; but the successive migrations of civilization, the variety of its developments and the indispensable influence of local circumstances are a sufficient explanation of that phenomenon. The gracious and pure songs of the youth of the world are no longer appropriate to its decadence; the brilliant paintings and the harmonious scenes of a privileged climate will be displaced to a more severe zone, and the days will perhaps not be long delayed when Apollo, long exiled by the barbarians from the cheerful Parnassus of the Greeks, will settle the chorus of the Muses in the midst of the ice of the North.

However, this apology for a certain genre of literature that is less to be disdained than one might think, will not be subject to a large number of applications; and I am convinced that the one whose last opuscules I am publishing would attach too little value to them to dare to make common cause with his models. He often admitted that the agitations of his life and the strange obstinacy of his woes had given an audacious and bizarre character to his mind and a gigantic and unusual form to his sensations. When new misfortunes surprised him, he ripened, in the calm of his retreat, writings that might have obtained the suffrage of taste; and those, cast at hazard in the brief intervals of repose left to him by his errant and persecuted life, are scarcely worthy of indulgence. Wild fruits of an impetuous and sick imagination that has forgotten even the most common rules of human language, and which heap up confusedly in the first frame to come along all the ideas that distress him, they can only have charm for certain souls avid for powerful emotions and capable of appreciating sensibility even in its aberrations.

For those of you, however, who like to shed glad tears, approved by intelligence and reason, enough of your contemporaries will enable you to savor those precious enjoyments, inexhaustible in mildness.

Read the pastoral amours of Paul and Virginie, and bless in the patriarch who has depicted them the interpreter of innocence and virtue.

Read the immortal productions of Chateaubriand, who has spoken about religion in the style of Isaiah, Milton and Bossuet; and if it is true, as he has said somewhere, that great men have recounted their history in their works, dare to recognize him in the sad and sublime *René*, which, admirable as it is, remains only a faint sketch in itself.

Read the beautiful pages of Ballanche[1] and the *Nuits éliséennes* of Gleizes,[2] almost formless fragments of that rich conception that is prepared in their heart; and do not disdain a sketch by Michelangelo because it is only a sketch.

Read the *Obermann* and the *Rêveries* of Sénancour,[3] and feel sorry for a writer, who has sensed nature so well, for not having sensed God.

Read the *Lina* of Droz,[4] so interesting and too little known. Read the delightful romances of the likes of Flahault, Genlis

---

1 The philosopher Pierre-Simon Ballanche (1776-1847), whom Nodier met during his first sojourn in Paris and remained a friend for the rest of his life, even though Nodier dissented from his theory of social palingenesis and wrote essays contradicting it. The first time Nodier felt compelled to challenge a journalist who had insulted him to a duel, in the 1820s, he wrote to Ballanche asking him to look after his wife and daughter if he were killed, but it proved unnecessary.

2 *Les Nuits éliséenees*, signed J. A. G. (Jean-Antoine Gleizes, 1773-1843), published in Paris in 1800, is a kind of sentimental travelogue, which employs descriptions of landscapes in a fashion similar to other pioneers of romanticism. Gleizes is primarily remembered now as a fervent advocate of vegetarianism, based on his particular theory of the harmony of nature.

3 Étienne Pivert de Sénancour (1770-1846) was an important precursor of French romanticism, particularly for the earlier of the two philosophical works cited, whose full title is *Rêveries sur the primitive nature de l'homme, sur ses sensations, sur le moyens de Bonheur qu'elles lui indiquent, sur le mode social qui conserverait le plus de ses formes primordiale*s (1797), whose quasi-Rousseauesque theses are reproduced continually in Nodier's own philosophical rhapsodies on primitive society. The discussions conducted in the wide-ranging "letters" constituting *Obermann* (1804) are also echoed in many of Nodier's essays. Sénancour went to Switzerland in 1789, apparently to avoid pressure from his family to enter the priesthood and in order to marry, but he was automatically classed by the National Government as an *émigré* and a *proscrit*. He was living in Paris in 1801 while writing *Obermann*, and Nodier met him there.

4 Like Nodier, Joseph Droz (1773-1850) was born in Besançon into a family of lawyers, and he was one of Nodier's teachers there at the École Centrale; in 1803 he moved to Paris, and there, in addition to his numerous works on ethics, politics and religion, he produced the romance *Lina* (1805).

and Montolieu,[1] fresh inventions, as regular and as delightful as the graces that inspired them.

Such a just tribute of eulogies would not be disavowed by the author of these miscellanies. The majority of those names would remind him of his masters; others would remind him of his friends; and if that latter feature proves nothing for his talent, it can at least testify to qualities of which talent can never redeem the absence.

I do not recommend this book to the benevolence of critics; if it were worthy of their attention, I would not try to hide it from their censure; but if it causes a few tears to flow, if it excites some interest, if a single woman—a good and sensitive woman—takes pleasure in perusing it occasionally, if the anguish of an unfortunate who has only described herein afflictions far inferior to his own in bitterness and duration, draws a single sigh from him, that is enough for his memory; he would not have aspired to any other success.

1 The references are to three female writers: Adélaïde de Filleul, Comtesse de Flahault, author of *Adèle de Senange* (1798), which is prefaced by an analytical essay on the history of *romans*; the prolific Comtesse de Genlis (1746-1830), best known for her educational theories and fiction for children, who returned to Paris in 1799 after a long exile and formed a close friendship with Napoléon's wife, Joséphine de Beauharnais; and the prolific Swiss novelist Isabelle de Montolieu (1751-1832), who published a three-volume set of *Contes* in 1803.

The New Werthera[1]

A year ago my botanical research took me to the environs of a small village not far from London. A woman of about forty encountered me on the hill and imagined that I was collecting simples. I observed that she wanted to talk to me, and, without divining what could have given rise to that desire, I opened the conversation myself. She told me then that she was very unhappy, that she had a young daughter who was her only consolation, that she cherished her more than herself, and that she was near to losing her, for she was ill and had been abandoned by the physicians. After that, weeping, she begged me to visit her and not to refuse her my help. It would have been pointless to forbid myself to do it, and why, in any case, rob her of the charm of a momentary hope, a sterile but sweet compensation for several months of uncertainty and tears?

I walked behind her through the flowering gorse and bushes of the heath until we reached the hamlet. Finally, she showed me the threshold of the hut and I went into the room where her daughter was reposing on an old camp bed between two green curtains.

---

1 In *Les Tristes* (1806) this story is entitled "La nouvelle Werthèrie," which echoes Rousseau's "La nouvelle Héloïse" obliquely and eccentrically, but when it was appended to a new edition of *Les Proscrits* in 1820 , and in subsequent reprints, it was re-titled "La filleule du Seigneur" [The Lord's God-daghter"].

She was leaning on one arm; her eyes were haggard, her cheeks red and hot, her mouth panting and pale. She appeared to be sixteen or seventeen years old, but her features lacked charm; only the touching and passionate expression that has the power to embellish anyone was evident there.

"Suzanne," her mother said to her, "this is a gentleman of great knowledge who will surely cure your illness."

She turned to the wall, smiling softly.

"Suzanne," I continued, taking possession of her hand, "don't abandon yourself to an unjust suspicion; there are remedies for everything."

She raised her head and stared at me.

"By examining the characteristics of your malady for some time, I shall doubtless find a means of soothing it."

She smiled again and withdrew her hand from mine with a slight effort.

Her mother went out.

I don't know what disturbance took hold of me. I paced back and forth in the cottage, and my imagination only seized thoughts devoid of harmony and order.

The young woman interested me.

I came back to her bedside and sat down, I heard a sigh.

I sought the hand that had quit me. Mine was ardent. She squeezed it.

"Suzanne," I said, placing it on her heart, "it's here that you're suffering."

Her eyelids lowered with a melancholy calm; they were swollen and taut. The lashes met in sheaves, still shiny with the moistness of tears.

"You're in love," I added, in a low voice. Her breast swelled.

She slid her fingers into a curl of her black hair and brought it back over her face.

I enveloped her with one of my arms. I drew her toward my breast with a chaste interest. My breath brushed her lips.

She spoke; I could scarcely hear her. “It’s not him,” she said.

“No, it’s not him,” I replied. “But won’t he come?”

Suzanne waved her hand around her head.

“Perhaps he’ll come to see you tomorrow.”

She did not reply.

I feared having aggravated her pain and I remained silent. She was still looking at me, and I was weeping.

There was a tear on my cheek; she wiped it away with the back of her hand.

Another had fallen on my hand; she collected it with her mouth.

“You’re very fortunate,” she said to me. “I believe that you’ve wept.”

Then, still observing me, she added: “I could love you, for you have the soul of an angel. Tell me, though, whether you’re noble.”

I hesitated to admit it. It cost to say it before virtue lying on the bed of poverty.

“Oh,” she went on, “noble and good; there’s a misunderstanding. But you’re still too young. I’m content to see you blush.”

Explain to me . . .

I did not pronounce those words aloud; what need had I of a dolorous enlightenment to give her my pity? We understood one another well enough like that.

A little later, I saw her mother again, and she awaited the words that were going to escape from me like an oracle of salvation.

“Has she loved?” I asked her.

“Never, alas. Rich parties have offered themselves, and in spite of our indigence, the amour of my Suzanne has been solicited ardently; she was indifferent to all of them. She would have liked there to be cloisters in order to bury her youth therein, because the world importuned her, and she found life long and difficult. I don't believe that any man has obtained a single kiss from Suzanne, except for her godfather. He's twelve years older than her and the son of the former village lord. When he was absent on the king's service she said: 'I know that my godfather will come back, because God has promised me that; and when he comes back, my Frederick, I shall give him a white lamb with blue and pink ribbons, and tresses of flowers, in accordance with the season.' She did, in fact, go to meet him, and when he saw her he dismounted from his horse in order to kiss her forehead. 'See how pretty Suzanne has become!' he said 'I don't want her to lead the flocks along the hedgerows and tan her complexion in the ardor of the sun, for I love her like my sister.'"

The next day I came back at daybreak. I found her illness worse.

"Listen," she said to me, embracing me. "You must be as good as you are handsome, and I'm going to ask you for something better than life. Ask my mother to give me my white dress, my muslin head-dress and my crystal cross. Pick me a cornflower in the garden and an iris from the bank of the stream. Today is the anniversary of my birth."

I did what she asked of me, and her mother dressed her; but as she got out of bed she fell, weakly.

A bell rang nearby, for the cottage faced the church. Her mother said to her: "Come and see; it's Frederick's wedding; if you weren't ill you could dance like the other young women in the halls of the manor house. Why can't you be brave?"

She could no longer hear, poor Suzanne. She told us that she was better.

Her mother and I went to the door to see the bride and groom passing by. The wife chose, with a fearful intention, the places where she ought to place her feet, in order not to damage the embroidery of her shoes. All her movements were awkward and affected, all her gestures superb and disdainful.

In her footsteps, her gaze, the arrangement of her hair and the creases of her garments there was nothing but symmetry. Oh, how the cares of a simple celebration and a common ceremony inspired her with disgust!

Frederick came after; his large eyebrows were lowered, his attire negligent, his stride slow and careful. As they went past the house he darted a glance at it with a somber and discontented expression; he took half a step back, biting his lips, shredding a bouquet that he was holding, and then he resumed his route, and the church opened.

I was left alone, and I was reflecting on that when I heard a long cry.

I ran. The mother was on her knees. The daughter was lying down.

"Are you sure?"

"Look," said the mother.

Suzanne was dead, stiff, colorless, already quite inanimate. I touched her; she was cold. I lent an ear, to make sure that she was no longer breathing.

That is what I saw in the village in the environs of London.

The Gardens of Oberheim

THE PASSER-BY

It's here. God help me. I feel my heart ready to burst, and I'm not mistaken about its beating. There is the belfry on the hill and the willows in the valley. You told me about those rocks suspended like vaults, those woods in an amphitheatre and that lake of verdure that fades away between the hamlets. Have you seen that leaning cross?

THE FARMER'S WIFE

Look, my son, how troubled that passer-by seems. His eyes are shedding tears. Look!

THE PASSER-BY

Tell me the name of this village.

THE WOMAN

Oberheim.

THE PASSER-BY

I wanted to be told that again. How far is it from here to the city?

THE WOMAN

Two leagues.

THE PASSER-BY

And from here to the torrent?

THE WOMAN

When you've passed to your left that woman dressed in white whose garment you can see floating over the mountain grass, you'll hear the sound of waves close by, and the water of the torrent will be seething at your feet.

THE PASSER-BY

Let me rest on the threshold of your house, and bring me the milk of that black goat, for my breast is ardent and my lips are dry.

THE WOMAN

You've come far, then?

THE PASSER-BY

Very far.

THE WOMAN

And will your journey end soon?

THE PASSER-BY

When the water of the torrent is seething at my feet.

THE WOMAN

Take this jar of milk and break a little bread here. Sweat is running from your hair and your mouth is trembling. Why are you looking at me without speaking?

THE PASSER-BY

Tell me who owned that deserted house and those abandoned gardens. Grass is growing in the courtyards and the wind whistling through the windows.

THE WOMAN

What do those things matter to a traveler? You never knew Lucile.

THE PASSER-BY

Go on.

THE WOMAN

Those gardens flourished under her hand, and her presence seemed to maintain the spring. That tree with such sad foliage, which never loses its mourning dress, she planted. Beneath it she had consecrated two graves to two illustrious strangers whom she called her friends. One was a marble square on which she had sculpted, in large letters, a few verses of an old poet from the North; the other was charged with an urn of black stone, all burned, which she dedicated to the memory of an unfortunate youth who killed himself for love. Those monuments no longer exist, but on the bark of the cypress that covered them, you can still find the names of her Ossian and her Werther.

THE PASSER-BY

Lucile was a good friend.

THE WOMAN

She was an angel on earth. It seems to me that I can still see her with her black dress and her dark red kerchief, over which her long hair floated. She walked, pale and pensive, and her gaze was as sad and grave as the night. But if a pauper was in her passage, if a child ran to her side, if the spirit of charity took her by the hand to the bed of an invalid, a merciful smile blossomed on her lips, and she was embellished by her virtue.

THE PASSER-BY

That's enough. You don't know how you're hurting me.

THE WOMAN

She died so far away. Her mother was alone here. I wept.

THE PASSER-BY

Excellent heart! You wept when she died!

THE WOMAN

I wept for a long time. When my eyes arrested on the gardens, I looked for Lucile, and was astonished not to find her. Then I wept more bitterly; my children also wept.

THE PASSER-BY

Your children also wept! This one too!

THE WOMAN

This one most of all; she had held him over the baptismal font. See how he still weeps.

THE PASSER-BY

Come, I want to kiss your tears. He's more beautiful than before; I would never have thought that he was so beautiful.

THE CHILD

You don't know that she gave me a rosary of glass beads, on which I say the *Pater* and the *Ave* every day, and another prayer.

THE PASSER-BY

Teach me that other prayer.

THE CHILD

My God, be good to Lucile, as she was to everyone.

THE PASSER-BY

I want to give you a jewel too. It's a silver cross that I received from my mother, which you can suspend from your glass rosary in memory of the traveler.

THE CHILD

In memory of the man who loved Lucile.

THE WOMAN

You haven't drunk your milk, and you're still standing there . . . perhaps you're ill.

THE PASSER-BY

It's all right.

THE WOMAN

Wait . . . your eyes are bloodshot and you're not letting me see your tears.

THE PASSER-BY

Have me conducted to the torrent.

THE WOMAN

What are you doing, insensate youth? You're throwing me a gold coin for a few drops of milk. There's nothing in the cabin to give you its value.

THE PASSER-BY

Have me conducted to the torrent.

THE WOMAN

Oh well! You're going out without listening to me. May God render your benefit; I'll pray for you often.

THE PASSER-BY

Pray for Lucile and for me.

THE CHILD

Don't go so rapidly past that house; that's Lucile's window.

THE PASSER-BY

Which one?

THE CHILD

The second.

THE PASSER-BY

It's worm-eaten and dirty.

THE CHILD

No one opens it any longer.

THE PASSER-BY

What is that bird that resembles the swift of old walls, and is perching on the linden tree, gazing with a somber air at that silent house? Its breast is a dull white and its back is black; its tail terminates in trailing threads like the rear of a window's dress, and its song has something sinister, like the laments of a woman in a forest.

THE CHILD

That's the cemetery bird; it's sacred to bird-catchers, because it only appears at long intervals to announce disastrous adventures. But the eye can't follow its flight, and children have never found its nest. One has just flown over your head.

THE PASSER-BY

I didn't see it, but the flutter of its wings stirred my hair.

THE CHILD

Can you hear the sound of the torrent?

THE PASSER-BY

I can hear the sound of the torrent. I can already see the water spring up in white spray and falling back in silvery rain. Do you know if the water is deep?

THE CHILD

No one has ever seen the bottom. A traveler was going by with his horse; the horse slipped and they both disappeared.

THE PASSER-BY

Go back to your mother. The sun is behind the mountain, and the day is advanced.

THE CHILD

Adieu, good stranger; don't go far today.

THE PASSER-BY

Adieu, my son; love Lucile and your mother; and Heaven will enable you to prosper.

The Tomb on the Lake Shore

ALBERT

Where are you going, young women, with your hair scattered in a sign of mourning and garlands of flowers in your hands?

ONE OF THE YOUNG WOMEN

These flowers are consecrated to sadness; here is the bloody hyacinth, the lugubrious marigold, and the columbine, daughter of the rocks and friend of tombs. We are going to put them on the sepulcher of the unknown woman on the lake shore.

ALBERT

Who was that unknown woman whose monument you are honoring?

THE YOUNG WOMAN

She was a young woman like us, but she was a hundred times more beautiful; she had a gaze so tender and so soft that it would have made you smile in despair. Virtue descended to earth would not have taken any other form.

ALBERT

Continue, for your words are agreeable to my ear and I sense my heart gripped by a disturbance as delectable as the purest joy.

THE YOUNG WOMAN

Four months ago she arrived in the hamlet; it was at the end of the great snows. She went into a cottage and fainted with dolor. A fire of fir-wood was lit, and her limbs, which were icy at first, gradually warmed up; her temples were washed with salutary water. We gathered around her and waited impatiently for her to come back to life. Finally, she sighed, and her eyes, as they had opened, filled with tears. We could see that she was suffering, but we respected the mystery of her misfortune. She only told us that her travels had ended, and that she wanted to stay in that isolated house at the top of the mountain. She had a few items of rustic furniture transported there, and no longer showed herself.

ALBERT

You soon ceased to see her?

THE YOUNG WOMAN

Her benefits always rendered her present to us; the most sympathetic and most pious souls could not compete with her; there was no indigent person who did not receive aid, no unfortunate who did not obtain consolation, no invalid who did not know the efficacy of her remedies, no family that did not have to praise her prudence and her advice, no tears that she was not prompt to wipe away. All the mothers gave her as an example to their daughters; but her virtue was too perfect to inspire emulation. What soul would have dared to believe itself to be of the same stripe as hers?

ALBERT

Fortunate society! Will you find panegyrists who can outbid that funeral oration?

THE YOUNG WOMAN

The pastor cited her as a saint and we had no doubt that she was of a nature even more elevated. You might think that idea too exaggerated, but it is not without plausibility. Who could have attributed to regrets of the same species as mortal regrets the sublime and more than human sorrow that appeared on her face? And was anyone among us worthy to occupy the divine sensibility with which her creator had endowed her? Are the celestial spirits exempt from sins and punishments, then? They once sinned by ambition; perhaps she had sinned by amour. This was the place of her exile, and the melancholy that weighed upon her was the impatience of her original homeland.

ALBERT

Tell me about that banished angel; I too was made to love her.

THE YOUNG WOMAN

When she descended into the plain at the commencement of fine days in order to behold the graces of the nascent spring and the rejuvenated year, we suddenly surrounded her, and we gave her bouquets of violets and anemones. Then she embraced all of us, but she seemed most affectionate with those who were less rich and less pretty. She preferred me, however, because I knew the arts of the city and I had seen their marvels at close range. She was able to talk to me about the great models in which admiration discovers new beauties every day, and as soon as she began to talk about painters or poets whose masterpieces she had meditated her genius, exalted by her memories, no longer thought of veiling itself, and was revealed unconsciously. She only perceived her superiority by my astonishment, and then she wept in order to make me believe that she was a woman.

ALBERT

What! Were no imperfections remarked in that divine masterpiece?

THE YOUNG WOMAN

She affected a few in order not to humiliate us; but we knew full well that she was deceiving us.

ALBERT

If you had an idea of the uncertainty into which you're plunging me, you'd have pity on me. Has the Avenger sent you already, in order to irritate my remorse?

THE YOUNG WOMAN

What are you saying there in a low and halting voice? It is only the wicked who have remorse.

ALBERT

Did you not form any conjecture regarding the veritable motive of her solitude and her chagrins?

THE YOUNG WOMAN

Only once . . . but that ought to be buried in eternal secrecy . . .

ALBERT

Speak, and it will die in my heart.

THE YOUNG WOMAN

Only once . . . I was coming back from the next village, and cheerfully following the edge of that little wood, singing old ballads, and I recognized from afar her simple orange tunic floating close to that clump of larches . . .

ALBERT

Yes, a simple tunic, a floating tunic, and the color that she loved . . .

THE YOUNG WOMAN

She was thus dressed . . . I approached slowly . . . she was speaking . . .

ALBERT

She was speaking, you say?

THE YOUNG WOMAN

And gazing beyond the lake at the roofs of those palaces . . .

ALBERT

I know a great deal already; I know everything.

THE YOUNG WOMAN

"Albert!" she cried

ALBERT

She still named him!

THE YOUNG WOMAN

"Albert, why have you deceived me?"

ALBERT

He deceived her, that's true.

THE YOUNG WOMAN

She perceived me; I saw her go pale and totter; but why is it that you are tottering and going pale like her?

ALBERT

She died soon after?

THE YOUNG WOMAN

She died the next day. I put my arm under her head as she was about to expire. "I want you," she said, "to bury me in that place from which one can see the city and the roofs of those palaces, on the lake shore."

ALBERT

This is the lake shore.

THE YOUNG WOMAN

"Albert," she added. Then she died.

ALBERT

Where is she?

THE YOUNG WOMAN

Her tomb is at your feet.

ALBERT

I can't see it.

THE YOUNG WOMAN

Look, it's there.

ALBERT

This is really her tomb?

THE YOUNG WOMAN

Yes. Your hands are gripping it, your lips attaching themselves to it furiously. Who are you, to love that unknown woman so ardently.

ALBERT

Eléonore!

THE YOUNG WOMAN

He is no longer calling to her; he is as motionless as death. His eyes are closed, and they will be forever. Approach, my sisters, and look at the friend of the unknown woman. He is lying on her tomb, and his heart has broken.

One o'clock; or, The Vision

I had a heart full of bitterness and I sought solitude and the night. My walk had scarcely extended beyond Chaillot's gardens, and I usually only began it after eleven o'clock in the evening had chimed; but I was obsessed by such sad thoughts, my imagination was nourished by so many dire reveries, that often, in the state of involuntary excitement that is familiar to souls in pain, I had had to repel I know not how many illusions at which a moment's reflection would have caused me to blush.

One day, I had gone, later than usual, to the accustomed place; and, ether because the more obscure darkness had deceived my design, or because the succession of my ideas, more unequal and more fortuitous, had caused me to lose sight of the goal of my nocturnal course, the bell of the village church was striking one o'clock when I perceived that I was no longer following my familiar route, and that my distraction had taken me into an unknown path. I hastened my steps toward the place from which the sound had come. At a turning in a narrow passage, a shadow rose up before my feet and disappeared into the hedge. I stopped, shivering, and I saw a long stone in the form of a tomb. I heard a sigh; the foliage trembled.

The following day, preoccupied with that adventure, I sought the same place at almost the same hour; the apparition was reiterated, and the phantom brushed me in passing; its footsteps resounded on the stone; the dry grass rustled behind it, and at intervals, I saw it fleeing, like a dark cloud, between the nearby willows or at the corner of a path. Always following the light and uncertain trace, I arrived at the old monastery of Sainte-Marie; but, wandering from one heap of rubble to another, I no longer found anything.[1]

That dilapidated convent offers one of the saddest sights that can strike the human eye. Nothing remains of the church but large isolated pilasters which bear the debris of a destroyed vault in places. When the moon lets its light fall through those columns and owls ululate on the cornices, as one reaches the summits of the uncultivated terraces and advanced among the high walls, stumbling among the ditches, and descending the broken stairways overgrown by poisonous plants, such as henbane and celandine, one ends up at buildings that are utterly degraded, of which nothing subsists but menacing sections of wall and eaves suspended in an almost-miraculous manner. When one is conducted by hazard to that funereal avenue, which leads via a rocky slope beneath damp arches to the ancient catacombs, and by the light of some dying lamp one can read on the scattered stones the names of the chaste women whose bones were deposited there . . . there is no human strength that can resist similar emotions. They absorbed all my faculties to such an extent that I forgot, in a way, the strange motive of my research; it was not until the next day that I felt the desire reborn more vividly to penetrate the mystery of the being whose encounter had troubled me, and which had made the great sepulcher a habitation as mysterious as itself.

At one o'clock, holding my breath and walking silently, I arrived at the tomb, and I recognized the specter.

He was sitting, with his eyes fixed on a certain point in the sky. It was a young man, thin and very pale, clad in poor

1 The ruins of the convent of Sainte-Marie, near Chaillot on the road to Passy, have long been swallowed up by the expansion of Paris, but in the 1820s the area was still rural.

rags, whose unkempt hair fell back in thick waves. On seeing his gaping mouth, his extended neck, his stiff arms and his entire occupied attitude, one might have thought that he was delivering himself to a grave contemplation; but a sob escaped him, and I presumed that he had not seen what he appeared to be seeking.

He perceived me then, and leapt up in order to flee. Then, stopping immediately and looking at me mildly, he said: "What do you want with me?"

"To know you, and perhaps to console you."

"You're a man," he said, "and your heart is made like theirs. I don't like that species; there were some in my early days who were sympathetic to the suffering of others; they were noble hearts loved by God; things are very different now."

He shook his head and wiped his eyelids.

"There are still some now," I said. "Don't close your heart to your brothers."

"I no longer have brothers; do the unfortunate have any? Look how wan and withered I am; Look how soiled I am. I'm hungry during the day; during the night I lay my bones in the mud and the water of marshes. God has given me bad days. There are moments when my eyes are troubled, when my teeth join effortfully. My breast rises, my nerves vibrate like the strings of a harp; I sense tears that are trying to escape, a chill that runs through my limbs, and an inexplicable malaise that grips me by the throat. It's said that I'm a maniac and an epileptic, and people pass by, letting a smile of disdain fall upon me. That is what I am."

He sat down on the tomb, and I sat down beside him.

"I can recount to you . . ." he said, suddenly. "She won't come tonight, anyway. Do you see that black cupola rising up there in the blue depths of the sky? And that star, shining above, floating in such a pure light. Do you see it? She's there, in truth, since she told me so; but she no longer descends.

"I was almost as rich as Octavie, but the heir of a great house presented himself, and her parents refused me. Two days before the wedding, I was walking under the trees of the Luxembourg and I was embracing my dolor. What dreams did I not have! 'I shall take a sharp dagger into the banqueting hall,' I said, 'and I shall give eternity to my beloved and myself; or I shall throw fear into the temple and I shall abduct Octavie from the midst of her consternated friends; or I shall mingle the horrors of a conflagration with the preparations for her hymen; and in the trouble of that scene of terror, I shall steal her, dead or alive, from the crime of a new amour.'

"She passed by. The satin of her dress rustled. I shivered all over; a red cloud obscured my sight; all my blood flowed to my heart. She had recognized me, my Octavie. 'I'll come back soon,' she said to those surrounding her. 'The calm of midnight must be more delightful here. I'll come back soon; perhaps I'll come tomorrow.'

"They resound like such sweet music, the words of the woman one loves. They resound for a long time. All the faculties are gripped by them; the soul identifies with them; it seems that in carrying away her last thought, one is bearing her away entirely.

"I went away repeating: *I'll come back soon, perhaps I'll come tomorrow*. Perhaps tomorrow, she had said. But she didn't come.

"One o'clock chimed. Then a lugubrious bell, struck at long intervals, filled the air with a symphony of death.

"I would not have been able to define the emotion by which my senses were surprised, but it was as if it emanated from the sky. Whatever it was, an action of will of which I had not taken account drew me to Octavie's house; and, cleaving through the crowd of domestics, I stopped at the disarray of the apartment that she occupied.

The windows were open. Behind the curtains, shadows and torches could be seen passing by turns, and I know not what stifled cries were rising from the depths of the room.

"'She's dead!' I cried.

"'No,' replied her father, clutching me convulsively in his arms. 'She's asleep.'

"She was lying on her bed of red damask; there was a candle on her nightstand, a book at her feet; a priest was motionless beside the bed; her mother had fainted on the floor. Eulalie was weeping copiously, and a man dressed in black said with a ferocious sang-froid: 'There's no more hope; I knew full well that she wouldn't get out of it."

"I have forgotten the entire year that followed that evening, for I was ill, people said, and my malady excited repugnance and horror. Since Octavie's death, there was no longer anyone who loved me.

"A year later, to the day, I was going up the Rue de Tournon by the light of the illuminations of a public festival; I had passed slowly through twenty groups who afflicted me with the outbursts of their vulgar joy when one o'clock chimed. If the stroke of the clapper had hit me, it would have wounded me less rudely than it did in making that bell groan. Why was that hour—the hour whose last murmur had covered the sounds of your agony—not removed from the cycle of time?

"Then an adolescent with an angelic face saluted me with a moist and luminous gaze, and disappeared into the crowd, indicating the Luxembourg to me.

"I hesitated; I could still see him; a tear slid down his face, glistened and fell.

"I went into the gardens, very emotional—me, who had never known fear—and the dust that rose up in my passage, and the rays of moonlight that sprang forth between the leaves, and the distant tumult of the crowd returning home, all filled me with disquiet and alarm.

"She finally appeared to me, dressed and veiled in white, as on the beautiful evening when we had traversed all the quais of the Seine on foot, and I saw distinctly that she was floating in a vapor as gentle as the dawn. I lost consciousness, and Octavie did not draw away from me. She leaned over my motionless body, and her hot breath warmed my breast. Her kisses fluttered from my mouth to my eyelids and from my eyelids to my hair. Her arms enveloped me softly and rocked me in a region full of light and perfumes. There was a burden of voluptuousness upon all my organs. But when my reassured mind began to enjoy more fully that scene of intoxication; when my anxious eyes sought Octavie around me, I could no longer distinguish anything but the trace of her flight, a pale and trembling furrow that extended all the way to that star, and which gradually faded away.

"I don't know why she no longer comes, but if she doesn't come, I shall go . . . I believe I shall go," he repeated, in a low voice.

Such was the story that the epileptic told me, and after that, I enquired at length, but fruitlessly, regarding his fate. I had despaired of seeing him again, when hazard informed me that someone similar had been seen in the infirmary at Bicêtre. I went there, and had myself taken to his bed. He was little more than a cadaver, almost totally fleshless, and frightfully livid. His eyes still had a little fire and moved quite rapidly in their sunken orbits, but his gaze made one feel ill.

After having reflected for a few minutes with the air of a man trying to fix confused reminiscences, a bitter smile creased his lips slightly and he leaned gently in my direction.

"I knew full well," he said, "that I would go. I shall probably go tomorrow. Octavie came to invite me there, and I've already received a pledge from her of imminent alliance—for it's good," he added, "Octavie's hand, which extends thus toward me at any hour; it isn't a hand desiccated by death. It isn't a black and hideous hand like those of skeletons that have grown old in the tomb; its form is sweeter than the hands of angels. It's true that I can't touch her yet, but when the moment is ready to be accomplished, that hand will seize me and draw me beyond the sky."

As he finished speaking, he started staring at his pillow with a fearful joy, and cried out in a muted and alarmed voice: "There she is, there she still is, and there's her oval onyx with a little circle of gold.

"I shall go tomorrow," he said, smiling.

Capricious aberrations of a vivid or credulous imagination! He did not seem to see the straw on which his head was resting, and the coarse sheet that covered him was depressed by the weight of Octavie's hand, conserving its imprint.

How do I know, an unfortunate they call mad, whether that pretended infirmity was not the symptom of a more energetic sensibility, a more complete organization, and whether nature, in stimulating all your faculties, does not render them more apt to perceive the unknown?

That idea still occupied me when I arrived the next day. I approached the epileptic's bed and I did not see him, but a shroud thrown over him allowed me to divine his body. There was also a little candle burning there, and everything else was as it ordinarily was.

When the evening had advanced somewhat I went to the place where I had encountered him previously and I sat down on the tomb where we had sat together. It had been disturbed, perhaps with the intention of taking it away in order to form the boundary-marker of a field or the cornerstone of a building. I heard one o'clock chime and I calculated that that night would be the second anniversary of Octavie's death.

The sky was not pure; at first, a dull and stormy cloud hid the star where her friend had so often looked for her, but it emerged slowly from the darkness, and seemed more resplendent.

"Poor madman!" I said aloud. "What is the price of your discoveries now, vain science of the earth? There is nothing obscure for you in so many marvels that make the astonishment of sages; and if some cloud has veiled your days, you are freed therefrom, like that star, in order to resume in a new life your primal grace and your original beauty."

Sanchette; or, The Oleander

We were born near to one another.

While still very young, I called him my friend.

I was not as beautiful as him, but I was beautiful.

When he put his arm around me, my voice died on my lips and my heart was squeezed. I felt a frisson that ran all the way to my hair, and I wept with pleasure.

One day, he said to me: "You will be my wife, and I shall be able to kiss your neck without anyone being able to say anything about it. You will no longer reject me by making me afraid of your mother; and when I hear footsteps behind me, I shall not turn round to see whether it is her."

While speaking thus we gave one another intoxicating kisses, and I did not know why I was troubled.

After that he departed for a great voyage, and he brought me an oleander in a box of veined wood. The oleander was in flower.

"You see," he said to me, "these cups of such a soft crimson hue have the freshness and the color of your mouth; they will soon wither, and my heart will wither like them, in the chagrin of your absence. They will be reborn with the first fires of spring, and my heart will also be reborn when your hand comes to press it."

However, your oleander has flowered again, and my hand will not press your heart again.

The cups of your oleander no longer have such a soft crimson hue; they are violet and bruised, because I have watered them with my tears, and my tears burn.

My mouth has lost its color and its freshness; has it not lost your kisses? The flowers of the oleander fade so quickly when they are deprived of the zephyr.

"Sanchette," my mother said to me, "it is necessary to make another choice, since your Emmanuel is dead." My mother said that to me.

Shall I say to my oleander*: It's necessary to take another soil, and to flower in the midst of the mountain snows?*

Listen, Emmanuel, my Emmanuel, it is necessary to die here. At least I shall be near to you; and when I hear the hollow earth resounding a little beneath my feet, I shall say: *Perhaps that's him*; and I will transplant my oleander there.

How can I know where your grave is, and whether anyone has sown flowers there?

They will soon have fallen, the flowers of the oleander; there are only one, two and three now. But there are still a great many leaves, and its leaves are mortal.

Meditations in the Cloister

The existence of an undeceived man is a long torture; his days are sown with anguish and his memories are full of regrets.

He nourishes himself on absinthe and bile; the commerce of his peers has become odious to him; the succession of the hours fatigues him; scrupulous cares obsess him, importune him and revolt him; his own faculties are a burden to him, and like Job, he curses the moment when he was conceived.

Tottering under the weight of the sadness that overwhelms him, he sits down on the edge of his grave, and in the effusion of the most bitter dolor, he raises his eyes toward the heavens and asks God whether his providence has abandoned him.

Still so young and so unfortunate, disillusioned with life and society by a precocious experience, a stranger to men who had withered my heart and deprived of all the hopes that had disappointed me, I sought a refuge in my misery and I have not found one.

I asked myself whether the present state of civilization was so desperate, whether there was no longer a remedy to the calamities of the species, and whether the institutions most solemnly consecrated by the suffrage of the people had felt the effects of a universal corruption.

I walked at hazard far from frequented paths, for I avoided encountering those whom nature had given me as brothers, and I feared that the blood running from my lacerated feet might reveal my passage to them.

One day, at a bend in a sunken road, in the depths of a somber agrarian valley, I perceived an old edifice of a simple but imposing architecture, and the mere aspect of that place caused meditation and peace to descend into my senses.

I reached the ancient walls, lending a curious ear to the sounds of that solitude, but I only heard the north wind moaning feebly in the interior courtyards and the cries of birds of prey soaring over the towers. I only found within broken doors on their rusty hinges, a large vestibule in which human feet had not left traces, and deserted cells. Then, descending by means of narrow steps by the light of a ventilation shaft into the subterrains of the monastery, I advanced slowly through the debris of death with which they were cluttered and, in haste to deliver myself without distraction to the vague and almost pleasant distraction that the solemnity of the retreat inspired in me, I sat down on the planks of a shattered coffin.

When I recall these venerable associations, which I was to see for such a short time and regret so frequently; while I reflect on the unexampled revolution that had devoured them in its fiery course, as if to steal from good men even the hope of possible consolation, I say to myself, in the intimacy of my heart: *This place might have become your refuge, but it has not been left to you; to suffer and to die, that is your destiny.* How beautiful and touching they appear to me, the great thoughts that presided over the inauguration of cloisters! With what delights I delivered myself to the majestic meditations that they were about to suggest to me!

In the epoch when society passed from the horrors of an excessive civilization to the infinitely more tolerable horrors of barbarity, and in the hypothesis in which a return to a state of nature, or even patriarchal government, was no longer the chimera of a few exalted minds, men of an austere virtue and august character established, as the deposit of all human morality, the first monastic constitutions.

Those conservatory hospices were as many monuments dedicated to religion, justice and truth.

Their founders were not of a common stripe.

The mania of perfectibility, from which all our aberrations and errors derive, was already close to rebirth; the world was about to civilize itself for a second time. All generous thoughts and all primitive affections were about to be effaced again, and those obscure monks had foreseen it.

Modest and sublime in their vocation, they watched over the sacred fire, and they also brought the tradition of good morality, lost to the rest of the world.

The man who was rich makes his wealth the patrimony of the poor.

The man who was powerful, and who imposed inviolable orders around him, puts on a rude cilice and enters submissively into the paths prescribed for him.

The man who was burning with amour and desires renounces the promised pleasures and hollows out an abyss between his heart and the heart of the creature.

The slightest sacrifice of the weakest of those anchorites would be the glory of a hero.

Let us examine, however, with a scrupulous attention what that sacred militia might have had that is so revolting for the sages of our century, by what crimes humble cenobites might have attracted that furious animadversion, unique in the annals of fanaticism.

They were angels of peace who gave themselves in silence and solitude and the practice of an excellent and pure morality, and who only appeared in the midst of men in order to bring them some benefit.

Even their leisures were devoted to prayer and charity.

They directed the conscience of fathers; they presided over the education of children; like fays, they protected the first days of the new-born child; they summoned upon him the gifts of Heaven and the light of faith. Later, they guided his steps in the difficult paths of life, and when it reached its supreme period, they sustained the debilitated travelers in the avenues of the tomb and opened eternity for him.

Let no one say any longer that the unfortunate man is a broken link in the chain of beings.

The pauper expiring on the straw was at least surrounded by their exhortations and their aid.

They enchanted with their consolations the agony of the sick and the sadness of prisoners.

They embraced all the afflicted with an equal compassion. Their ardent charity sought information less of sin than of woe, and if the innocent was dear to them, the culpable was not odious. Crime also has need of pity.

When the law had chosen a victim, and the patient, abandoned by the entire earth, advanced slowly toward his scaffold, he found at his side those divine emissaries of religion, and his eyes, ready to be extinguished, read in their resigned eyes the promise of salvation.

Their modest splendors were nevertheless enriched by the most illustrious memories. They had seen powerful monarchs abdicate the purple before their altars, and they kept in their reliquaries the scepter of Amédée[1] and the double crown of Charles Quint,

They had given chiefs to the Christian world, fathers and orators to the Church, and interpreters and martyrs to the truth.

Their founders were the elect that God had inspired; their reformers courageous enthusiasts whom misfortune had instructed.

It is in their midst that the genius matured of Abelard,[2] whose memory is linked to all the sentiments of piety and amour.

---

1 Amadeus VIII, the prince of Savoy who became the antipope Felix V, but renounced the tiara in 1449 to end the western schism,

2 Peter Abelard (1079-1142), the scholastic philosopher whose love affair with Héloïse d'Argenteuil became legendary.

It is in the obscurity of their cells that Rancé[1] hid his regrets, and that ingenious mind, which had divined at twelve years the delicate beauties of Anacreon, freely embraced, at the age of pleasure, austerities by which our weakness is astonished.

Finally, their habitudes, their mores and even their garments participated in the noble and severe character of their mission.

Almost contemporary with the true worship, their origin went back to the Essenes of Syria and the Therapeutes of Lake Moeris.

The deserts of Africa and Asia spoke of their grottoes and their thébaïds.

They lived in common, like the people of Lycurgus, and treated one another as brothers like the young Theban warriors.

They had remedies like the psylles[2] and secrets like the priests of Isis.

Some abstained from the flesh of animals and the usage of speech, like the pupils of Pythagoras. There were some who wore the tunic and bonnet of Phrygians and others who wore loincloths like the men of ancient days.

The orders of women presented harmonies no less marvelous.

Their life was as chaste as that of the Muses. They sang in melodious voices and lived in retired places, like them.

Some had veils and headbands like the vestals, or trailing robes like Roman widows, or helmets and armor like the Sarmatian women.[3]

---

1 Armand-Jean de Bouthillier de Rancé (1626-1700), abbot of La Trappe, the founder of the strict monastic sect known in consequence as Trappists.

2 The psylles were a North African people who acquired a reputation as snake charmers, with the result that the term was applied more generally to men of that dubious profession, whose alleged immunity to venoms sometimes led to their being consulted as healers.

3 The third-century Roman emperor Proculus was reputed to have sent a hundred young Sarmatian women into battle, but the legend is a distortion

Some were seen who took care of neglected little children, like as many new mothers given by Providence, and others who bandaged the wounds of the brave, like the princesses of the heroic centuries and the chatelaines of the old wars.

They retained the memory of the likes of Héloïse, Chantal[1] and Louise de La Vallière;[2] they included the names of several daughters and several lovers of kings who had exchanged between them sumptuous clothes and the illusions of sensuality against the habit and the labors of penitence.

In sum, the more I fathomed the history of those decried monks, the more the extent of their labors imposed admiration and respect on me.

Knights of the faith at Rhodes and Jerusalem; holocausts of the faith among the idolaters; conservers of enlightenment throughout Europe and propagators of morality over the two hemispheres; artists and literates in China; legislators in Paraguay; instructors of youth in great cities and patrons of pilgrims in the woods; hospitalers on Mont Saint-Bernard and redeemers of captives under the cloth of the Mercy, I do not know whether the wrongs for which they are reproached can balance so many services, but it is demonstrated to me that a perfect institution would be contrary to our essence, and that if it is true that monastic associations are not without inconvenience, it is because the genius of evil has imprinted his seal on all human creations.

What do you hope for, then, of your proud attempts, seditious innovator? Annihilation or perfection? The first of those designs is perhaps a crime, the second is surely only the vainest

---

of a letter that was probably a fake.

1 Saint Jane Frances de Chantal (1572-1641), the widowed founder of a religious order and grandmother of the famous Madame de Sévigné.

2 I have corrected a misprint in the original, which refers to "Louise et La Vallière"; the reference is to one of Louis XIV's mistresses, who became a Carmelite nun, allegedly in order to do penance, when replaced as the king's favorite by Madame de Montespan.

and the most dangerous of errors. Carry, if you wish, the torch of Erostratos into the social edifice; my heart is bitter enough to approve; but since Heaven has wanted us to inhabit an imperfect earth, where nothing is achieved without dolor, do not try henceforth, at the expense of the experience of all times, these partial reforms that only ought to serve as monuments to nullity.

What! They have analyzed the human heart, they have sounded all its depths, they have studied all its movements, but they have not anticipated a single one of those excessively numerous occasions for which religion had invented cloisters! Terrors of a timid soul that lacks confidence in its own strength; expansion of an ardent soul that feels a need to isolate itself with its creator; indignation of a sickened soul that no longer believes in happiness; collapse of a worn-out soul that despair has vanquished; what specifics do they oppose to so many calamities? Ask the suicides.

Behold an entire generation for which political events have taken the place of the education of Achilles. It has had for aliments the marrow and the blood of lions; and now that a government that leaves nothing to hazard and which fixes the future, has restricted the dangerous development of its faculties; now that the narrow circle of Popilius has been traced around it,[1] and that someone has said, like the Almighty to the sea: you shall not pass these limits, does one know what so many idle passions and repressed energies might produce of the calamitous? Does one know how close an impetuous heart that is open to ennui is open to crime? I declare it with bitterness and with fear; Werther's pistol and the executioner's ax have already decimated us.

---

1 Livy and Polybius reported that the Roman military commander Gaius Popilius Laenas, in the second century B.C. drew a circle around Antiochus IV Epiphanes during the latter's invasion of Egypt when the latter was procrastinating with regard to an instruction from the Senate, and insisted that he remain within it until he had made a decision.

This generation is rising up, and demanding cloisters of you.[1]

Unalloyed peace to the fortunate of the earth! But malediction to anyone who contests a refuge to misfortune! The first people were sublime who consecrated in the number of its institutions a place of repose for the woeful. A good society provides for everything, even the needs of those who detach themselves from it by choice or by necessity.

I had returned to the superior buildings, and as I leaned against a Gothic pillar ornamented by sad emblems I remarked characters painfully engraved on one of the faces of its base. The following could be read there:

> *In seeing the blindness and the miseries of man, and the astonishing contrarieties that are discovered in his nature, and regarding all the mute universe, and man without light, abandoned to himself, as if gone astray in this corner of the universe, without knowing who put him there, what he has come to do there, what will become of him in dying, I enter into terror, like a man carried in his sleep to a frightful desert island, and who wakes up without knowing where he is, and without any means of leaving; and in that case, how I admire a man who does not enter into despair in such a dismal estate.*

It is Pascal who penciled in those lines the entire history of the human race.

---

1 The National Assembly had appropriated the wealth of the Church to the nation in 1789 and abolished monastic vows; all religious orders were officially abolished in 1790. Napoléon dissolved monastic orders in German, Italy and Spain as his conquests advanced and he held the pope captive, but some monasteries succeeded in resisting the persecution from the outset, and it relented even before the Emperor's defeat, in 1814, enabled a partial restitution of Church property and the revivification of religious institutions. The demand for cloisters was, therefore, soon answered.

On Romance

I regard *romance*[1] as the most precious tradition of our old poetry.

It is noteworthy that the genre belongs essentially to the melancholy centuries, and was almost unknown in antiquity.

It is, however, permissible to think that if *Ruth* is the most perfect of idylls, and the *Song of Songs* the most magnificent of epithalamiums, then the story of Dinah,[2] that of the Levite of Ephraim[3] and a part of the book of *Job* might be regarded as

---

1 With specific reference to music, to which the French term *romance* is usually confined, the word normally refers to ballads, and dictionaries of translation usually refuse it synonymy with the English word "romance," although it seems appropriate to me to defy that convention here and to transcribe the word as it stands. The author clearly is not using the word in this essay simply to refer to ballads, or even to music; he evidently means something much closer to what the word would imply in such English phrases as "Medieval romance." He did not preserve the term for his works of fiction, usually calling the longer ones *romans*, but that term too is more aptly translated into English in that instance as "romances" than "novels," and when Nodier and other French authors began talking about *romanticisme*, prompted by Madame de Staël, they meant something closely allied with the manner in which the word *romance* is used in this essay. The subsequent citations demonstrate that the entire essay, as well as the doggerel that it introduces (to which the unrhymed translation cannot do justice), was written tongue-in-cheek.

2 In *Genesis* 34 Dinah, a daughter of Jacob, becomes the pretext for a treacherous massacre after being requested in marriage by Schechem, on the grounds that the latter had defiled her.

3 In *Judges* 19—a rather enigmatic but extremely unsavory story about a

the first models of romance.

The somber mythology of the Caledonians seemed invented for the romance. The poems of Ossian are inimitable romances.

The romance flourished with chivalric mores in the epoch of the civilization of the Occident. It was the war song of the Muses, the war song of the Moors and the love song of the troubadours.

It is the monument of all "romantic" memories. One could reference with romances the entire history of the Crusades. Tasso and Ariosto are perhaps only fortunate compilers of romances.

The romance is a poem that has an action like the epic, and admits its means. But it can pass into a very narrow frame, from the elevation of the ode to the simplicity of the eclogue, to the mild gravity of the elegy. It does not disdain to arm itself sometimes with the point of an epigram or the dart of a madrigal.

Berquin has made pretty romances;[1] Fabre-d'Églantine[2] and Moncrif[3] have made beautiful ones. The romances in

---

man who delivers his concubine to a mob in order to be gang-raped, and then dismembers her body: an even more peculiar choice as a model for romance than the previous item.

1 The reference is presumably to Arnaud Berquin's *L'ami des enfans* (1782-83), although the stories it contains are naturalistic, deliberately opposed to the tradition of *contes*.

2 The self-styled Fabre d'Églantiine (Philippe Fabre, 1750-1794) was a Rousseau-inspired Jacobin guillotined during the Terror, best known as a satirical dramatist; the "romance" with which he is credited here is presumably *Étude de nature* (1783), but he adopted his pseudonym after receiving a silver eglantine as a prize at the Toulousan *Jeux Floraux*, in the name of their legendary patroness, Clémence Isaure.

3 François-Augustin de Paradis de Moncrif (1687-1770) became famous as a librettist for comedies, tragedies and ballets, but his prose work included *Les Aventures de Zeloïde et d'Amanzarifdine* (1715), parodying Antoine Galland's Arabian tales.

prose of Monsieur de Chateaubriand, and the pseudographical romances that are attributed to Clotilde, are sublime.[1]

I have heard better ones of which nature pays all the expense, and which are only sung in hamlets.

It requires more than intelligence to make a good romance; it requires sensibility—which is to say, genius.

I do not know anything, however, more pitiful than a mediocre romance, and I fear that this one might be even worse.

---

1 "Clotilde de Surville" was the supposed fifteenth-century author of a collection of poems published in 1803 by Charles Vanderbourg, who might have believed in their authenticity, having acquired them from the widow of the Marquis de Surville, an émigré killed in 1798 during an insurrection in Provence, who was thus unavailable to confirm or deny that he was their actual author

The Blonde Isaure

(Tune by Martini for the romance by Florian,
***Si nous vivons comme vivoient nos pères.*)**[1]

Young beauties, on my ebon harp
I'll sing the amorous dolors
And the pain of a heart betrays
And the sins it invents in its turn;
Lend an ear to the Troubadour's verse.

"You can sing the heroes, the battles
All that pleases the heart of a knight;
Noble Evrard awaits in his walls;
Prepare a war song for his feast,
I am Arthur; I am his squire.

The lovely Agnes, pearl of France
Has accorded her hand to Evrard
In this castle of fine appearance
The marriage will soon be made,
This varlet will show you the way."

---

1 The composer Jean-Paul Martini (1741-1816) wrote the music for the classic love song "Plaisir d'amour" (1783) to accompany a poem by Jean-Pierre Claris de Florian (1755-1794), who was best-known for his fables, but wrote in a variety of genres; he was elected to the Académie Française in 1788 and was spared the guillotine when Robespierre fell, only to die in prison of tuberculosis.

All was ready; the genteel bride
Was alone in the bosky shade;
Simple ribbons adorned her hair;
Simple jasmines were her bouquet.
"Come Troubadour, and take your place."

How pretty Evrard found her then!
Seeing her, what fire was ignited.
"Your smile is the rose embellished,
Where the zephyr loves to repose."
Then, to one side, he takes a kiss.

When they all sat down they were pressed;
Badinage flew all around;
Every gallant sought a mistress
Every gaze sought a sweet return;
Every guest was a Troubadour.

"A pilgrim is approaching the place;
Tender in age, ingenuous in gaze.
In the Crusade in the Holy Land
His father was known to you."
"Good," said Evrard, "he is welcome."

A thick felt hat disguises his face
His thin body is clad in linen.
Evrard, trembling at his passage,
Strives to appear serene.
What will he say to the pilgrim?

"Is it to Rome or to Galicia.
Good pilgrim that your steps are bound?
Are you not going to the place of torment
Of the Savior to deplore his death?"
The pilgrim made him no reply.

"Have you made some temeritous vow
On a ship harassed by danger?
Or do you pray for a father's health
That no secret can relieve?"
The stranger was heard to sigh.

Exquisite wine shines in light foam
Presaging the return of pleasure.
The pilgrim inundates his impetuosity:
"Agnes, I drink to your amour;
Take my cup and let's drink by turns."

She smiles and the cup is drained.
"Shiver," he said, "and know my plan.
A dire poison this nectar disguises
Will flow with it in your breast.
The pilgrim was your assassin!"

Agnes succumbs, dying and livid,
A sinister cry strikes the air.
"For that child whose death is rapid
Have you paid the evils I've suffered?
Then go to announce me in Hell!"

Evrard leaps; who would believe it!
The pilgrim's gaze confounds him.
She's a woman; and on her ivory back
Blonde hair escapes at hazard;
Bleak fear suspends Evrard's blows.

"I am" she says, "Isaure de Ancerre;
Palestine attests my ancestry;
In a tourney, Evrard pleased me;
God, what fervor shone in his eyes!
I adored him; he was the victor.

Covered with blood, sweat and dust,
Under his armor a God seemed hid;
With his exploits he filled the lists;
The most valiant were laid at his feet,
And the sand was strewn with crests.

The king said to me: 'Take this crown
Award him the prize of his valor.'
I whispered: 'It's love that gives it;
Of them and me fate has made you victor,
Return this even and think of my joy.

I loved him well, believed him faithful!
Of his love a son was born to me.
He no longer lives, under my cruel hand,
That son too dear died murdered
I punished him for the sin of his birth.

But 'tis done, my heart burns and shudders.
Enjoy, Evrard, the death that attains me.'
Those words said, strength abandons her
Whiteness of lilies spreads over her face;
Her blue eyes languish and roll, extinct.

At that sight, Evrard takes his sword
He pierces himself with its blade,
And three times, steeped in his blood,
Plunges it into his torn flank
And turns it with a desperate arm.

There is no wellbeing without frankness
No treason without trouble and regret.
Of our ancestors conserve this device:
Be constant, and then be discreet.
Those are the secrets of happiness.

Ophelia

(Translation of an English Ballad)

OPHELIA'S SERVANTS

There she is, Ophelia, who charmed all eyes; there she is, pale, distraught and desperate. She stops, sighs and weeps. O you, weep for Ophelia!

OPHELIA

I thought that I would not weep any more, and that I would be happy. Tell me whether it is true that I have to lament, and that you do not gaze sadly when I speak to you. My mind is troubled because you have abandoned me; I am also told that my father is dead, but he is doubtless not dead, although that is why I am weeping.

OPHELIA'S SERVANTS

Now she has fallen silent. She is contemplating the sky, and listening to the wind.

OPHELIA

How pure the sky is today! The sky is as pure as my heart. I have never seen the sun so beautiful and the murmur of the woods so sweet. If you want to follow me into the woods, we will find my father there and your lovers, who are sleeping tranquilly under the fire trees; it is a fête for Ophelia.

OPHELIA'S SERVANTS

We will follow Ophelia into the woods; we will search for her father who is sleeping tranquilly under the fir trees.

Let us flatter her dolor and take pity on her delirium. What soul would be cruel enough to undeceive the despair of an error that soothes?

We will follow you into the woods; we will search for your father who is sleeping tranquilly under the fir-trees, Ophelia, as you wish.

OPHELIA

No; I want you to leave me alone, and no longer listen to me. I shall not hide from you that I am waiting here for my lover, and that it is for him that I am crowned with the roses of May. The roses of May are fresh and brilliant; the drops of dew that roll over their leaves resemble tears. These flowers appear more beautiful when I attach them to my hair; but I mingle them there with the little pale flowers that grow on the edge of the stream.

OPHELIA'S SERVANTS

She is parting the reeds; she is leaning over the water in order to see her crown of roses and to mingle the flowers with it.

OPHELIA

The stream is calm in this place, because it is deep; and yet, it is troubled, it darkens at my approach. I don't know why I have come, and why I have ornamented myself, and why I have picked these flowers, and why I have plaited roses. Oh, how they importune me! What is the matter, poor Ophelia? You no longer love roses?

OPHELIA'S SERVANTS

She is gazing at the stream, she is extending her arms, she is trembling. Listen to what she is about to say!

OPHELIA

Silence, and walk no further! The wind is calming down and the stream smoothing over; the image of a young woman is painted on its motionless surface. Alas, I know that it is me; but why is my hair so scattered? Why am I wearing mourning? And why have I been weeping for so long?

OPHELIA'S SERVANTS

Sad Ophelia!

OPHELIA

My father!

OPHELIA'S SERVANTS

She can no longer be seen, and we part the reeds in vain in

order to search for her. She is not hidden behind the reeds; but there on the stream are her veil and her crown, and there is her body on the bank.

There she is, Ophelia who charmed all eyes; there she is, dead on the bank. What will you respond to those who ask you for her? You will turn your eyes away and you will not respond.

O you, weep for Ophelia.

Schiller's Last Judgment

Observation

A strange idea, that of Newton and Bossuet, who have commented on the Apocalypse.

Stranger still that of a scholar of our days who has only seen there an astronomical system.

The Apocalypse is the epic of judgment.

The poem is mystical, as obscure and marvelous as its subject. The poet has employed vague, and even bizarre, colors because he was painting the unknown. That idea alone reveals a rare genius.

Young is, very nearly, merely a pompous orator.

I do not know whether Klopstock succeeded very well in a poem on the Last Judgment. He was strong enough for his first enterprise, and the episodic persona of Abadonna is one of the finest inventions of the epic muse; but one could desire that the work were a more austere and chastely ornamented composition; the model is in the gospels.

The depiction that I have tried to pass into our language is sublime; let it not be judged by this miserable copy. Schiller has the Last Judgment dreamed by a reproved, and links to the story of that great catastrophe a striking and terrible action. Schiller's scene contains an entire poem. What man would undertake it? The Last Judgment has had its Michelangelo, but has not had its Homer.

Remember that it is a parricide who is speaking.

> I dreamed that, by joy and amour intoxicated,
> To the charms of sleep my senses were liberated,
> Tranquil, I was asleep beneath a tender shade;
> I was asleep; suddenly a noise was heard,
> And roaring in the distance in the shaken air.
> The thunder rumbled and fell in doubled lightning.
> I wake up. Suddenly, to the alarm of my sight.
> The horizon is covered in flame and smoke;
> And all the winds, launched forth at once
> Sweeping cities and woods before them
> Augment with their cries the tempest's horrors,
> Rolling volcanoes and seas over my head.
> And I see ONE appear in that bleak apparel
> Whose feet enclose the whole course of the sun.
> From the height of the firmament his balance extends
> Over pale humans remaining suspended.
> And his brow crowned with thunder and lightning,
> Under veils of fire is lost in the air.
> Children of days destroyed and races past,
> It is me, he cries, who judges thought.
> They crawl, suppliant, before their sovereign.
> And their teeth gnash like teeth of bronze.
> But then, preceded by a horrible silence,
> I believe I see an old man advancing.
> With odious bonds his limbs are charged;
> Hunger has mutilated his half-corroded arms,
> A slow agony has made his face leaden
> And fearful eyes are alarmed by his passage.
> At his frightful smile, his sad regard

I approach, and great God, I know that old man!
Slowly he cleaves through the frightened crowd.
Seizes a silvery curl of his hair.
Tears it out, throws it, and under that feeble weight
The balance descends, and the noise of his voice,
Filling the deserts of the sky and the abyss;
"Mercy," says the Avenger; "this crime absolves the crime;
It alone is condemned!"

Letter From the Maire Of C***, Near L***, to the Publisher of *Sorrows*

Monsieur,

I am forwarding to your address the manuscript that was found among the papers of the unknown man, whose last journal entries announced his deplorable end. While condemning the insensate despair that led him to kill himself, I cannot help recognizing in that event one of the views of Providence, which wanted to justify in some way to the claims of the unfortunate youth in favor of monastic institutions and to show that it is for want of such a resource that many men worthy of delivering themselves to virtue have terminated their days by a crime that revolts nature. Such a consideration does not seem to me to be of slight weight in that cause, and if it were submitted to the government by a writer who was able to support it with all the force of eloquence and reason, I have no doubt that it would produce a full effect. In any case, you will see that our author had only amassed on this subject a small number of materials and that his manuscript, although marred by faults of taste that are only too familiar to him that had not reached a suitable point of maturity. It is up to you to decide, you whose name is respectable by more than one entitlement, whether some ardor of sensibility that animates his style, and the tragic manner in which he has been removed from literature and amity, are sufficiently powerful vehicles of interest for you to dare to risk the impression of these fragments. Thus, I ought to limit myself to making you party to the circumstances of the suicide, such as I have collected them scrupulously, inasmuch as the employment I exercise and my particular inclination have impelled me to do so.

It was some three months ago that in the village of which I am the Maire, a passer-by was remarked with a rather distinguished physiognomy and more than mediocre stature, who appeared to be walking aimlessly, and as if afflicted by a profound melancholy. It was perceived after two days that he had no fixed habitation, and that he was living on the simplest aliments in the crudest of huts. It was believed that he slept in the woods, but no one can say why. Finally, he was no longer encountered.

I was informed a few weeks later that a man similar to the one that had been mentioned to me had retired to an old hermitage abandoned by everyone, in a situation so primitive that it was rare to reach it. It was added that he had been seen here and there in the forest, and that everything about him marked an alienation neighboring on delirium; but such touching details were reported in that regard, and such a tender enthusiasm was put into those stories that I desired to see him in my turn and to penetrate his secret.

Finally, a short while ago the rumor of a murder spread through the canton, and I went to the place indicated, with a number of witnesses, although the passages were dangerous and the hour was advanced.

It was at the entrance to a natural grotto, which is renowned locally for the curiosities it contains, and also for having often served as a refuge for malefactors. It was an hour after midnight, but the moon was shining very brightly, with the consequence that no objects could escape my research, and I thought it as well not to put off my visit until the next day. Having arrived at the mouth of the cavern, via paths entirely covered with stones, on which I was shown a few traces of blood, I had the cadaver that was still lying there picked up, and a careful search of the surroundings made.

After these precautions I went to one of the houses of the nearest hamlet and there I preceded with the examination of the body and the things that belonged to it.

The identity of the individual with the one of whom there was question above immediately appeared to be incontestable to all those who were accompanying me. He was a man twenty-four years old at the most, but his face was so horribly distorted that I could not recognize any feature of it, except that his beard was thick and brown. His hair was cut roundly, very stiff and soiled. At the moment when we found him, his two hands were raised behind his head and the rest of his body's posture was of a nature to permit the thought that he was asleep. He had half-boots, almost ragged, deerskin trousers that went all the way up to his chest, a red waistcoat surrounded by a little gold fringe, and a very short sky-blue coat. His cravat was red Indian linen, like his waistcoat and his right hand was wrapped in a similar handkerchief, marked with an M and an O in large capital letters.[1] In his hand he was holding a new file with a box-wood handle and his fingers, the handle and the iron were slightly bloodstained.

When we had removed his clothing we found beneath the left nipple a wound a few inches broad, bruised and blue-black.

A green silk ribbon suspended from his neck a velvet bag of the same color, very worn, which contained a lock of chestnut-brown hair and a little ebony box inlaid with gold and silver.

---

1 Hindsight allows us to suspect strongly that these initials might stand for Maxime Odin, even though the later fictitious memoirs attributed to that individual reveal that he did not commit suicide at twenty-four, any more than Charles Nodier did. "Odin" is an anagram of the first four letters of "Nodier," while "Maxime" might be a wry acknowledgement of the author's liking for exaggeration and excess.

After having opened it, with difficulty, it seemed to us that we glimpsed a brown substance ready to fall into dust, which I assumed to be long-dried blood. On a folded piece of paper that enveloped it, someone had written CAMILLE.

In one of the fob pockets there was a steel cross and two small silver coins. We took a wad of papers from his pocket consisting of three letters, from which he had torn off the address and signature; and two notebooks, one of which was bound in green cardboard and the other covered with marbled pink paper. On the envelope of the former, which I am sending to you, your name and place of residence were inscribed. You will see that the opuscules it contains, partly written in pencil, all very negligently, do not appear to have been written in order to be published. The erasures and the numerous insertions with which they are covered testify that he had never deigned to make a copy of them.

The other contained various extracts from his favorite books, for example, a part of the story of Job, *Le Profession de foi du vicaire savoyard*;[1] a chapter from Montaigne: *to be a philosopher is to learn to die*; two of Werther's letters; several scenes from Racine; several of Pascal's *Pensées*; and several lines from Shakespeare. One of those, which he had probably made his motto, was frequently repeated:

To be or not to be, that is the question.

That, Monsieur, is the information that I promised you, and with which I have doubtless entertained your dolor for too long. I know that particularities of this species, fatal as they are, always have a great price for amity, and if I have been too prolix in detailing them, that consideration will be my excuse.

---

1 *Le Profession de foi du vicaire savoyard* is an extract, often reprinted separately, from *Émile, ou De l'éducation* (1762) by Jean-Jacques Rousseau.

A PARTIAL LIST OF SNUGGLY BOOKS

G. ALBERT AURIER *Elsewhere and Other Stories*
CHARLES BARBARA *My Lunatic Asylum*
S. HENRY BERTHOUD *Misanthropic Tales*
LÉON BLOY *The Tarantulas' Parlor and Other Unkind Tales*
ÉLÉMIR BOURGES *The Twilight of the Gods*
JAMES CHAMPAGNE *Harlem Smoke*
FÉLICIEN CHAMPSAUR *The Latin Orgy*
FÉLICIEN CHAMPSAUR
The Emerald Princess and Other Decadent Fantasies
BRENDAN CONNELL *Unofficial History of Pi Wei*
BRENDAN CONNELL *The Metapheromenoi*
RAFAELA CONTRERAS *The Turquoise Ring and Other Stories*
ADOLFO COUVE *When I Think of My Missing Head*
QUENTIN S. CRISP *Aiaigasa*
QUENTIN S. CRISP *Graves*
LADY DILKE *The Outcast Spirit and Other Stories*
CATHERINE DOUSTEYSSIER-KHOZE *The Beauty of the Death Cap*
ÉDOUARD DUJARDIN *Hauntings*
BERIT ELLINGSEN *Now We Can See the Moon*
BERIT ELLINGSEN *Vessel and Solsvart*
ERCKMANN-CHATRIAN *A Malediction*
ENRIQUE GÓMEZ CARRILLO *Sentimental Stories*
EDMOND AND JULES DE GONCOURT *Manette Salomon*
REMY DE GOURMONT *From a Faraway Land*
GUIDO GOZZANO *Alcina and Other Stories*
EDWARD HERON-ALLEN *The Complete Shorter Fiction*
EDWARD HERON-ALLEN *Three Ghost-Written Novels*
RHYS HUGHES *Cloud Farming in Wales*
J.-K. HUYSMANS *The Crowds of Lourdes*
J.-K. HUYSMANS *Knapsacks*
COLIN INSOLE *Valerie and Other Stories*
JUSTIN ISIS *Pleasant Tales II*
JUSTIN ISIS AND DANIEL CORRICK (editors)
Drowning in Beauty: The Neo-Decadent Anthology
VICTOR JOLY *The Unknown Collaborator and Other Legendary Tales*

MARIE KRYSINSKA *The Path of Amour*
BERNARD LAZARE *The Mirror of Legends*
BERNARD LAZARE *The Torch-Bearers*
MAURICE LEVEL *The Shadow*
JEAN LORRAIN *Errant Vice*
JEAN LORRAIN *Fards and Poisons*
JEAN LORRAIN *Masks in the Tapestry*
JEAN LORRAIN *Monsieur de Bougrelon and Other Stories*
JEAN LORRAIN *Nightmares of an Ether-Drinker*
JEAN LORRAIN *The Soul-Drinker and Other Decadent Fantasies*
ARTHUR MACHEN *N*
ARTHUR MACHEN *Ornaments in Jade*
CAMILLE MAUCLAIR *The Frail Soul and Other Stories*
CATULLE MENDÈS *Bluebirds*
CATULLE MENDÈS *For Reading in the Bath*
CATULLE MENDÈS *Mephistophela*
ÉPHRAÏM MIKHAËL *Halyartes and Other Poems in Prose*
LUIS DE MIRANDA *Who Killed the Poet?*
OCTAVE MIRBEAU *The Death of Balzac*
CHARLES MORICE *Babels, Balloons and Innocent Eyes*
GABRIEL MOUREY *Monada*
DAMIAN MURPHY *Daughters of Apostasy*
DAMIAN MURPHY *The Star of Gnosia*
KRISTINE ONG MUSLIM *Butterfly Dream*
PHILOTHÉE O'NEDDY *The Enchanted Ring*
YARROW PAISLEY *Mendicant City*
URSULA PFLUG *Down From*
JEREMY REED *When a Girl Loves a Girl*
JEREMY REED *Bad Boys*
ADOLPHE RETTÉ *Misty Thule*
JEAN RICHEPIN *The Bull-Man and the Grasshopper*
DAVID RIX *A Blast of Hunters*
DAVID RIX *A Suite in Four Windows*
FREDERICK ROLFE (Baron Corvo) *Amico di Sandro*
FREDERICK ROLFE (Baron Corvo)
An Ossuary of the North Lagoon and Other Stories
JASON ROLFE *An Archive of Human Nonsense*

MARCEL SCHWOB *The Assassins and Other Stories*
BRIAN STABLEFORD (editor)
Decadence and Symbolism: A Showcase Anthology
BRIAN STABLEFORD (editor) *The Snuggly Satyricon*
BRIAN STABLEFORD (editor) *The Snuggly Satanicon*
BRIAN STABLEFORD (editor) *Snuggly Tales of Hashish and Opium*
BRIAN STABLEFORD *The Insubstantial Pageant*
BRIAN STABLEFORD *Spirits of the Vasty Deep*
BRIAN STABLEFORD *The Truths of Darkness*
COUNT ERIC STENBOCK *Love, Sleep & Dreams*
COUNT ERIC STENBOCK *Myrtle, Rue & Cypress*
COUNT ERIC STENBOCK *The Shadow of Death*
COUNT ERIC STENBOCK *Studies of Death*
MONTAGUE SUMMERS *The Bride of Christ and Other Fictions*
MONTAGUE SUMMERS *Six Ghost Stories*
GILBERT-AUGUSTIN THIERRY *The Blonde Tress and The Mask*
GILBERT-AUGUSTIN THIERRY *Reincarnation and Redemption*
DOUGLAS THOMPSON *The Fallen West*
TOADHOUSE *Gone Fishing with Samy Rosenstock*
TOADHOUSE *Living and Dying in a Mind Field*
TOADHOUSE *What Makes the Wave Break?*
LÉO TRÉZENIK *Decadent Prose Pieces*
RUGGERO VASARI *Raun*
JANE DE LA VAUDÈRE *The Demi-Sexes and The Androgynes*
JANE DE LA VAUDÈRE *The Double Star and Other Occult Fantasies*
JANE DE LA VAUDÈRE *The Mystery of Kama and Brahma's Courtesans*
JANE DE LA VAUDÈRE *The Priestesses of Mylitta*
JANE DE LA VAUDÈRE *Three Flowers and The King of Siam's Amazon*
JANE DE LA VAUDÈRE *The Witch of Ecbatana and The Virgin of Israel*
AUGUSTE VILLIERS DE L'ISLE-ADAM *Isis*
RENÉE VIVIEN AND HÉLÈNE DE ZUYLEN DE NYEVELT
Faustina and Other Stories
RENÉE VIVIEN *Lilith's Legacy*
RENÉE VIVIEN *A Woman Appeared to Me*
TERESA WILMS MONTT *In the Stillness of Marble*
TERESA WILMS MONTT *Sentimental Doubts*
KAREL VAN DE WOESTIJNE *The Dying Peasant*

CPSIA information can be obtained
at www.ICGtesting.com
Printed in the USA
BVHW030228150920
588843BV00001B/255

9 781645 250487